D0282690

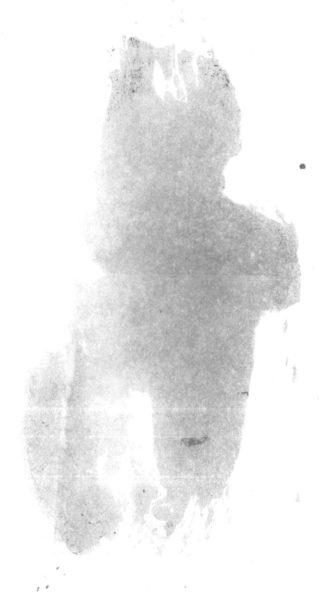

By the same author:

Killed in the Ratings
(winner of the Mystery Writers of America's Edgar Allan Poe
Award for the best first novel of 1978)

The Hog Murders
(winner of the Mystery Writers of America's Edgar Allan Poe
Award for the best paperback original of 1979)

The Lunatic Fringe

Killed in the Act

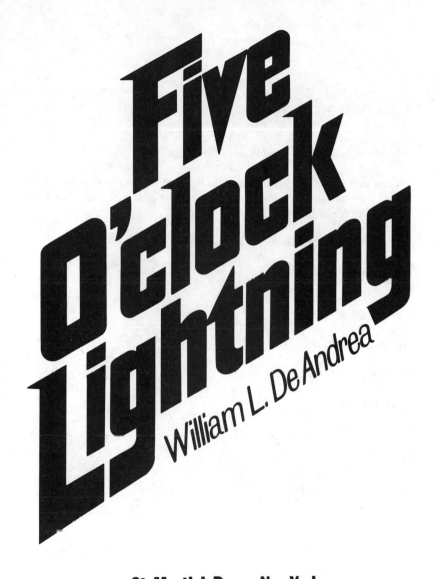

Five O'clock Lightning

William L. DeAndrea

St. Martin's Press, New York

Library of Congress Cataloging in Publication Data

DeAndrea, William L.
  Five o'clock lightning.

  I. Title.
PS3554.E174F5   813'.54   81-21534
ISBN 0-312-29498-0   AACR2

10 9 8 7 6 5 4 3 2 1

First Edition

For Dr. Lewis J. Orphanof, scientist and friend.

Author's Note

This is a work of fiction. A work of history must be as true as the author can make it; a historical novel, because it is a work of fiction, can be as false as the author needs it to be. Geography and architecture, as well as time itself, can (and have) been changed to suit the needs of the story.

In writing this novel, I have incorporated some well-known real people as characters and certain public events, such as baseball games, into the narrative. However, no implication should be drawn (and certainly none is intended) that any of these real people used as characters said, did, or were involved in the things written in the novel. My purpose was solely to evoke an era and create a real-seeming 1953, not to report events.

I hasten to add that most of the characters (including *all* the bad guys) are totally fictitious. Therefore, simply because a character may have been portrayed in the novel as occupying a certain position or job, the reader should not construe this to mean that the character was meant to represent in any way whatsoever the person who actually held that position or job at the time described in the novel; any resemblance is entirely coincidental.

Finally, I'd like to take this opportunity to thank some people: Carol Brener, Read Evans, and Steve Fabian, for making the contents of their libraries available to me; Janice Young Brooks, for showing me Kansas City; and especially Meredith Bernstein, who stayed with the pitch until she connected.

Chapter One
Warm-up

His hands were trembling as he lowered them from his face. Slowly, he raised his head to look at himself in the small shaving mirror that hung crookedly from a nail above the only sink in the cottage.

As he had last night, he nearly jumped at his own reflection—it had been so long since he'd seen it. Like an amnesiac, he was surprised to recognize himself. But there it was, looking back at him from the flawed circle of silvered glass. His eyes; his coloring; his very own bone structure. This was his face, the face of David Laird. He turned his head slowly, letting the sunlight that poured through the open windows strike his head at constantly changing angles. It put his face through phases, like the moon's.

He raised his rough, red hands again and touched his face. He touched lightly, as though he were afraid to break it. Gently, he traced the line of his high cheekbones; his strong, square jaw. He brushed a lock of hair the color of cornmeal from his forehead. He was mesmerized.

This is a good face, he told himself. An honest face. Jenny used to tell him it was a beautiful face. Since just before midnight, it had been a killer's face.

He couldn't pull his eyes away from the reflection, at least not yet. For years now he'd avoided mirrors, had needed to make a conscious effort to look at one. Now it looked as if he'd have to make an effort to turn away.

He hadn't even *owned* a mirror until yesterday. He'd

driven his old, prewar—World War II, that is—Chevrolet (the driving mirrors adjusted so they never showed him his own reflection) to a town fifteen miles to the north, to one of those big, impersonal, modern drugstores. He almost gave up and drove right back. For some reason he couldn't understand even now, Laird had just stood around pretending to read a promotional leaflet for Sal Hepatica. When a clerk had asked him what he wanted, he'd coughed and stammered like a teenager trying to work up the nerve to ask for his first box of condoms. He was literally unable to say the word—he had to point to get what he wanted.

It was a truth that had become an instinct: mirrors were his enemy. Like a vampire. No, like a zombie.

He smiled. He felt a mixture of joy and anguish at seeing it was his old smile again, David Laird's smile.

A zombie. That was very good. A walking corpse, resurrected through the power of black voodoo and sent to kill at the whim of its master. Laird's smile widened. *This* zombie had a will of his own.

His "master" would not even know, for example, about the first murder, the one last night, not until it was too late. Killing Ed Bristow had been easier than Laird had anticipated. Bristow had been a friend; but he'd turned out to be a coward and a traitor. He'd gotten nothing worse than he deserved.

Besides, Laird needed to see how the gun worked and how the silencer affected it. Dr. Bristow, alive and dead, had been very helpful. And with any luck his body wouldn't be found, or at least identified, until Laird was back among the dead and out of reach.

The clock-radio blared to life, startling Laird and breaking the mirror's spell. The radio was Laird's one and only extravagance, the most expensive thing by quite a bit in the one-room cottage that passed for his home. It was an Emerson, sleek and shiny, the streamlined cabinet laminated with two shades of wood. It had a lighted dial, and its tubes' humming was hardly audible. Laird had bought it brand new two years ago, took it with him all during his wanderings.

He'd never regretted it—1951 had apparently been a great year for radios.

He'd set the alarm last night before going to meet Bristow, believing, like a fool, that he'd be able to sleep when he returned.

It was a good thing, though, that he *had* set the alarm, Laird decided. He might have stood at the mirror for hours and destroyed his schedule. Now he'd be sure to stay right on time.

The ten o'clock news began. Laird played the radio constantly, when his headache subsided enough to let him stand it. He paid little attention to the drama programs, or Fred Allen, or those new "disc jockey" programs, but he always listened closely to the news.

"The first story this August Saturday is the riots in Iran," the announcer said. "Thousands of Iranians took to the streets again today to demand the return of the young Shah Mohammed Riza Pahlevi and the ouster of General Mossadegh, the man who deposed him. United States Government officials said . . ."

Laird reloaded the pistol his "comrade" had given him, the one Dr. Bristow had helped him learn so intimately. It was a target pistol, .22 caliber—a light weapon but easily sufficient to kill a man if properly used.

The newscast cut away to an advertisement that tried to convince the listener that frozen peas were as tasty and nutritious as fresh or canned. Laird knew as much about frozen food already as he would ever care to and turned his full attention to his work.

The newscast resumed. ". . . House Un-American Activities Committee member Rex Simmons is in New York City today, on the trail of what he calls irrefutable evidence of the most shocking infiltration by the International Communist Conspiracy into a beloved American institution yet discovered. Our reporter, Roger Milbank, asked the Missouri Republican what that evidence might show. Here is the congressman's transcribed reply:

"'Well [Simmons's voice began], like my fellow Re-

4

publican and patriot, Senator McCarthy, I prefer to do my speaking where it counts, on the floor of the House, with my evidence before me. But I will say this: when once the American people have heard of this new threat, they will be shocked; they will call on their Government to save the beloved American Way of Life from those who would . . .'"

The congressman went on. And on. Laird had been expecting—even hoping, to hear this statement, in these very words, but the sound of Simmons's voice seemed to burn him like air from a blast furnace.

Laird ground the heels of his hands against his head, trying to crush the pains that grew there. Then, with a wordless scream, he took the mirror off the wall and raised it high over his head. He'd shut that evil, conniving bastard's mouth, smash the mirror and radio together, crush the hateful sound of Simmons between them, and . . .

Simmons said, ". . . but this afternoon, all I plan to do is go to a ball game. Thank you, young man." The announcer went on to give the weather—hazy, hot, very humid, with a chance of thundershowers late tonight.

The pains subsided. Breathing like an asthma victim, Laird lowered the mirror. Carefully, almost lovingly, he placed it far to the back of a drawer in a cheap fiberboard bureau. He might have a need for that mirror again.

There were better ways to use his hatred, better things to smash. He'd made such progress already; his plan was working well, so far—the time lag he'd caused by sending his anonymous letter to Simmons's Kansas City headquarters instead of his Washington office had given Laird a chance to know his weapon and perfect his plan.

Laird took a deep breath now and forced himself to stay calm. He attached the homemade silencer (basically a stiff rubber tube) to the muzzle of the target pistol and held it in his hand and admired it. He'd never been the type of man who was given to a passion for firearms, but he was beginning to understand the feeling. The pistol looked clean; looked efficient; looked simple and right for what it was designed to do. Laird placed the weapon on top of some clothing in a small canvas travel bag.

Laird slung the bag over his shoulder and left the cottage. He didn't bother to lock the door behind him—he had nothing of value but the radio, and even that wouldn't matter for long.

Besides, no one stopped here anymore. Laird's cottage was the last habitation for humans in the middle of what was becoming a technological ghost town—this part of New Jersey's shore had been given over to great silvered tanks and the piped-in surreal skylines of oil refineries. It was the perfect place for Laird to live—it looked beautiful, and it stank. It was a symbol, he thought, of the entire nation.

It didn't matter, he told himself. He couldn't even smell it anymore.

He hugged the bag to him and was reassured by the feel of the gun metal inside. Then he got in his car and pulled off his little patch of grass and sand onto the highway. He had a long drive ahead of him; across the George Washington Bridge, across the northern end of Manhattan, then across the Harlem River into the Bronx.

It would only be wise to leave early—this way he could check all his getaway cars and still make it to Yankee Stadium in plenty of time. Laird patted the bag on the seat beside him. He didn't know about anyone else, but he was going to enjoy this afternoon's ball game.

Chapter Two
Hit and Run

1

It was either a ritual or an ordeal; Russ Garrett wasn't sure which. But he was painfully aware that whichever it was, it had been his own idea, and it was only his own stonelike stubbornness that kept him to it.

It wasn't even noon yet, but already Garrett felt like he'd spent years in some enormous Turkish bath. Still, Garrett ran up and down his selected stretch of twenty steep, gray-painted Yankee Stadium stairs, slapping his sneakers on the cement in the precise rhythm of "How Much Is That Doggie in the Window," as recently recorded by Miss Patti Page.

Garrett was sick of that song. He wished mightily that he could come up with something different to time his stair-climbing, but it was too late. Now every time he started to run he heard Patti's voice echoing inside his head, and every time he heard the lady singing three-part harmony with herself on the "Make-Believe Ballroom," his knees started to tremble. And his feet got cold.

Jesus, he used to think that song was *cute!* Now it was nonstop background music, and sometimes it drove him crazy.

Garrett reached his three-hundredth step; he tapped the railing with his hand, turned clumsily in the narrow aisle between the banks of reserved seats, and started back up the stairs.

Just five more times up and back (just!) and Garrett could stop. Until tomorrow. If the pain went away by then. Or the cold.

The cold worried him even more than the pain did. A

catcher learned to live with sore legs the way a housewife learned to live with rough hands—if they didn't hurt, you weren't doing the job right.

Besides, nothing Garrett would ever feel could be worse than the pain he'd suffered when the slugs from the Red Chinese soldier's Russian-made machine gun tore through the flesh and bone just below his knees.

In a way he'd been lucky. Two inches higher and he'd have been a hopeless cripple for life. The closest he could have come to baseball then would have been when they pushed his wheelchair close to the railing by the Yankee dugout so all the fans could clap for him between games of the doubleheader on Memorial Day.

All right, then, Garrett could still walk. He could also run, for short distances, at least; make love as well as he ever could; and even (God knew) climb stairs.

But his feet got cold. Frequently. And that meant the doctors were right. They'd told Garrett just before he was discharged from the army hospital (and, simultaneously, the army itself) that he'd suffered nerve damage and circulatory damage. He would have some discomfort, but, "Corporal, we want to assure you you've sustained absolutely no injury that could prevent you from leading a perfectly normal life."

Garrett had snorted in the doctor's face. He would have snorted again now, but he didn't have enough breath.

Russ Garrett didn't *want* a normal life; wasn't about to settle for one. Russ Garrett was going to be a major-league ball player.

Top of the stairs. Plant the foot. Turn. Do the knees feel strong? Better than they were? Well, don't worry about it. Down the stairs again.

It was easier going down the stairs than it was to climb them, and not just because of gravity. Going up, all he could see were stairs, seats, exit signs, and a few early-bird fans. And a wall, the one he sometimes felt he might as well be beating his head against. The one he sometimes felt he *had* been beating his head against since he broke up with Annie and dropped out of Columbia.

But going down the stairs he could just lift his head and see the whole thing over the rim of the mezzanine. Yankee

Stadium, the House That Ruth Built. The bleachers, with the scoreboard towering on stilts above them, its red-white-and-blue Uncle Sam hat symbol telling amnesiacs and little green men from outer space whose home this was. He could see the elegant, lacy facade that rimmed the stadium roof; once bronze, it had weathered to the same pale green as the Statue of Liberty.

He could see the Bronx over the left center field wall, and the roofs lucky tenants could sit on to watch ball games for free.

Looking down, he could see the ball field itself. A thing of beauty, impossibly green, with the rich brown dirt of the diamond cut into it like a symbol of something, a hieroglyph designed for only birds or angels to read.

Goddammit, he *belonged* down there. Sometimes (and Garrett would have died if anyone ever found this out) he'd ease the tedium of training by imagining himself on a bubble-gum card. He'd picture himself, clean-cut and earnest, gazing into the camera from the half-crouch of his batting stance. Or maybe smiling, with his Yankees' hat turned backward, squatting to catch some imaginary fastball.

That part of it didn't take much imagination—the pictures had already been taken a couple of years ago at spring training in St. Petersburg, by the man from the gum company. The photographer, a gruff and garrulous old character who wore incredibly loud flowered shirts, had called Garrett over during wind sprints. Garrett had wanted to kiss him—he'd figured it could only mean that sooner or later he'd make the Yankees. The bubble-gum people didn't need pictures of career minor leaguers.

Of course, that was before Harry Truman had sent him his greetings, and before General MacArthur had sent him a couple of parallels farther north than it was safe to go.

But he'd promised himself he wouldn't brood about the past today. For a change. Right, Garrett? You're not going to brood about the past, are you? Of course not. Flip the card over, that powdery, sweet-smelling bubble-gum card you carry around in your mind. Read about yourself:

RUSSELL ANDREW GARRETT
New York YANKEES catcher/outfield
6'0" 205 lbs. bats—left throws—right
Born—June 30, 1929, Port Chester, New
York Nickname—"RAGS"

Reading along (in his mind), Garrett skimmed over his career record, which consisted of not quite one whole season with the Kansas City Blues, the Yankees' top minor league farm team.

"Along with Mickey Mantle," the fantasy-card read, "'Rags' is counted as a 'can't miss' prospect by the 'Bombers' for either the 1951 or '52 season."

Of course, since this was 1953 (and late August at that) the message was a little outdated. Mantle wasn't a prospect anymore, he was a star—his batting power had pitchers terrorized around the league.

Garrett wondered what his card would say now.

Plant the foot. Spin. Jesus, that one hurt.

Garrett decided he'd do Topps or Fleer a favor and think of some interesting stuff about himself.

"Garrett is a rarity among major leaguers . . ." That's a good start, he thought. He tried to ignore the sick, dull throbbing in his legs. His feet were colder than ever, but sweat covered the rest of him like thin, warm jelly.

". . . A rarity among major leaguers, being both a college graduate and a combat veteran. 'Rags' (the name comes from his initials) left college for a baseball career, but completed his studies in a military hospital—" Garrett stopped for a second, then decided this was reporting, not brooding, and allowed himself to go on. "—hospital after being severely wounded while fighting with United Nations forces during the Korean Confl—"

On the three hundred eighty-seventh step, just before Patti Page could finish the verse, Garrett's right leg gave out, and he fell hard on the concrete steps.

"*Son of a bitch!*" he hissed. His legs were getting worse, not better. He wanted to cry. Next time he'd arrange it so he fell running *down* the stairs. Then he could just roll right through the railing and fall to his death in the lower deck.

Garrett closed his eyes and took a slow, ragged breath. He hauled himself into a seat. It wasn't difficult. Months on crutches had given him arms and shoulders almost as powerful as Mickey Mantle's.

With his hands, he literally lifted his legs and propped them against the rail. He looked at them in the sunlight, felt them as though they were being offered for sale by a dishonest butcher. His head felt hot enough to glow, but his legs were cool under his fingers. It was as though the bullet holes had let in the Korean winter, and nothing was ever going to get it out again.

Well, too bad, he thought. He was suddenly very angry. He'd just have to find a better doctor or think of a better way to get these goddam legs in shape. He couldn't put up with this kind of nonsense—he had to be ready to play ball next spring. Oh, not for the Big Club; of course not there—maybe back in K.C. or farther down in the minors, to get his timing back, and to prove he was as good as ever . . .

Garrett sighed and started groaning quietly to himself. He shook his head slowly from side to side and tried to figure out who the hell he thought he was kidding.

2

Russ Garrett did a lot of his best thinking in the shower. It was a habit he'd gotten into in the minor leagues; what with living in a rooming house or in a cheap hotel with at least one roommate, traveling on crowded buses, playing ball or practicing, the shower was the only place he could count on a little privacy.

So Garrett stood under the hot water and thought.

One thing was becoming obvious—his training program wasn't getting him anything but tired. And he was starting to look foolish. He had his B.A.; he could apply to law school back at Columbia or NYU or maybe Fordham. He'd saved a lot of his army salary; hadn't had much chance to spend it while he was in the hospital. He had all his GI benefits coming, too.

It was costing him practically nothing to live, for the time being. He'd moved back in with his parents when he left the hospital, and it was only after a loud and bitter argument that he'd gotten them to accept even token money for room and board.

He even had a job of sorts—adviser to the Commissioner of Baseball for Veterans' Affairs (minor-league division). Mostly that meant answering letters from guys whose lives and careers had been jerked out from under them by the war. He'd qualified for the job by having been a ball player, by being able to write an effective letter and sound as if he knew what he was talking about on the telephone, and by having nothing better to do. He was his own first successful project.

He'd been able to fix a few men up with jobs or arrange some tryouts with new teams, but Garrett's job was mostly make-work, and he knew it. He didn't like the idea. There were altogether too many people supporting him. He might as well have been a Communist. He laughed at that. A knee buckled; he lost his balance for a second and dropped the soap.

Christ, he thought, I'd better get out of baseball fast.

He'd give it, he decided, one more day. If tomorrow's workout left him as depressed and as beat as today's, he'd have to let it go. Maybe he could tape himself differently, or take a shorter flight of stairs, or a shallower one . . .

Garrett told himself to shut up. He reached for his towel and stepped out of the shower.

No one could do enough for a veteran, especially a wounded one. That was why he had his job, and that was why the Yankees let him use their stadium and the home-team locker room when he worked out—the coaches' room, actually. Still, Garrett tried to be out of the way before any of the *real* ball players showed up. When they were around, Garrett felt like an impostor, a gate-crasher. Collins, McDougald, Raschi, Reynolds, Rizzuto—these guys had proven themselves. Garrett might never get the chance to do the same. Besides, he was no longer the same self he had started out to prove.

The first thing he had to do was to stop feeling sorry for

himself. He did that by walking past Yogi Berra's locker. There you go, kid, he told himself. That's an even bigger handicap than cold legs. Yogi is the best damned catcher in the game, and he's likely to play forever. Why knock yourself out for the chance to spend your career on the bench or playing in the American Association or down in Mexico?

He'd keep the dream one more day. It was hard to let go of a dream on a sunny Saturday with a ball game coming up.

Garrett finished buttoning his shirt, then tied his tie—his second favorite one, dark gray, with a discreet red stripe. His first favorite tie happened to be navy and white; the commissioner had cautioned him not to wear it around any baseball-related activity. Navy and white were the Yankees' colors, and Garrett was to do nothing to indicate that the adviser to the Commissioner for Veterans' Affairs (minor-league division) might be partial to the team he still hoped to play for.

There had been a time Garrett had been able to attend baseball games in sport shirts, but no more. That was another reason to quit—if he couldn't be a player, at least he could be an honest fan.

Garrett laughed and shook his head. Who *are* you kidding, you hopeless bullshit artist? You'd watch a game in a suit of armor lined with excelsior. He made sure his tie was straight, put on his jacket (though that wouldn't last long in this heat), and went back out into the stadium to watch batting practice. He wanted to have a few words with Mickey before the game began.

3

David Laird handed in his ticket and entered Yankee Stadium. There were ushers to direct him to his seat, in Section 21, upper deck, first-base side, but Laird knew the way. It was stadium policy to let people in several hours early, because a real die-hard fan liked to sit in the sun and settle gradually into baseball's artificial universe. It took time to reduce the world to a wedge of grass and dirt surrounded by uncomfortable seats, where every event, no matter how bizarre, could be recorded with a few arcane symbols and reduced to statistics.

Then, too, the real baseball fan liked to watch the players warm up, to see if Noren was stinging the ball, to find out how Reynolds's injured shoulder was doing.

The real fan could watch a player run and judge the condition of the field. If the visiting team depended on their base-running speed, the grounds keepers would water down the infield, softening it and slowing the runners down. If the visitors liked to bunt, the groundhogs would bank the foul lines just enough so that a bunt that might otherwise work would roll harmlessly foul.

The real fan noticed things like that, appreciated them, liked to see them.

David Laird was not a real fan.

He'd never really cared much for baseball. Rowing was more to his taste, or had been. It was true that Laird had attended almost all the Yankee home games over the last five weeks or so, but that had been a matter of planning and logistics, not enthusiasm.

Laird had picked Section 21 for several reasons, none of which had to do with his view of the playing field. For one thing, it was relatively deserted during the hours before a game. When he'd originally taken his seat, he'd had only a few loud-mouthed beer drinkers and some fool torturing himself by running up and down stairs to keep him company.

Another reason for choosing Section 21 was that it got a good portion of the afternoon shade. No one had seen David Laird's face in quite a while, any more than he had himself, but there had been a time when that face was well known. Not as famous as Secretary of State Dulles's face, say, or Desi Arnaz's, but David Laird had been recognized on the street more than once. He wanted to be recognized today, but only by one person, and only when he chose the time. Until then he'd keep to the shadows. He'd gotten to be quite good at that.

A third item in Section 21's favor was the excellent view it commanded of the lower-deck box seats, the high-priced accommodations, three dollars each. The seats he'd reserved for the congressman and his party were easily visible. He'd be able to see how well the congressman was following his instructions.

But the fourth reason was the most important. If it weren't for the young vendor, Section 21 could have been paradise itself, but it still would have been useless for his plan.

David Laird looked at his watch. Ten before one. He'd be face to face with his fourth reason in less than a quarter hour.

4

Any time he happened to find himself in New York City (something he tried to avoid as much as possible), Congressman Rex Harwood Simmons (R-Missouri) stayed at a small hotel on East Thirty-ninth Street. He could have stayed in a plush, or more prestigious place—hell, he was on an expense account, wasn't he?—but he didn't give a good goddam about plushness or prestige.

If you asked him, Rex Simmons would inform you that he brought his own prestige with him. As he liked to tell reporters, he bought his suits off the rack, his shoes from J. C. Penney, and his ties from his brother Tad.

No, the Bentley was just a good, solid, American place (something damnation hard to find in New York), and that suited the congressman just fine—he was nothing if he wasn't a good, solid one-hundred-percent genu-wine American.

Simmons also preferred the Bentley because it was the only decently clean big-city hotel (outside of Kansas City, of course) that would take his breakfast order the night before, then wake him next morning with the knock on the door that said it had arrived.

Oh, the Plaza, the Statler, and the rest would *do* it all right, but Rex H. Simmons could tell when some stuck-up frog or spiggoty of a bellboy thought he was being put upon.

Here at the Bentley, though, there was no problem at all. They spoke his language here. They knew that the hunger of Rex Harwood Simmons was nothing to trifle with.

What the congressman didn't know (and was never given the opportunity to find out) was that the hotel's night manager, head cashier, and chef had all belonged to the Communist Party back in the early thirties, when being a Communist had been fashionable. They'd outgrown it years ago, but they were all scared witless that if anything happened to displease the Honorable Gentleman from Missouri, he'd check up on them and have them up before his subcommittee, and they'd soon be unemployed, or worse.

Simmons was dreaming sweet dreams of the consternation the very mention of his name caused at the Kremlin and how he had that bunch of Commie bastards quivering in their fur-lined boots. He liked that dream; dreamed it often.

The knock on the door woke him. Simmons sprang out of bed and stood in his A-shirt and boxer shorts, looking for his pants. He finally found them on the back of a chair, under his jacket. Cheryl must have picked them up and draped them there before she let herself out last night. Simmons grinned. A tiger-woman in the sack, and neat, too. What a doll. He was lucky to have her.

Simmons went to answer the door.

"Here you are, Congressman," the bellhop said. "Hope you like it."

"Sure. Here." He handed over a dime.

The bellhop's face was stone. "Thank you, sir," he said and left. The hell with him, Simmons thought. Am I supposed to make him rich on the taxpayers' money? Besides, the bellhop was never going to be voting in Missouri.

The congressman shed his pants, sat, wolfed down his bacon, eggs, and home fries (crappy ones, if you asked him), then started his morning exercises. Someone had once tried to tell him that so-called "experts" said you should do the exercises *before* you ate. That was the trouble with experts—common sense was too easy for them. If you did the exercises before you put some fuel in your tank, where the hell did you get the strength to finish? Rex Simmons stopped listening to "experts" years ago—half of them, at a charitable estimate, were pink around the edges, anyway.

Fifty push-ups, a hundred straddle hops, and a hundred sit-ups later, the congressman felt great. His muscles bulged under his freckled skin, pumped up with blood from the strenuous work he'd put them to. Sweat gleamed on him; drops of it slid across his scalp and down his neck, unaffected by the bristles of his trademark red-brown crew cut.

Simmons opened the bathroom door and looked in the full-length mirror behind it. He shed his underwear and let it fall wetly to the floor. He stood and admired himself.

He would always be squat and a little bowlegged, but he was still powerful. He grinned and slapped his taut stomach. An American had a duty to keep himself in shape. It was a disgrace the way some of his colleagues on the Hill had let themselves go to seed. America—and especially those who were to *lead* America during the struggles ahead—couldn't afford to get soft, mentally or physically. A man who was too out of shape to fight the Reds with fists would be the most likely to flinch during a duel of ideas.

Rex Simmons would never flinch. "I'd like to see the son of a bitch who could make me, too," he said aloud as he stepped into the shower.

He was the avenging sword of the American people. He'd visited their wrath on entertainers, and writers, and educators, and government officials. No target was too big. Ask Wilma Bascombe, the actress. Ask David Laird, that pinko college professor. Ask any of the fellow travelers he'd run out of the Interior Department for their communistic plans to deprive American businesses of their right to make use of forests in the Northwest.

Simmons turned around in the shower and let the hot water splash over his back.

Of course, the congressman had to share credit for his previous triumphs. Joe McCarthy and others were working the same territory. But this was his very own.

In a way, it was funny. When he'd first been elected to Congress, Simmons himself had no idea how pervasive Communist influence had become in this country. But the closer you looked, the easier it was to see the network—a web of friendships and family ties, and trips abroad at very suspiciously convenient times, and memberships in (cough, cough) *liberal* organizations. Obvious, devious, and ominous.

They had infiltrated every part of American life—that became more apparent by the day—but they withered under purifying light of investigation.

Already the pink tinge was beginning to fade from show business—things had been fixed so that the traitors and fellow travelers in that neck of the woods would find it hard to find work from now on.

Simmons bent to wash his knees, scrubbing them until they hurt.

But the Red Menace was like athlete's foot—get rid of it one place, and it pops up somewhere else. Now the Reds had moved in on something that would allow them access to the cream of America's young people. They were in sports.

Fungus in sports. *Exactly* like athlete's foot. Simmons liked that one. He smiled. He had to remember to use it in his next speech.

But clever remarks wouldn't make the danger go away. Kids worshipped athletes—what if they were worshipping traitors? What if the coaches, in the schools and the Little Leagues, started slipping some un-American poison into the middle of their pep talks? The kids, eager to learn how to be winners, would soak it right up. Simmons knew how influential a coach could be to a boy. Back when Pa had run off and Ma had started her drinking, it was Coach Steinmark at Central High who had single-handedly kept the young Rex in school. God only knew what might have become of this country if Rex Simmons hadn't finished his education and gone on to the halls of Congress.

The sports people were starting to wake up to the problem. Congressman Simmons had sent the owners of the Cincinnati baseball team a certificate of commendation when they'd changed the name of the club from the "Reds" to the "Redlegs." It was a small thing, sure, but a symbol of a commitment to the bigger fight.

The congressman had always been sports-minded. In '51 he'd protected the reputations of all professional athletes in this country by making sure none of them had been able to duck his fair share of the fighting in Korea, and he'd stuck with that job right up through the shameful surrender the White House had had the nerve to call a truce. Sure, a few had been able to come up with phoney injuries or diseases and fool a draft board or two, but for the most part Americans could rest easy that the athletes they loved weren't going to get special privileges as long as Rex Simmons sat in the House.

Then, last winter, the idea of the sports subcommittee hit him. As he did everything, Simmons had talked the idea over with Tad. Tad had been enthusiastic.

Simmons grinned and shook his head, spraying the door of the shower with drops of water from his crew cut. Leave it to little brother, he thought. Tad had seen the possible political dividends of such an investigation, something that had never crossed Rex's mind. A few words to the right folks on the Hill, and the subcommittee had been in business.

The only trouble was they hadn't been *finding* anything. Oh, sure, the staff had turned up a few half-assed sympathizers in some Ivy League programs, but finding Commies in the Ivy League was about as surprising as finding juice in an orange.

Trouble was, most athletes were too naive to spot a pinko unless he came up and bit them. They were concentrating on the game, striving to excel—which was right, the American way and all that, but it made protecting them from un-American influences a lot more work.

There was pressure to make some progress. Just before the first letter had come into his Kansas City office, Rex had had a conversation with Tad.

"Rex," his brother had said, "we've got to get moving on this sports thing or move on to something else. It's beginning to be embarrassing."

Simmons hadn't liked hearing that. "These things take time, Tad; you know that yourself."

"Of course I do, Rex. It's just that we can't risk jeopardizing the whole destalinization process by making ourselves look foolish with a stalled investigation."

"Hmmm," the congressman mused. "If we only weren't

so damned understaffed . . . Well, I guess we'll just have to do it on our own again. Tell Cheryl to set up a meeting with Mrs. Klimber on . . ." he went to consult his calendar but never got to lift a page.

"Mrs. Klimber won't help us this time, Rex. She's getting impatient, too. She told Cheryl she wasn't sure she was getting her money's worth lately."

The congressman was astounded. "Why, that fat old bitch! Just who the hell does she think she is?"

"Dam-dam-dammit, Rex!" Tad had a tendency to stammer when he got worked up. It was the only thing that kept him from running for office himself.

Tad was worked up at the moment because he knew exactly who Mrs. Klimber thought she was, and he knew Rex knew it, too. Mrs. Klimber was the congressman's secret sponsor. Her husband had accumulated some ridiculous number of millions during World War Two by manufacturing the nuts that held the propellers on airplanes. He died in 1947 upon hearing the news that his only son had been slaughtered by Communist Huk rebels in the Philippines.

Mrs. Klimber had inherited both her husband's fortune and his blazing hatred of Communists. She'd been more than willing to underwrite the campaign of a young man who felt the same way. And since they were doing the Lord's work, so to speak, she saw nothing wrong with continuing to support him *after* the election, either with money or with the services of the more-or-less-legal information-gathering system her husband had put together during the war. He'd built it to guard his manufacturing secrets both from enemy agents and from the rest of the industry. Wartime cooperation was all well and good, but the war wasn't going to last for ever, and after that it would be every man for himself. Of course, if Mr. Klimber's agents *happened* to uncover a secret or two that belonged to somebody else, he wasn't going to complain.

The little spy network was good for finding Commies, too. Mrs. Klimber always said her husband would have been pleased at the use Congressman Simmons had made of it. She was disappointed at Tad's insistence that the organization's tie to his brother remain secret but went along because he said it worked more effectively that way.

But it made her impatient.

Tad didn't have to tell his brother any of this—all he'd had to say was, "Come on, Rex. We still need her." The congressman had gotten the message. He didn't have quite enough power *yet* to do without Mrs. Klimber. But it was coming.

The letter would do it. He was sure of it; he had an infallible nose, and that nondescript little envelope had the smell of Fate. The letter had hinted at great secrets to be revealed, linking "someone who is a switch-hitter in his politics as well as in his playing" to un-American activities in baseball.

Simmons soaped his chest and prayed it was true. He'd love to nail that draft-dodging son of a bitch.

A later letter contained four tickets to a ball game (three together in a field-level box and a single in the upper deck) and a plan for a safe meeting, isolated in the midst of thousands, to exchange the evidence for one thousand dollars of Mrs. Klimber's money.

Then he'd shake this country up a little, by God. He'd hold hearings as soon as Congress reconvened. Maybe sooner, if he could convince Eisenhower to call a special session. Get the hearings on television, too. He'd tell Tad to arrange it. It shouldn't be too hard. It would be a great show for the public.

In fact, the public would get a great show even if all they got out of it was a look at Cheryl Tilton. Cheryl was by miles the smartest and best-looking secretary in politics. The best lay, too, but the voters wouldn't learn *that* out on TV. That part of Cheryl was for private times like last night . . .

The Honorable Rex Harwood Simmons blushed through his suds when he became aware of where he'd started washing himself as soon as he thought of last night and Cheryl. Hastily he grabbed the hot-water handle and twisted, standing under a spray that turned first cool, then icy.

He'd been satisfied—and more—last night. He didn't need to do things like that. It was beneath him, and it took away from what he and Cheryl had together. He was going to make it official as soon as possible, though Cheryl didn't know it yet.

Simmons stood under the stinging cold water until his passion cooled. Then he continued to take the icy needles until he could control his shivering.

Finally, happy with himself and clean of purpose, body, and mind, Simmons stepped from the shower ready to face the day.

5

The smartest and best-looking secretary in politics had spent perhaps thirty minutes in her own room in the Bentley that night; just long enough to wash the congressman off her and redo her makeup before sneaking off to his brother's room down the hall. It was something they'd been doing a lot lately. For Tad it was a chance to do his big brother in the eye without the congressman's knowing about it. Tad hated his brother. Cheryl supposed she was the only person who knew that.

It made Tad a whole new person. The first time she'd played this kind of doubleheader, Tad had been a virtual madman, laughing and touching as if he couldn't get enough of it. Forbidden fruit and all that.

Cheryl didn't know what *she* got out of it. She guessed it was the *decadence* of it that she liked. It was sinful, and forbidden, and ostentatiously lewd. It was exciting.

That was the first time. Things did not excite Cheryl Tilton for long. Now sneaking off to Tad was a habit, like the after-sex cigarette smoldering in the bedside ashtray.

". . . Now, to throw a fastball," Tad was saying, "you grip it like this." He reached out a smooth, manicured hand to demonstrate.

Cheryl's voice was icy. "Telford," she began. She knew that the younger Simmons brother hated his nickname—Tad was for kids, in his opinion—and that he put up with it only because his given name was worse.

"Telford," she said, "take your hand off my breast."

Tad grinned at her. Damn him, Cheryl thought, he has a good face for grinning. A fox's face, bright-eyed and sly enough to get the joke everyone else misses.

Tad didn't move his hand. "I thought you wanted to learn something about baseball," he said. "Don't you want to enjoy the game this afternoon?"

Cheryl looked at him. Tad liked games. He laid out his life like a bridge hand or a chess game. There was a family resemblance between the Simmons brothers—features, coloring, things like that—but when it came to attitudes and behavior, they might as well have belonged to different species.

Cheryl was one of Tad's favorite games—he'd been playing with her one way or another ever since the day five years ago when Cheryl had walked into the office of the brand-new congressman, crossed her long legs, and asked him in a silky voice if she might apply for a job as the congressman's secretary.

Tad had told her she might. Cheryl had class, and that was a very important qualification. Congressman Simmons was unpolished and volatile (it wasn't smart to say *crude*); he needed someone cool and smooth to run the office.

Cheryl was cool and smooth, all right, and looked it. She had skin like ivory; hair like jet, cut in the silky dome of a page boy that never seemed anything but perfect; and glittering deep blue eyes.

She'd come to the job with excellent references, even though she was only twenty-five at the time. She'd proven herself to be as competent as she was lovely. She was smart enough to read political angles for herself, and she was willing to use *all* her talents to further the interests of her employer.

It had been inevitable that Congressman Simmons would fall in love with her. And Cheryl had gone along—it made things cozier all the way around, and it increased Cheryl's fringe benefits enormously. It occurred to her sometimes that with the influence she had on Rex, she was, next to Mrs. Klimber, probably the most powerful woman in the United States.

Tad had been delighted to share Cheryl with his

brother—and with anyone else, for that matter. He knew more political power is gained or lost in bed than in all the legislatures in the world.

Besides, Cheryl made it easier to keep an eye on Rex. Rex was ten years older than Tad's thirty-four, but Rex had to be watched. Rex would find something he wanted to believe, embrace it with the zeal of a missionary, then crush anyone or anything that tried to make him believe it wasn't true.

Not that there was anything wrong with that. Hell, Tad thought, it was his brother's number-one political asset. Rex had a special mission: to expose and destroy Commies in this country, wherever they might be found. The country needed Rex to continue his work. Therefore, nothing could be allowed to get him out of office. As far as Rex was concerned, it was exactly that simple. It fell to Tad to think of ways to carry the plan out.

Not that the election part had been much of a worry. Rex was up for his fourth term a year from November, and the voters of his congressional district had sent him back to Washington with bigger majorities every time. There was no reason to think that wasn't going to continue. They might even make it unanimous, if this baseball thing was as big a sensation as it seemed it might be.

Cheryl was talking about baseball.

"Telford, dearest," she said. Lightly she scratched with strawberry-color nails the back of the hand that cupped her breast. "I *never* said I wanted to learn about baseball. I have no interest in that asinine *game* this afternoon. I said I don't know anything about baseball, and I wish I could skip the whole damned thing!"

As she spoke, she caught a piece of skin between the nails of her thumb and middle finger. Then she pinched him, hard.

Tad yowled and put his hand to his mouth, sucking the sore spot. Cheryl shot him a triumphant look, threw the sheet aside, and walked naked to the dressing table, where she stubbed out her cigarette so fiercely she twisted it to shreds.

Tad Simmons wanted to be furious, but as he looked at

her standing naked, angry, and unashamed, all he could notice was how damned sexy she was.

But he was irritated. "How the hell," he demanded, "do you get off acting so damned pro-pro-proprietary over your goddam *bosom* all of a sudden?"

"When I tell you to stop touching me, you'd better do it."

Tad snorted. "A half-hour ago you were begging me to touch you. And telling me where."

Cheryl put on the robe she'd been wearing when she'd crept into the room last night. It was made of a thick, velvety material, the same color as her eyes. She wore it now like armor.

The robe gapped at the chest to show the tops of her small, firm breasts. Cheryl jabbed her pointed red nails against her white chest.

"This is *my* body, Tad," she said. "*Mine.* Alone. I lend it to you; to your brother. I'll use it as a bribe when someone we need can't be reached any other way. But those are *my* decisions. I decide who's going to touch me. And where. And when!

"And I *don't* like," she went on, "being treated like an idiot, or like a . . . a toy!" She stormed out of the room without giving Tad a chance to apologize or even decide if he wanted to.

And *that* was something Tad didn't like. Cheryl was getting a little too big for her lacy britches, no matter how sweetly she filled them. Maybe she'd have to be taught a lesson.

6

Philadelphia was using a lefty pitcher today, so Mantle concentrated on hitting right-handed in batting practice. He'd wait for the pitch to come in, a straight ball, not too fast—this was batting practice, after all, nobody was trying to get anybody out—then the mechanics would take over. He'd take a quick step forward with his left foot and tighten his grip on the bottom of his thirty-five-ounce bat. Then, smoothly, his whole body would participate in shifting his weight to his front foot; thighs, hips, shoulders all gliding forward to build momentum for the instant when those powerful arms would whip the bat around like a war club and send the ball sailing out of sight.

Mantle swung mightily and produced a feeble dribbler down the third-base line. Mantle tightened his lips and kicked the dirt.

Elvin Mantle, Mickey's daddy, always loved baseball. Mickey was named after his father's favorite ball player, Mickey Cochrane, whose real first name was Gordon, but who had been called Mickey because he was Irish.

But Mickey was Mantle's real name, as you could see for yourself, printed right there in black and white on the scorecard you couldn't tell the players without. Mutt Mantle (that was Elvin's nickname) had seen the day when ball players would be platooned, with right-handed batters playing only against left-handed pitchers and vice versa. The idea was each batter would get a better look at the ball. It was getting more and more common in baseball all the time these days.

Mutt Mantle had seen all this coming, so he'd taken a lot of time and trouble to teach his son to switch-hit, to bat with equal skill from either side of the plate. It was supposed to keep Mickey in the lineup.

Tell that to Casey, Mantle thought.

The next practice pitch was low. Mantle lined it to center. Probably be good for a single in the game.

If he got in the game. As Casey kept telling everyone in his inimitable Stengelese, with the Yankees so far out in front, which they were with a nineteen game lead on the rest of the American League, it would be silly to use Mantles (Casey always called him Mantles) except as a pinch-hitter, which he does real good, until his leg, which is always giving him trouble, gets a good chance to heal normal.

All Mickey Mantle knew was that he felt fine and he wanted to play. What was the sense in saving him for the World Series if he was going to be so rusty when he got there he'd strike out every time he came to the plate? Mantle was a free-swinger; he struck out enough as it was. He needed to get in the game.

Mantle was a ball player. That's what he was. As his daddy had known it would be, baseball had been Mickey's ticket out of Commerce, Oklahoma, away from a life of back-breaking, spirit-killing work in the lead mines.

Mickey had already clocked some time in the mines, and he had to admit that swinging a pick through those long, dark days in Blue Mine Number Six had helped develop the powerful arms and shoulders everybody talked about. But Lord, that was no way to spend your *life*.

It was Mickey Mantle's considered belief that the mines had killed his daddy; Elvin Mantle had died last year at the age of thirty-nine. Mickey was twenty-one. He was glad his daddy had gotten a chance to see his son play in the major leagues before he passed on. Maybe he could see him still, from wherever he was.

Mantle bore down, and the next three pitches disappeared into various parts of the stands. One landed in a portion of the upper deck so remote the crowd, which usually oohed or ahhed after a good shot in batting practice, broke into actual cheers.

That'll do it, he thought. Mantle felt good when he was hitting. He started to trot back to the Yankees' dugout.

"Hey, Mick," said a voice.

Mantle saw the owner of the voice leaning over the railing of a field-level box next to the Yankees' dugout. Mantle's face broke into a warm, country-boy grin.

"Rags!" he said and ran to where Russ Garrett waited. They shook hands. "Russ, you old son of a gun. How're they treating you in the commissioner's office?"

Garrett grinned. "Not bad. Mostly they forget I'm there. The only time Mr. Frick notices me is when I do something stupid." Ford C. Frick, a former newspaperman and former president of the National League, was the new Commissioner of Baseball.

A few kids came over with baseballs or scorecards they wanted signed. Mantle signed them while he talked to Garrett.

"Hell, then I don't expect you get noticed too much. Maybe you could never hit a sinker ball for spit, but you always were a smart ball player."

Mantle realized what he'd said, and a worried look replaced his smile. "Not that you ain't still," he added hastily. "How're your legs?"

Garrett shrugged it off; Mantle understood perfectly. Ball players hated to talk about injuries. The worse the injury, the more they hated to talk about it. Mickey was just as glad not to talk about Garrett's legs, to tell the truth. He knew it was dumb, but he felt kind of guilty about them.

"I'm still standing," Garrett said. "How are *your* legs doing? Casey got you in the lineup today?"

"No, dammit, and I'm ready, too."

Garrett made a thoughtful noise. "Maybe," he said, "it's just as well you don't play today."

Mantle scowled and pushed his Yankee cap back on his head with a thumb. "And what the hell is *that* supposed to mean, Rags old pal?"

Garrett grinned at him. "Easy, Greasy," he said. "Mick didn't you hear the radio this morning?"

"No, I slept as late as I could, then came right to the ball park."

"Late night with Whitey and Billy—don't answer that. If the commissioner ever asks me anything about the social life you guys lead, I want to be able to tell him I don't know a thing."

Garrett knew that New York was a very exciting place to a kid like Mantle. It was part nightmare, part wonderland. Let him enjoy it.

"Somebody's coming to the game today," Garrett said.

"Who's that?"

"The honorable gentleman from Missouri."

Mantle couldn't believe it. "That hot dog? That *skunk?*"

Hot dog is baseball slang for someone who goes out of his way to attract attention to himself. *Skunk* was a substitute for the word Mantle actually wanted to say. He'd stifled it because he knew Mr. George Weiss, who ran the Yankees, frowned on players cussing in front of fans, especially kids. It was a shame. *Skunk* didn't come close to describing what Mickey Mantle thought of Congressman Simmons.

Garrett nodded. "That's who it is, all right, and he says—*heads up!*"

Garrett ducked, at the same time grabbing Mantle by the shirt and pulling him out of the way of a screaming line foul off the bat of Irv Noren, who was taking his batting practice now. The ball whistled like a bullet through the space that a split-second earlier had been occupied by Mantle's head.

One of the autograph seekers, a little gap-toothed kid in a Yankees' cap and a striped shirt, raised a baseball glove about half his size and made a catch that would have been worthy of Joe DiMaggio if he hadn't been knocked on his rump by the force of the ball.

Still squeezing the glove around the ball, the kid stood up, crying, and rubbed where it hurt.

"Hey," Mantle said, "don't let Casey catch you rubbin.' Ball players ain't supposed to let on they been hurt."

The kid sniffled and looked at him. "No?"

"Nope. And I can tell you've got the makin's of a hell of—I mean a real fine ball player."

Irv Noren yelled from the batting cage to see if everyone was all right. Garrett reassured him.

Meanwhile Mantle had taken the ball from the kid. "What's your name?" he asked.

"Gary Danziger," the kid said. "What's yours?"

Mantle laughed. "My name is Mickey. Why'd you want my autograph if you didn't know who I was?"

"I knew you were a Yankee. I just followed the other kids."

Mantle took Gary's pen and wrote on the ball. *"To Gary. Nice catch. Don't rub. Best wishes, Mickey Mantle."* He gave the ball and pen back to the boy. "This is so you won't forget who I am."

Gary thanked him and retreated to a distance of about five feet, where he watched Mantle with big round eyes.

Russ Garrett said, "You've made a fan for life. That kid's feet aren't going to touch the ground for a week. Think we ought to tell Irv to watch where he goes firing off his artillery?"

"Irv can't help it," Mantle said. "Besides, he never hit the ball so good before."

Garrett smiled. "You're a lot quicker with the needle these days than you used to be back in Kansas City. And a lot less of an *RA*."

RA stood for Red Ass. It was Stengelese for a player with a bad temper.

"Mine is red," Mantle told Garrett. "When it comes to that Simmons, it's redder than the devil's. What's he want to come here for? I don't need him makin' trouble for me. Why doesn't he go back to Washington and chase Communists the way he's supposed to?"

Garrett told his friend to take it easy. He didn't know about the rest of Mantle's anatomy, but his handsome, boyish face was sure red enough.

The Honorable Rex Harwood Simmons was a memory for Mantle, a bad one from 1951, a year that had held more than its share of bad memories.

Things had started out fine. 'Fifty-one was Mantle's first year with the Yankees. He had shown up at Casey's instructional camp for rookies in Phoenix and tore the place up. He hit baseballs over buildings, and as soon as the Yankee brass decided to move him from shortstop to the outfield, it became apparent that Mantle was going to do something the experts considered almost impossible—jump from Class-C ball right to the major leagues.

The camp was where Mantle had met Russ Garrett. Garrett was trying to do something equally impossible—make like Lou Gehrig and walk off the campus of Columbia University and onto the Yankee roster, talked into the effort by Hal Keating, a former ball player who was now a businessman and a part-time Yankee scout. Garrett had nearly as good a camp as Mantle but failed to make the big club because the Yankees were already stocked with high-quality catchers.

Still, the people in charge were impressed enough to let

Garrett begin his professional baseball career in the triple-A American Association. It boded well for his career.

As Stengel put it, "He'll be wearin' the pinstripes before you know it, as this is a college boy which can hit and also throw the baseball, though he is wild at times throwin' to second, but he can run, which is rare in catchers, and he is smart, and can handle a pitcher, which is the most important thing for a catcher to do, which is why Berra is so great, and besides, like this kid Mantles, he's got what I consider a great-soundin' baseball name."

What that meant when it was all deciphered was that Mantle joined the Yankees and Garrett went to Kansas City.

The pressure of New York on the young boy from Oklahoma was enormous.

New York was too big a jump from the places he'd played ball before; just too damn much bigger than Independence, or Joplin, or Commerce. The fans wanted too much, and they wanted it immediately. Mantle brooded, then lashed out. He was booed.

Then there were the draft problems. Mantle was exempt from the draft; 4-F. He had osteomyelitis, a degenerative bone disease. The disease was in remission, but any one of baseball's constant bumps and injuries could bring it back.

Still, people talked. If he was well enough to play baseball, why wasn't he well enough to go and fight for his country?

Favoritism, they said. Draft dodging.

Rex Simmons did a lot of talking along those lines. The congressman got a lot of mileage out of Mickey Mantle's draft status. He threatened congressional investigations. The Yankees flew Mantle back to Oklahoma for another physical. He was again declared 4-F. The congressman proposed a law that would remove the exemption for osteomyelitis victims who had gone a certain length of time with the disease in remission.

Soon the boos Mantle heard were being mixed with taunts. Draft dodger, they said. Coward.

It was too much. What did they want from him, anyway? As hard as he tried to keep his mind on the game, he still heard the taunts. His play suffered badly.

By June Casey had stopped playing Mantle every day. Soon he didn't use him at all. On July 12 Mantle was sent to Kansas City.

He didn't play so well in Kansas City at first, either. Congressman Simmons would come to the games now. People would cheer for him; he'd bring doctors around, try to get them to say Mantle was faking.

Mantle was ready to quit baseball until his daddy, who'd come up from Commerce to see him play, read him the riot act one night in the hotel.

"I thought I'd raised a man," Elvin Mantle said in disgust. "You're nothing but a baby." He got out his son's suitcase. "Come back and work in the mines."

Mickey was shocked, said he wasn't going to quit that easily. His father clapped him on the back, said he knew all along he'd raised a man. He told his son to go play ball the best he knew how and forget everything else.

So Mickey went out and played ball. He made a shambles of the American Association for the rest of July and August and was called back to the Yanks at the beginning of September.

Not that he ignored his troubles completely. That wouldn't have been human. He talked to people, including Russ Garrett.

Garrett, a little older and, as a city boy and a college boy, a lot more sophisticated, was glad to listen to the miner's son's problems. He became sort of a not-too-big-brother, though he had his troubles, too. Something about a gal—he never got too specific.

Garrett was playing some kind of baseball, too. The rumor got around Mickey and Russ would travel to New York together.

Then Garrett got his draft notice.

He came in from practice and found it waiting for him in the Blues' locker room.

Garrett had been expecting it, but he'd been praying it wouldn't come until he'd at least had a chance to show *some* of what he could do in the big leagues. That wouldn't happen now for two years, unless he got stateside duty or. . . .

It was useless. Frustration led him to make a remark to Mantle, a remark he would have signed away seventy-five points off his lifetime batting average to have back.

"Hey, Mick," Garrett had said, "how do I arrange to get a case of osteomyelitis?"

He had meant nothing by it—it was supposed to be a fatalistic wisecrack to show he could take a tough break like a man.

But in the summer of 1951 Mickey Mantle was laughing at no jokes about osteomyelitis. Especially from guys who called themselves his friends.

Mantle lashed out. "I hope," he told Garrett, "I just hope someday you have to spend your nights worryin' if you're gonna be a cripple when you wake up in the mornin'!" Then he stormed out of the clubhouse.

The next day he was on his way to join the Yankees. Garrett played out the week with the Blues (and the blues), then reported for his army physical.

The next Mantle heard of his old pal Rags, there was a very good chance that he *would* be a cripple.

Of course, that hadn't happened, but everybody but Garrett seemed to know he was through as a ball player, and in a foolish, nagging way Mantle felt guilty about it. He'd jinxed his friend, put a curse on him. And now Garrett was out of the hospital and back around baseball. Mantle had to see him and be reminded. Somehow it only made him feel worse that Rags seemed to hold no hard feelings at all over the incident.

". . . and I don't know what he's up to, Mick," Garrett was saying. "He's got that Reds-in-sports subcommittee, but that's ridiculous. Everybody in baseball is too rich, too independent, or too damn grateful to be a Communist—he can't be here for that."

Mantle nodded. He'd heard Garrett say that before.

"Anyway," Garrett went on, "we know he used to have it in for you—you were the biggest target he could find, the way to get the most newspaper space. Maybe now that he's a *Time* magazine cover boy he'll lay off."

Mantle snorted. "I doubt that," he said.

"Well, for your own good and for the good of the Yankees—for the good of baseball, actually . . ." Garrett grinned. Mr. Frick was always giving orders that started with "For the good of baseball." ". . . For the good of baseball, don't let him get your goat, no matter what he says or does, all right?"

Mantle sighed as he signed the last autograph. "It ain't gonna be easy, Rags. I remember I used to sometimes find myself formin' violent intentions toward that man. I wanted to . . ." Mantle stopped and grinned. "Hear me talkin'. I ain't like that usually, but I get mad just thinkin' about Simmons." He made the congressman's name sound like spitting.

"Take it out on the Athletics," Garrett suggested.

"Okay, Slick, it's a promise. The A's are in for it from me today." After a few seconds he added, "If Casey lets me in the darn game."

"Good enough for me," Garrett said.

"I'll do my best. Take care of yourself, okay, Rags? I mean it."

"Sure, Mick. Thanks." Mantle punched Garrett on the shoulder, then went to do a little running in the outfield to loosen up.

Garrett watched him go, trying not to be jealous. At last he turned to go and saw little Gary Danziger crying quietly against the railing.

"Hey," Garrett said softly. "What's wrong, Champ?"

"I don't remember where my Grandpa is."

Garrett told him not to worry. He took a look at the kid's ticket stub and directed him to his seat.

7

Cheryl Tilton never got a thrill out of the way men looked at her. They looked; she went about her business. That was it, unless she happened to feel like doing a little looking herself.

Right now, though, she wouldn't have noticed if Jeff Chandler walked by, or even Rock Hudson. She was too angry at the raucous beer-swilling louts who were making idiotic remarks as she passed among them.

There were so many other things she could have been doing. She could have been shopping at Bloomingdale's or Lord and Taylor. All the stores in New York were staying open Saturdays during the summer—Cheryl could have been bringing her wardrobe up to date in air-conditioned comfort instead of sitting in the broiling sunshine wearing the last outfit she hadn't mortgaged to a cleaner.

She was wearing what she usually wore at the office— white silk blouse, close-fitting dark gray skirt, and pearls. As a concession to the sun (which would probably burn her fair skin to a cinder), she had on her dark glasses.

Tad had warned her to wear flat-sole shoes, but she'd been too angry to listen to him. Now she was trying to negotiate the concrete stairs in spike-heeled pumps. It wouldn't have been so bad if the steps had all been the same width, but every fourth or fifth one would be a new landing, which she'd have to stretch a leg to clear. This inevitably caused her skirt to ride up, giving anyone who happened to be looking her way a quick glimpse of soft thigh wrapped in shimmering nylon.

A lot of men happened to be looking her way; it became a sort of game. The men would whistle every time Cheryl's skirt rose. Click, click, click, and all together, boys, whistle. A consensus arose that after the brunet with the legs, the game was likely to be an anticlimax.

Cheryl was angry and tried walking faster so she could escape these animals. It was a mistake. She stumbled, and her tight skirt rode up her legs. This really gave the boys a show. Cheryl fumed. Rex Simmons sprang to her aid. "Cheryl, are you all right?"

"She's all right," Tad said between his teeth. "Pull yourself together, Cheryl, before the photographers notice you."

That amused the congressman. "Heh, heh. That's right, Cheryl. We don't want the New York *Mirror* damaging my dignity."

Tad said, "Let's go. The game is about to start." Cheryl,

even through her anger, wondered how he knew that. There wasn't a player to be seen on the field.

Eager as an eight-year-old, the congressman scurried to be in place before "The Star-Spangled Banner" started. Cheryl and Tad lagged behind. Baby Brother leaned forward and grumbled into the secretary's hairdo where he figured her ear might be. "Next time I give you advice about what to wear, maybe you'll listen."

Cheryl ignored him, but she'd heard him fine. Cheryl had had about enough. Working for the Simmons brothers had been exciting at first. They'd raised a demon for the public, then ridden its scaly back to power. But now she knew that they were too small, too petty, too unimaginative to expand their influence or even to hang onto what they had.

Oh, Tad had possibilities, maybe, but he was hopelessly loyal to his brother; and Rex was just plain hopeless. The boys had gotten lucky for a while, but Cheryl was tired of watching them try to figure out what to do next.

Cheryl planned her future while she sang the national anthem. She had experience now. She knew people. She'd be able to pick a likely winner out of the Washington dogfight. Somebody with teeth. Somebody who knew what he wanted more than two days in advance.

Sure, she thought, I can think of a candidate already. He's got his father's money and ambition behind him, and he's just gotten married to that thin-blooded heiress. Damned attractive, too. Cheryl would look him up, find out if marriage had changed his love life any, though she doubted it had. Find out if there was an opening on his staff. If not, it didn't really matter. She'd find a job with *somebody*. But she was going to shed herself of these no-class Simmons boys as soon as she got back to D.C. Cheryl sang the last four bars of the anthem with a smile on her face. By the time the umpire shouted "Play ball," she was positively beaming.

8

It was a long game but an eventful one. To say the least. Russ Garrett watched from the official scorer's booth in the press box, on the rim of the second deck behind home plate. The scorer that day was a sportswriter from the *World, Telegram & Sun*. The American League paid sportswriters a few extra bucks to score games, and the reporters were usually glad to get them. Garrett was forbidden to sit in the stands and root for the Yankees the way he wanted to, so he shared the booth with his fellow employee of the baseball administration.

When he leaned back in his folding chair and touched his head to the partition, Garrett could hear the smooth Alabama tones of Mel Allen drifting across from another part of the press box. Mel always sounded as though he could talk about baseball forever and do it so well you'd want to listen just as long.

The Yankees started the scoring, picking up two cheap runs in the bottom of the first inning on two walks and a pop fly a fielder lost in the sun.

Garrett was pleased but not surprised. The Yanks were champs, the Athletics near the bottom of the standings, and this sort of thing was to be expected. The majority of the 31,647 fans felt the same way. Some were less pleased—the transplanted Philadelphians, for example. Or the Yankee-haters.

There was always a significant number of people who'd pay for a ticket to a ball game hoping to see the Yankees get beat. They claimed the New York team was arrogant or that it was boring to see the same team win the World Series four year in a row (as the Yankees had), or possibly five (as they showed every sign of being capable of doing this year).

Liberals often rooted against the Yankees. Five years ago Jackie Robinson had joined the Yankees' perennial rivals, the Brooklyn Dodgers, to become the first Negro to play in the major leagues. By now most teams had realized that most fans, no matter how prejudiced they might be in everyday life, became color-blind when someone wearing the home colors could pitch like Satchel Paige or hit, run, and field like Willie Mays.

But the Yankees kept playing (and, more maddeningly, *winning*) with a lily-white lineup. They had bowed to pressure sufficiently to have some colored players on their

Kansas City team. Congressman Rex Simmons had seen them play.

About the fourth inning the congressman reflected it might not be a bad move by the Yankees to call one or two of them up. They could run like watermelon thieves; one thing about those boys, they were fast. He was thinking about this because the Athletics had just tied the game on a run that scored all the way from first on a single to left center. Okay, it was the deepest part of the park, but that run never would have happened if DiMaggio were still out there. Or even that draft dodger, Mantle.

The Yankee pitcher walked the next two men, then hung a curveball to Gus Zernial, who proceeded to park it in the upper deck for a home run.

The congressman turned to his companions. "Seems Ford just doesn't have it today."

Cheryl said nothing; Tad said, "Right, Rex."

Tad looked at Cheryl's impassive features, then at the Band-Aid on the back at his hand. The little bitch had drawn his blood. If it got infected, he promised himself he'd have her taken out and shot. Finally he thought, to hell with her. He had more important things to worry about. Like what Mrs. Klimber might be up to. He hadn't liked the sound of her voice the last time they'd spoken.

Mrs. Klimber *had* expressed impatience with the progress of the Sports Subcommittee's investigation, just as Tad had told his brother. What he hadn't told Rex was how the widow had gone on to smile that horrible motherly smile of hers and tell Tad not to worry, something would happen very soon.

When Tad asked her what that was supposed to mean, she'd grinned a grin that pulled her chins back even farther and said Tad and Rex were too busy to worry over things like that.

Tad shook his head. The last time Mrs. Klimber had made a similar promise, Tad wound up having to help cook up evidence that ruined the reputations of six (as far as Tad could tell) perfectly innocent persons, one of whom, a college professor, committed suicide shortly after the hearings.

Tad had to admit, though, that it was a masterpiece of political drama. The public ate it up. The six *looked* as red as ketchup, and Rex came across as a hero saving America yet again.

Rex had never known they weren't really card-carrying Communists.

Sometimes Tad didn't know who was worse, Mrs. Klimber or that big buck nigger she kept around to do the dirty work, a fellow by the name of Gennarro Kennedy. He had been an army buddy of Mrs. Klimber's son. He'd come to pay his condolences one day and had just sort of stayed around. Mrs. Klimber had the money and the spy network, but it was Kennedy who had the brains to make them work.

It was Tad Simmons's opinion that if he weren't a Negro, Gennarro Kennedy could be President, or a millionaire, or whatever he wanted. Hell, for all Tad knew, he *was* a millionaire. He could probably get whatever he wanted out of the old lady.

Not a drop of white blood in him, either. His skin was like pencil lead, his nose was flat, and his hair was like tight little springs hugging close to his head. He was six feet two inches tall and weighed two hundred and fifteen perfectly toned pounds. He had imagination, daring, and ruthlessness. Tad would be a lot less nervous about angering Mrs. Klimber if she didn't have the brain and body of Gennarro Kennedy to unleash on those who did.

He tried to put it out of his mind. Instead he tried to figure out what was wrong with Rex. Rex was in an aisle seat, a first. Sitting on the aisle meant Rex had to be the one to call vendors for hot dogs and beer. It meant Rex had to handle money, had to watch out for people walking by slopping things on him. Rex normally demanded to be protected from things like that—they were beneath his dignity.

It was all pretty remarkable. Even Cheryl had come out of her snit long enough to comment on it.

9

The Yankees scored a run in the bottom of the sixth but still trailed by two when the inning ended. It wasn't that they hadn't had their chances. Russ Garrett took a peek at the scorekeeper's card and saw they'd left nine men on base already. He groaned.

David Laird, sitting quietly in his seat in Section 21, had no idea the Yankees had stranded nine men. He didn't care, wasn't even watching the game. The reactions of people around him gave him a vague awareness the home team was behind, but that was all.

Laird was watching Salvatore Vitiello. Salvatore Vitiello worked in his uncle's liquor store on East Tremont Avenue in the Bronx. Salvatore's uncle was a kindly man, understanding about most things—for example, he had no comprehension of baseball, but he indulged his nephew's passion for it. He himself was a dedicated supporter of Inter-Milano in the Italian Football League. Consequently, Salvatore was let off work in the liquor store to pursue a second career—hot-dog butcher at Yankee Stadium.

A hot-dog butcher has nothing to do with the manufacture of the sausage itself; any vendor who roams among the crowd at a sporting or entertainment event is called a butcher. A candy butcher sells candy, a hot-dog butcher sells hot dogs.

Except for the fact that he hated the baggy white uniform and silly paper-and-cheesecloth hat he had to wear, being a hot-dog butcher was an ideal job for Salvatore Vitiello. Not only did it give him a chance to see all the Yankee games (over his shoulder, sure, but at least it was free), it gave him a chance to practice his projection.

He was doing it now. "Getcha red-red-red-red *hot* dogs here!" Beautiful. You could hear it over a tidal wave. The maestro would be pleased. Because, in addition to being a liquor-store clerk and a hot-dog butcher, Salvatore Vitiello was in training to become the finest operatic tenor New York

City had ever produced. His uncle said so, and more important, so did his teacher.

Section 21 was part of Salvatore Vitiello's territory. The young vendor was the fourth reason David Laird had chosen the seat he now occupied.

10

It had been the original murder, the murder David Laird was *supposed* to be committing, that had led him to Yankee Stadium in the first place. He hadn't had anything special in mind, just going through the motions in case anyone had been monitoring him. (He was sure now that no one was.)

Once he'd sat through a few games, though, it had dawned on Laird what a wonderful place a ball park would be for an assassination—provided, of course, the assassin had anything like a brain in his head. Laird had no worries on that score. He had a brain—it was, in fact, nearly all he had left.

So he had started thinking, way back in July when the matter had first come up. He'd gone to every Yankee game at the stadium until he was sure he'd gotten a look at all the vendors. As soon as he saw Salvatore Vitiello, with his medium build, high cheekbones, square jaw, and sandy hair, Laird knew he didn't have to look any farther.

Laird studied the young man. He watched his routine; where he went to get his frankfurters, and when. He watched the way the young man moved. He learned his name. He listened to his voice. Vitiello had a marvelous voice.

David Laird was confident the impersonation would carry if he avoided situations where he had to speak. Laird's voice wasn't what it once was, and it had *never* been likely to be mistaken for an opera singer's.

It didn't matter. The masquerade wouldn't last too long.

It was time to begin.

One thing Laird had learned over the course of the summer was that fans bought hot dogs and peanuts and the rest much more slowly during an exciting game than during a dull one.

Apparently this game was very exciting. Laird's target

had gone off for a refill just twice since he'd started selling, unless he'd made a trip during the time Laird had slipped out to attend to a closet door in the corridor. Even so, if Vitiello didn't leave the stands soon, Laird would have to try to force the issue.

Laird could feel himself starting to panic. He realized suddenly that he had no idea of how he might force the vendor to do anything. The pains returned to his head. He pressed his hands to his forehead to squeeze them out. He cursed himself, told himself to think.

He could buy out the vendor's stock. He . . . he could say it was his birthday, and he was going to treat everyone in his section to a frankfurter.

But that would call attention to him. It didn't matter if people remembered him afterward—it was part of the plan, in fact, that they should—but he had to remain unnoticed until the job was done.

Maybe he could tell the vendor there was an urgent message for him—no, that wouldn't work, either. Fool. It was inexcusable not to have learned more about the boy than just his name. That kind of careless stupidity deserved to fail.

Laird pressed harder against the pain and almost told himself aloud to shut up. He wasn't going to fail!

He thought of bribing a stranger to use the birthday ploy for him, but that would be as bad as doing it himself—the stranger would have too much reason to notice him. Laird didn't want to have to kill a total stranger . . . But still, he was not going to waste months of preparation (to say nothing of the murder he'd already committed) because people weren't buying enough frankfurters!

Then all the worry suddenly became unnecessary. Vitiello was in the act of selling his last two frankfurters to a teenage couple who, apparently, could not exist if their heads were to stop touching. Laird had been so close to panic, he'd nearly missed seeing it.

Vitiello completed the sale and headed up the aisle. Laird closed his eyes and counted to five while he gathered his resolve. Then he left his seat and followed.

The walkways around the rim of the second deck were

quiet but not deserted—there were always people making their way to or from the rest rooms or souvenir stands. Laird had foreseen that and had decided not to let it worry him. He had to time his attack to take place just outside the door of the broom closet, the door he'd gimmicked earlier. He stopped at it briefly, placing his travel bag inside. Laird wanted to have both hands free for what was coming.

Salvatore Vitiello reached the concessionaire's kitchen, handed in his receipts, and filled his basket with more frankfurters, buns, and mustard. "Well, let me head on back to the stands," Laird heard him say. "There's still a few bucks to be made."

Laird waited outside the door. When Vitiello emerged, Laird made a fist around a roll of nickels and followed the vendor, much more closely this time. About five paces before Vitiello would reach the broom closet, Laird darted forward and tapped the young man on the shoulder. Things were perfect—no people were around. Laird didn't think they would have noticed if they had been, since people tended to be preoccupied with getting back to their seats and not missing any of the game. Still, it was better this way.

"Excuse me," Laird said. His voice was an ugly rasp.

"Yeah?" Vitiello said pleasantly. "You want a hot dog?"

Laird nodded, and the young man turned. He put his basket down so he could reach into it more easily. That was when Laird rammed his nickel-filled fist into Vitiello's abdomen. He wanted to incapacitate both Vitiello and his great voice. It would have been safer for Laird to have punched him in the throat, but that would almost certainly have ruptured Vitiello's windpipe, and Laird didn't want anyone to die who didn't deserve to. His research had shown that the blow to the belly would be sufficient.

Vitiello didn't know what had happened to him. A heart attack, he thought, with that tiny portion of his brain not filled with pain or fear or the desire to breathe. His eyes bugged out. He choked. He began to sink to his knees.

Laird worked quickly. He caught Vitiello under the arms and dragged him into the broom closet. Working in the dark with hands made skillful by practice, Laird bound and gagged the vendor. When he was sure the knots were tight enough, he grabbed Vitiello's belt buckle and pulled it slowly and firmly to get him breathing again.

After three or four tugs Laird heard air hissing into the young man's nostrils. A few more; Laird stopped tugging, and Vitiello kept breathing on his own.

Laird smiled. Things were working well.

Quickly he found his travel bag. He took out shirt and pants of food-service white, just like Vitiello's. He stripped off his regular clothes, stuffed them in the bag and put on the whites.

Then he took out the .22. He checked to see if the silencer was still firmly attached. He opened the basket and placed the weapon gently among the frankfurter buns. Finally he took the paper-and-cheesecloth cap off the young man's head and placed it on his own.

Then, this time without even bothering to listen for footsteps on the concourse (why *shouldn't* a stadium employee be coming out of one of those doors?), David Laird stepped out of the broom closet and went to attend to his butchering in Section 21.

11

Congressman Rex Harwood Simmons astounded Tad and Cheryl by leaving his seat as Philadelphia came to bat in the eighth inning.

"I should be back before the game ends," he told them. "Wait here for me if I'm not."

"Where are you going?" his brother demanded.

The congressman gave him a knowing smile. "Not far, Tad. I'm just going to get some evidence."

"What are you talking about?"

"You remember the letter we got, don't you?"

"There was a letter hinting someone you and Tad apparently could recognize was a Red, but that's all I remember it saying. There was supposed to be another letter."

The congressman was grinning so hard he could barely

move his lips to shape words. "There was," he said. "I happened to get to it first. I thought it best to keep it to myself. For security. It's not that I don't trust Cheryl and you—"

"Bullshit, Rex!" Tad snapped. "You want to have another of your comic-book adventures, that's all. This could be a trap, dammit. Now sit down and watch the game."

Congressman Simmons frowned stubbornly at his brother. "No. I'm going."

"Goddammit!" Tad exploded. A fan a few rows back requested that he shut his foul mouth.

Tad spoke more quietly, but not much. "All right, let's go and get this idiocy over with."

Again the congressman told him, "No. The letter said I had to be alone."

Tad forced himself to be patient. "Rex—" he began.

His brother cut him off. "I *know* there's a risk involved, Tad. But it's important to my work; to our country." The congressman squared his shoulders. "I'm ready to take a risk for the good of my country." He turned and started to go.

Tad was upset. "Cheryl, he'll listen to you. For God's sake talk him out of this. There'll probably be no one there but a photographer from the leftist press waiting to take a picture so they can laugh at how they fooled the great Rex Simmons."

The congressman hesitated.

"Cheryl," Tad said, "tell him, all right?"

Cheryl took off her dark glasses and looked with soft eyes in the congressman's face. "I wouldn't dream," she said, "of questioning Rex's judgment."

"That's the spirit!" Rex Simmons said. "If you want to help me, Tad, watch me as I leave and see nobody follows me. I don't want my man scared off." He strode up the stairs, looking exactly like a man with a mission.

Tad sat down angrily. To hell with him. Let him make a fool of himself. He couldn't trust anybody today.

"Thanks a lot, Cheryl," he said. "That's *two* you've got coming."

Cheryl took some paraphernalia from her bag and placed it on Rex's now-empty seat. She began doing her nails.

12

The pace of Congressman Simmons's climb to the second deck proved the value of his morning exercises. He was in the reserved seat the second letter had directed him to before the first Philadelphia player was retired; struck out by Allie Reynolds, who was pitching in relief of Whitey Ford. Rex had his breath back before the player had sat down in the dugout.

In a short time he'd have what he needed to fire up his hearings. Carefully he examined the people in the seats around him, trying to decide which of them might be his correspondent.

He had an aisle seat, so there was no one to his left. There was no one, in fact, anywhere around him. Rex figured the person he was meeting had bought a block of tickets so that their meeting could take place with a certain amount of privacy. The congressman approved.

Simmons's closest neighbor, on this side of the aisle, at least, was a kid about five years old. The kid wore a striped polo shirt and a Yankee cap. He was sitting with a paunchy, balding guy who chewed a fat, wet cigar and who was too tolerant of the kid's demands for food and souvenirs to be anything but his grandfather. That was one spoiled kid. Rex would have belted him one long before now if he were in charge.

The next two Philadelphia players grounded out to Rizzuto at short, and the congressman was starting to get annoyed. He'd expected the transaction to be over with by now. Tad was going to be unbearable if this turned out to be a hoax.

Meanwhile vendors went by. The kid wanted another cotton candy; the bald guy bought him a cotton candy. The kid wanted a Coke; the bald guy bought him a Coke. The kid wanted popcorn; the bald guy said, "Gary, you're gonna *explode!*" but he bought him popcorn.

The only thing the boy wanted that he couldn't get was a hot dog.

"Lookit," the grandfather said patiently, "the hot-dog guy ain't here now—he's over there a ways, see him?"

The kid stood up on his seat to look. Simmons noticed the kid wore a fielder's glove and held a ball tightly in it. "Hey, come here, hot-dog man!" the kid piped up.

"That won't do no good, Champ," the bald man said around his cigar. "He's too far away. The people in them seats got to get their hot dogs, too. I'll call him soon as he comes close enough. Okay?"

The kid looked suspicious, but he decided it was okay.

The bald man was happy. His smile seemed to say, see, kids can learn; all you got to do is be patient and reason with them.

He said to the boy, "Good for you, Champ, because— *run, you dago bastard!*"

The boy jumped; so did Congressman Simmons.

The yells had been directed toward the field, at Yankee shortstop Phil Rizzuto, who led off the bottom of the eighth for the Yankees. The Scooter's throwing arm might have been shot, and he might have lost a few steps off the speed that had earned him his nickname, but he was still the best bunter in baseball.

Rizzuto was now chugging down to first after executing a perfect push bunt. He'd placed the ball so precisely the pitcher and first baseman could do nothing but watch the ball dribble along the ground, just out of reach of both.

There were some stirrings among the crowd, the first in several innings. Charlie Keller pinch-hit for the next batter and drilled a single to right. Rizzuto went to third on the play.

The crowd started to buzz. Simmons became involved in the game and almost forgot his original mission. The bald man started yelling for the hot-dog man, though he really didn't have to. The vendor seemed to be heading in that direction in any case.

Down on the field Mickey Mantle walked out of the

Yankee dugout, swinging two bats. The crowd let Casey know it approved. Mantle was pinch-hitting for Reynolds. Reynolds was an excellent hitter for a pitcher, but Mantle could put the home team ahead with one swing of the bat.

Mantle had to wait while Philadelphia made a pitching change. The Athletics brought in Alex Kelner, their best reliever. Kelner was a lefty; Mantle would be batting right-handed against him.

Kelner was ready; Mantle stepped into the batter's box. The noise grew.

In the press box Russ Garrett opened the door of the scorer's booth so he could hear Mel Allen's play by play better.

" . . . bottom of the eighth, Yankees trail by two runs. The Bombers are hoping for a little of the old five o'clock lightning, with Mickey Mantle at the plate . . ."

Garrett looked at his watch. *Five o'clock lightning* was sportswriters' shorthand for the way the Yankees would storm back to win with late-inning rallies capped by dramatic home runs. The five o'clock part, though, was usually poetic license. Most games started at two in the afternoon, so the lightning, if it came, usually struck around four thirty or so.

The game today had been a slow one. It was four forty-seven by Garrett's watch. Close enough, he figured.

He watched Mantle take a prodigious swing at a Kelner curveball and miss.

Back in Section 21 the kid finally had his hot dog. The vendor left him and turned to the Honorable Rex Harwood Simmons.

13

David Laird said, "Hello, Congressman. Do you remember me?" He raised his head, letting Simmons see his face. His smiling face.

Simmons moved his lips.

"I can see you do," Laird told him. "Don't say anything: just listen." He lifted a white rag he had draped over his hand

and arm and showed the congressman his gun. He replaced the rag.

Simmons was too confused to follow instructions. "Wha—what are you doing here?"

Oh, this is wonderful, Laird thought; better than I expected.

The crowd was screaming now with every pitch. Mickey Mantle took a change-up low for a ball.

"Put that gun awa-awa-away." Good God, he was stammering! He'd never done it before in his life. *Tad* was the stammerer, he wasn't. "Put that gun away," he said again. Much better. "You can't—all these people—nobody could—"

"They're watching the game. They're cheering. They don't see us now; don't even hear us. Look around you."

Simmons did. Laird waited while his predicament sank in. Two men, literally having to scream to be heard by each other, invisible. They could have turned into beef cows and no one would notice, unless they happened to be blocking someone's view.

"You're surrounded by thousands of people, Congressman," Laird shouted. "But you're all alone. Just the way I was. Anyone who does see us will think you're buying a frankfurter. No one can help you. Just as no one could help me."

Simmons had trouble breathing. This couldn't be happening. He wouldn't let it. The noise was incredible: it filled his whole mind. Besides, it was impossible, because, dammit, Laird was—

He screamed it at his tormentor. *"You're dead!"*

Mantle got a fastball, waist high. He strode into it and whipped the bat forward. There was a loud crack, and the ball took off like a jet plane.

The congressman's scream was lost in the roar of the crowd, but David Laird had read his lips. Laird had been hoping Simmons would say that, that he would be trite and traditional to the very end. This made it a perfect day.

"No, Congressman," he replied as the excitement around him grew. "Not *me*."

With a quick push Laird knocked the bewildered Simmons back to his seat. Then he placed the muzzle of the gun, still draped in the rag, against Simmons's neck, just where the muscular throat joined the shoulders. He squeezed the trigger.

That ought to do it, Laird thought. Lots of important organs in that bullet's path. Lungs. Heart. Stomach. Intestine. Maybe even the liver or a kidney, with luck. Still, you never knew. He moved the muzzle a few inches, reset the automatic's mechanism, and fired again.

A short way around the curve of the stadium, Mel Allen went into his patented home run call. " . . . going, going, that ball is . . . *gone!* Into the upper deck, in left field. A Ballantine Blast for Mickey Mantle . . . Rizzuto scores . . . Here comes Charlie Keller around to score . . . and here comes Mantle. How *about* that! The Yankees take a five–four lead . . ."

The crowd continued in happy bedlam all the while Mantle trotted around the bases. No one would want a frankfurter for the next minute or so.

David Laird moved quickly. He climbed to the concourse. He stopped briefly at the broom closet. His captive seemed to be fine; that pleased him. He put down the hot-dog hamper, picked up his travel bag, stuffed the gun in with the clothes he'd worn to the stadium, and left. He ignored the angry, muffled sounds Salvatore Vitiello was making behind his gag.

David Laird left Yankee Stadium, reclaimed the car he'd arrived in—a Nash Rambler Airflyte stolen last night especially for this occasion—and struck out across the Bronx.

Chapter Three
Squeeze

1

Johnny Sain came on to pitch the ninth inning for the Yankees. The disheartened A's bowed meekly before him, ending the game with two grounders and a pop foul to Berra.

Berra. Russ Garrett sighed. One more workout and it would be over. Tomorrow one dream would die.

The official scorer had to total up the statistics for the game, and he asked Garrett to please get lost while he did the arithmetic.

Garrett nodded and wandered around the press box. The guys from the morning papers—the *Daily News*, the *Mirror*, the *Times*, the *Journal-American*—were all typing away madly, trying to make deadlines for the bulldog editions of the Sunday papers. The afternoon guys were shooting the breeze—most of their papers didn't publish Sunday, so they wouldn't have to write anything but a weekend wrap-up for the Monday sheet.

Garrett thought about sitting in on the bull session for a while, but he'd been written up once this season, in the *Telegram*, and he felt funny about talking to reporters. A person's innermost secrets and desires sure looked funny written down for the public to gape at.

Garrett slipped into the television booth, where Mel Allen was taking a bottle out of a little icebox and pouring his traditional postgame Ballantine, telling the folks in the audience how great it was going to taste. It sounded like a good idea to Garrett. He made a mental note to stop on the way home for a few beers.

What a pro Allen was, Garrett thought. He could simultaneously recreate the highlights of the game from the hieroglyphics on his scorecard, wink at Garrett, point to a chair for him to sit on, and never miss a beat of the smooth, Dixie-flavored patter for the fans. And all the while the Voice of the Yankees would keep an eye on the small TV monitor on the desk before him. Every now and then Allen would toss off amusing comments about what the ground crew was doing or the antics of the pigeons who liked to stroll about the outfield grass anytime the Yankees weren't using it, or just about anything a cameraman could spot.

There was a honey of a shot on the monitor now. Allen looked up from his scorecard to see a picture of a stocky, middle-aged man sitting all alone in the middle of a dead forest of empty seats in the second deck. The man was slumped down in his chair, looking very drunk and very comfortable.

". . . There's a fan who seems immune to all the excitement," Allen ad-libbed, "and that's something the game had plenty of. Phil Rizzuto led off the bottom of the eighth . . ."

Garrett stopped hearing him. He was concentrating on the monitor. It wasn't that TV was the novelty to Garrett that it was to some people, either. His father had a thriving TV repair shop up in Westchester. It was the picture.

That guy wasn't just drunk. Something was trickling from the corner of his mouth. In the black-and-white picture it looked like motor oil or chocolate syrup. Besides, Garrett thought he recognized him. He just hoped he was wrong.

Garrett bolted from the booth. He didn't care how much noise he made. He scrambled from the press box and looked around the mezzanine. He spotted the fan, still slumped down, sitting in Section 21. Garrett ran to him.

Garrett touched the body, and the red-haired head slipped from its balance on a shoulder and swung back and forth across the man's chest. There were two holes, black-rimmed with centers of dark red at the place where his neck joined his left shoulder. The weight of the moving head opened and closed them like obscene mouths.

Russell Andrew Garrett caught his breath.

This was Simmons, Congressman Rex Simmons, and he was extremely dead—no one in Korea had ever looked as dead as this, and if Garrett wanted a beer, he'd better go get it *now*, because the police would keep him busy for a long time.

2

Siren screaming, removable light flashing, the unmarked car sped along the Grand Concourse.

The driver was a handsome Negro who'd just made detective last July. He was excited, and more nervous than he liked to show. "Ooh, mama! My first VIP murder. And Simmons, no less. Think the FBI is going to try to take the case away from us, Vish—I mean Captain?"

The man in the passenger seat grunted. He adjusted the sun visor to cut down the glare, and when that wasn't enough, tugged the brim of the brown fedora he always wore lower on his forehead. He grunted again.

"If the FBI wants this case, Martin, I want you to promise me something."

The driver swerved to avoid a kid who'd wanted to get a closer look at the car. It figured that when the department finally broke down for a new car, it would be a brand-new Packard that attracted as much attention as an auto show all by its shiny new self. "Damn," Martin said. "Sorry about that Boss. You wanted me to promise something?"

The passenger growled. His name was Aloysius Murphy, and he was a captain of detectives, Bronx Homicide. He had a vast repertoire of grunts, groans, and assorted semi-human noises which he used as other people might use commas and semicolons. The noises were a large part of the reason for the nickname that was used by everyone but his wife: "Vicious."

He had grown resigned to the name. It was his belief that it got him in the newspapers a lot more frequently than he would have been otherwise. The *Mirror*, especially, liked to attribute quotes to "Captain Al 'Vicious Aloysius' Murphy" almost as much as they liked running Cholly Knickerbocker's column or cheesecake pictures on page 3.

"For one thing," Murphy growled, "I want you to knock off that 'Boss' crap. This is a police department, not a goddam plantation."

Dectective Martin grinned.

"For another thing, I want you to promise me, if the FBI wants this goddam case, *let them have it*. Immediately. Don't kick the dirt and say aw shucks. Don't make a face. Just get out. If you don't know the way, just follow me."

"They'll make you an inspector if you solve it."

"Oh, sure. And they'll put me in charge of traffic detail on Staten Island if I step on any toes to do it. Do you know who I talked to on the phone before we left the shop?"

"The commissioner?"

"The mayor. I guess someone woke him up and explained why this was an important case. Look out for the goddam truck."

"I see him," Martin said. "Well, I'm glad I'm not the only one who's edgy about this case."

Murphy snorted and let it go at that. *Edgy* was a pretty feeble word for it. His baby, the mayor had said. The hotshot of Bronx Homicide.

Sure, Vicious Aloysius could deal with crooks and pimps and mob guys, and sure, he had a feel for what to look for when otherwise honest citizens were hiding something, but this wasn't his kind of case.

This was going to be politics, and not at the ward level, either. Communists, for God's sake. And Commie hunters. Murphy didn't know the left or right wing from Raymond Gram Swing. And here he was with the mayor on his back. And soon it would be the papers, and the FBI, and God knew who else.

Hell, for all he knew at this early date, the Russians *had* done it. He could just see himself knocking on the door of the Kremlin, trying to get Stalin—no, Stalin was dead—trying to talk whatever the hell his name was now into giving himself up.

Murphy sighed. His only consolation was that this was Saturday and not Sunday. Sunday afternoon was for opera—he'd either be at the Met with his wife, Alice (a rare treat on a cop's salary), or he'd be home listening to Milton Cross and the Texaco Opera Broadcasts on WQXR or to something by Rossini on his recordings. *Guglielmo Tell*, maybe, the way the brass was expecting him to come on like the Lone Ranger and make an instant arrest.

Murphy was saving five dollars a week to buy one of those new kind of Victrolas, the ones that spun slowly enough to get a whole opera on one record. LP, it was called, or hi-fi, or something like that.

Martin broke into his reverie. "Funny you getting assigned to a murder at a ball game, isn't it?" Murphy was a legend in the NYPD—he had no interest in any sport whatever.

A grunt. "Damn good thing, if you ask me. Simmons was looking for Commies in sports, right? So we'll be talking to lots of these baseball guys. At least I won't spend my time getting autographs for my kids."

Martin grinned again. "Don't look at me: I'm a Giants fan. Now if I had a chance at Willie Mays's autograph—"

"Let's just concentrate on getting the killer's autograph. Preferably at the bottom of a confession. Because nobody's going to get any peace until we do."

"Here we are," Martin said. The siren groaned into silence, and the two policemen left the Packard and walked past a babbling crowd into the stadium. A uniformed patrolman led them to the Yankee offices.

"The witnesses are waiting for you, Captain," the patrolman said.

"Good, good. How many?"

"A few, sir. We're looking for more—we've made a radio appeal. Who would you like to talk to first?"

"Who found the body?"

"Fellow named Garrett. Works for the baseball commissioner's office. He seemed pretty—"

"Yeah, I'm sure he did. Let me talk to this guy Garrett."

3

The first time around with Garrett was uneventful; the police turned to other matters.

A few of the fans heard the radio appeal and returned to the stadium; they gave descriptions of the killer. Also someone had noticed a broken lock on a broom-closet door and discovered the real hot dog vendor trussed up like a Christmas turkey.

Captain Murphy asked Salvatore Vitiello if he could tell him what the assailant looked like.

"Sure," the young man told him. "I got a swell look at him," he said and gave a description.

"That could be you, for crying out loud," Detective Martin said.

Yeah, said some of the other witnesses, folks who'd been sitting in Section 21. It *could* be him. One or two even swore it *was* him, and Vitiello was starting to hint he ought to have a lawyer, but the consensus was that though the resemblance was marked, the killer was at least ten years older than the hot-dog butcher. Murphy was ready to accept that. Besides, Vitiello hadn't smashed himself in the solar plexus and bruised himself like that, or tied himself up, either.

So they put out an all-points bulletin, the full treatment—New York, New Jersey, Connecticut, Pennsylvania. Murphy had Vitiello stand in front of him, then described the young man, adding ten years to his age, and said, "Go and find him." Vitiello said he'd better stay out of sight or the cops would keep picking him up.

Murphy smiled at him. "You're a tenor, huh?"

Vitiello admitted it. He and Vicious Aloysius discussed the coming season at the Met while the other witnesses fidgeted, and Tad Simmons complained in a stammering roar to Murphy's subordinates. Murphy might have to avoid stepping on toes, but he was still in charge of the investigation, and he was going to make sure everybody had that straight from the start.

4

Their names were Olsen and Johnson; some now-forgotten wit in a position of authority with the New Jersey State Police had paired them in a car seven years ago. They were, like their namesakes, a good team. Olsen was bald, with a blond fringe and a soft-skinned baby face. Johnson was swarthy and always looked like his five o'clock shadow had checked in early. Johnson always drove.

They heard the all-points bulletin; noted it, because they were good cops; then went back to their routine duties, patrolling the New Jersey Turnpike between Elizabeth and New Brunswick.

This time of day on a Saturday evening was busy, but nothing like Friday or Sunday at the same time, when everyone seemed to be fleeing or returning to New York en route to or from a weekend in Atlantic City or Cape May. There were a few speeders tonight, a few dangerous lane changes, but mostly things were just dull.

They were talking about *Roman Holiday*, a movie both had seen recently (dragged, they protested, by their wives), and its young star, Audrey Hepburn.

"Did you see her in *Time* magazine?" Olsen wanted to know.

"Yeah. Nice eyes. But I'll tell you one thing—they better not use her in any 3D movies."

"Why not?"

"She's so skinny, nobody could tell it was supposed to be three dimensional."

"Partner, there's other things than boobs."

"Yeah, but my wife don't like me to see movies that show them. Now you take this Marilyn Monroe. *That's* my idea of a movie star."

"Lecher. I'm going to see *Stalag 17* this week whether Marie wants to or—hey, Johnson, look."

Olsen had happened to catch a glimpse of someone in the rearview mirror. For a second he'd wondered why he noticed the guy at all, but a cop developed instincts.

Johnson looked up from the road and checked the mirror. "I'll be damned," he said. "Blond hair, high cheek-bones, square jaw . . . hell, he's even wearing a restaurant-type shirt. Olsen, my boy, can we possibly be so lucky?"

Olsen grinned. "Are you kidding? Twenty minutes after we hear one of these last-ditch APBs out of New York, we spot the guy in a what is that? A '49 Studebaker? In a '49 Studebaker one car behind us and a lane to the right? No such luck."

Johnson suddenly got serious. "There's a '49 Studebaker on the hot sheet. Light blue, I think. Or light green." The car behind them was light green.

"Light green all right. Plate number doesn't match up, but that doesn't mean anything."

"Well," Johnson said, rubbing his stubble. "We've got *two* reasons to pull the fellow over now, haven't we?"

Olsen nodded and hit the switch for the flasher.

5

Laird couldn't stand it. He wasn't speeding. He was driving with deliberate caution. He'd taken care to keep the Studebaker out of sight since he'd stolen it last week in downtown Newark. He had carefully switched from one stolen car to another; cars he'd planted all across the Bronx to make his trail harder to follow. He was cursed. That was all it could be. They were *supposed* to find this car, and all the others. But not yet. Not yet.

He debated making a run for it. The Studebaker had a powerful engine. But so did police cars, especially the ones used by the State Police. He had to find some way to gain time.

The pains started coming back. He made them stop. It wasn't his fault, whatever happened now. It had been forced on him.

David Laird went through the useless charade of pre-tending to be surprised to learn he was the one they wanted to speak to. He pulled the car over, parked on the shoulder.

The police car stopped directly ahead. The passenger-side door opened, and the officer who stepped out seemed so boyish, Laird almost felt he might be able to talk his way out of this.

Then the officer unsnapped his holster.

Laird was ready. He unzipped the bag, removed the gun, yanked off the silencer, and tucked the weapon under him. He rolled down the window.

The policeman walked to the car. "What's the trouble, Officer?" Laird wanted to know.

"May I see your license and registration, please?"

"Surely. I have it right here." Laird took the gun from under him and shot Olsen twice. The policeman fell against the car, then spun crazily as Laird put the car in reverse and pressed the accelerator. When he had enough room to clear the police car, he shifted gears, and the Studebaker shot southward like a rocket.

Even as he passed, he saw the other officer draw his revolver and try to shoot him. When he gave up on that, he'd radio for help and go see to his friend. Or maybe he'd forget to radio for help.

It wouldn't matter. Within the next two miles David Laird would vanish from the face of the earth.

6

Johnson's reactions were sheer instinct. He ran to his partner. Olsen was bleeding but conscious.

"I'm fine," Olsen said. "Go get him."

"Are you all right?" Johnson asked. "I've called an ambulance."

"I'm fine," Olsen said again, "but I'll feel a hell of a lot better if you *catch* that bastard!"

"Right," Johnson said. "You just wait for the ambulance."

"I've got two fucking bullets in me, I swear I won't go anywhere. Move, goddammit!"

Johnson moved. Ignition. Lights. Siren. Hit the gas. The bastard would be caught, or Johnson would be very angry.

There was no way, Johnson reflected, that the Studebaker could get off the turnpike—by now his radio call would have brought men to every exit gate between here and whatever point a roadblock could be set up. The man in white would have troopers in front of him and more stationed anywhere he tried to get off the road. And he had Bob Johnson, in person, driving right up his ass.

The police car flew past trees and oil refineries. Signs went by too fast for Johnson to read more than a few words, but there was a rest area coming up. Johnson laughed. *He'd* give somebody a rest.

There it was now, the long, looping driveway that led to the combination diner-gas station building designed to save people the trouble of leaving the highway to eat or fill up. Or go to the bathroom, for that matter.

The Studebaker was just entering the drive. Johnson couldn't believe it. This guy shoots a cop, then stops off to take a leak? Johnson touched his gun in anticipation, then veered right to chase the suspect.

The man in white still had 150 yards or so on the police car, and the curves in the access road caused Johnson to lose sight of his quarry. Johnson hit the gas even harder to get back in eye contact.

He had to slam on the brakes when he did see it. The Studebaker was parked—sitting like a big, green boulder and blocking the drive just around the far side of the restaurant building.

The police car's tires squealed a protest. The car fishtailed, and Johnson fought the wheel to retain control. He came to a stop inches from the Studebaker.

Johnson drew his gun, took cover behind the car door, and ordered the suspect to come out with his hands up. Some people came out of the restaurant, a man and a woman. The man saw what was happening, gave a hoarse yell, and dragged the woman back inside.

There was no response from the Studebaker. If the gunman were still inside, he had to be hiding down behind the seat, because Johnson could see nothing of him. Johnson reached for the microphone and radioed for more help.

It came in seconds, since reinforcements had already been on the way. Two more cars arrived. The five State Policemen deployed themselves around the Studebaker, covering Johnson, who approached the car.

Johnson used the Studebaker itself for cover, running in a crouch to the rear bumper, than crawling alongside to the front door on the passenger side. Then he stood and aimed through the window, ready to fire.

There was no one in the car. There was a travel bag on the seat that contained some nondescript casual clothes and a .22-caliber target pistol. But the man in white was not there.

Johnson didn't outrank any of the other troopers at the scene, but he gave orders anyway. "You call in, tell all units to be looking for someone on foot. You two check the parking lot—he could be hiding under a car or something. You come with me."

Johnson and the other trooper went inside the diner.

Johnson was no sooner through the door than he saw a figure in restaurant white. He pointed his gun and said, "Don't move!"

There was a loud crash as the figure in white dropped a tray of dirty dishes. He raised his hands and, trembling, turned slowly at a command from Johnson to face him.

Johnson swallowed. It was a kid, with glasses and pimples on his face, and an Adam's apple as big as a walnut. Probably on a summer job.

I almost shot him, for God's sake, Johnson thought. I almost drilled this kid through the back of the head for shooting Olie. Johnson was disgusted with himself. This was a goddam *restaurant*. He'd find a lot of people wearing white.

And he did, too. Johnson, and everybody else from the various police agencies that soon joined him, found a whole lot of people in white clothes. Twice as many, in fact, as they might normally expect to find, because the excitement came to the Samuel Tilden rest area at six P.M., when the shifts were changing.

They found twelve waitresses and four cooks: two Negroes, one woman, and one shriveled old guy with an anchor tattooed on his hairy forearm. They found two dishwashers. The guy from the first shift weighed 350 pounds and was very upset at being kept from his big date; and the other guy had a puckered little mouth and big sad eyes. When anybody asked him a question, he would pull his head out of the cloud of soapy steam from the dishwater, brush some steam- and sweat-darkened spikes of wet brown hair from his forehead, and say in a voice that was more of a croak, "What?" When the question was repeated, he'd say, "I don't know," or "Maybe." They found two busboys, both high-school kids, the one Johnson had scared half to death and a little, dark, curly-haired kid who kept insisting that his uncle was a big shot in the Teamsters, and if they laid a hand on him, they'd regret it until their dying day. The kid seemed almost disappointed no one hit him.

They found only one porter, a Negro, the first-shift guy. Nobody knew what had happened to the other porter for a while.

That looked promising until they'd found him cowering in the ladies' room (of all places). His name was Dubcek, he was a refugee from Czechoslovakia, and he had gotten the diner job with a forged work permit. He couldn't be made to understand that the police weren't primarily interested in him; he would answer no questions at all. "Is my right," he kept saying. "Is America here!"

They gave him up as a lost cause and called Immigration.

About eight P.M. the news came in that Olsen would probably be all right.

And about ten o'clock that night everybody knew that the whole search—which by this time involved what seemed like half the police in New Jersey, along with dogs and helicopters—was a lost cause.

The man with the sandy blond hair, high cheekbones, and square jaw was simply not to be found. Johnson was very very angry.

7

Bells chimed. Russ Garrett groaned and buried his nose in his pillow. Port Chester was a nice town; the gateway to New England. Twenty-five thousand or so people lived in the village, a good mix of nationalities and races. There were factories, fields, swamps, and shoreline—the town had a pretty little harbor on Long Island Sound. Garrett had grown up there; and he'd gone back to let his boyhood surroundings wash the war and a woman from his memory.

But Port Chester was no place to try to sleep late on a Sunday morning. Not only did all the local churches have bells, but they all had slightly erratic clocks, so that clanging from one church or another filled a long ten minutes before and after the turn of each hour.

Our Lady of Mercy's bells faded out, to be replaced by those of the nearby North Baptist Church. Garrett sighed and gave up. He never should have left town—both his parents were sleeping peacefully down the hall. They hadn't had a chance to get unused to the sound of the bells.

Garrett heard his parents snoring musically as he padded past the door to their bedroom on the way to the toilet. Garrett hadn't gotten home until after midnight, but his parents were waiting up for him. They'd heard the news on the radio and taken it hard.

Sam Garrett, Russ's father, had been in his basement workshop, cursing silently at the guts of a big RCA table model TV. He'd asked his son if he was all right. Russ assured him he was.

"That's good. Goddamn Commies."

"They don't know that yet, Dad," Russ said softly.

"Who else would kill Congressman Simmons, will you tell me that?"

Russ said nothing, handed his father a Phillips screwdriver when the elder Garrett pointed to it.

"We lost a great American today. A real American."

Garrett suppressed a sigh. They'd talked about this before. "Dad—"

"Goddammit, Russ, I didn't drag my ass all over Europe in 1918 so some Commies could give it to the Russians. And my son leaves a gallon of blood and his baseball career in Korea for what? For 'peace talks!' You ask your pal, Hal Keating. He was in intelligence in World War II, right? He'll tell you. See if he don't. This country is in big trouble, and Simmons was one of the few guys in government who was doing something about it and getting results. And now they got him. Don't touch that, you'll get your ass blown through a wall. That's the high-voltage section—I took the cage off to test."

His son jerked his hand away from the innards of the set. "Sorry," he said. Russ used to be able to help his father in the shop, but no more. The technology had sped by him while he was in the hospital.

"Not as sorry as you would have been if I let you touch it," his father said. Both men laughed. Sam Garrett ran his hand over his wavy gray hair, embarrassed at what he was about to say. "I'm glad you're okay, son," he said. "I heard the cop say on the news that you were a good witness. I hope you help them catch the son of a bitch who did this."

"I'll have more than one chance," Russ said. His father asked him what he meant.

"Something the commissioner asked me to do." The younger man's mouth opened in a wide yawn. "Tired," he said.

"The police commissioner?" his father wanted to know.

Russ shook his head while he yawned again. "Mr. Frick. I'll tell you about it in the morning, okay, Dad?"

His father looked at him. Russ Garrett got the impression his father was looking into some kind of magic mirror, reliving something he saw in his son's face. Russ wished he knew what it was. At the same time the younger man saw in the lines of his father's face something of what it must be like to feel vaguely betrayed by all the things you'd believed in and all the people you'd trusted.

"Sure, son," the old man said. "I won't be far behind you. Just want to finish up this pig." He pointed at the set.

"Say good night to your mother. She's been waiting up for you, too."

"Okay, Dad. Good night."

Garrett's mother had held him and said she was glad he was safe and that she was afraid the Commies would be after him.

"All I did was find the body," he protested.

"Maybe they won't believe it," his mother said. "You just be careful."

"I will." His mother wanted to cook him something, but Garrett told her the cops had sent out for sandwiches, and what he mostly needed was sleep. "You, too," he scolded her. "You know what the doctor told you."

Garrett wiped some steam from the bathroom mirror (it was another hot, humid day) and reflected that what he *still* mostly needed was sleep. Fat chance. Not when he had that meeting with the cops at ten o'clock. He was a liaison—no, *official* liaison between the police and the Commissioner of Baseball for the investigation. "Ordinarily, Garrett," Mr. Frick had said on the phone last night, "I'd let our security people handle this, but I'm letting you do it because you have known the congressman, especially in his connection with the Game, and because you were on the scene." The commissioner went on to tell him that the whole thing had been Captain Murphy's idea.

Garrett neglected to thank either Mr. Frick *or* Vicious Aloysius (he'd heard a patrolman refer to the captain that way—it was one of the few laughs in an otherwise dismal evening) for the honor. It did explain, in a way, why Captain Murphy had kept Garrett around through all the interviews with the other witnesses.

Garrett winced as he applied styptic pencil to his various facial cuts. He always made a mess of himself if he shaved while he was tired. He took a quick hot shower, dried off, dressed, went downstairs, fixed himself an English muffin and a glass of orange juice (from a carton, not this newfangled concentrated frozen stuff), ate, and left the house.

Two steps down the green-painted wooden steps, he turned around, went back in, penciled a note to his parents, and left again, this time with a clear conscience. From early childhood his parents had trained him to let them know what he was up to so they wouldn't be worried.

Of course, Mom would be worried anyway when she found out her little boy wasn't going to be able to put this rotten business behind him. His father, on the other hand, would be proud his son was doing his bit to make America safe for Americans.

Garrett started his car, pulled out of the driveway of the family home, drove to the Boston Post Road, and took US 1 through its various names in various towns all the way to the Bronx.

Garrett leaned back into his seat and concentrated on not stamping his left foot against the floor in search of a non-existent clutch. Garrett had taken some of his accumulated back pay and helped Kaiser Motors finance its sixty-two-million-dollar expansion program by buying a brand-new green Kaiser with Hydra-Matic drive.

His parents had undoubtedly found his note by now. He wondered if he'd been right about the way they'd take it.

One thing was sure—Russ Garrett's parents had reacted a lot more visibly to the death of Congressman Simmons than the congressman's brother and secretary had. The brother, Telford (though Garrett remembered him from Kansas City as "Tad"), had come in with his nose very high. The cops had found him and the woman sitting around downstairs in a box seat, waiting for the congressman to return.

He'd demanded that the captain tell him what was going on. When he heard his brother had been shot, Telford Simmons had started to blurt something, like "I told him," or something like that, but he caught himself. Afterward he never came close to blurting anything. He'd answered a few questions, but refused to answer (or claimed he couldn't answer) a whole lot more, including who it was his brother had been meeting or just why he was meeting him. Captain Murphy had growled and grunted, but he'd eventually let it slide for the time being. Garrett noted that the cop at Murphy's side seemed astonished at that particular development.

Telford went on to say a few words of his own, though. He demanded that the killer of his brother be caught. He demanded to be led to a phone, because the Speaker of the House of Representatives and the Governor of the State of Missouri had to be notified at once. He demanded police protection for himself and Miss Tilton.

Garrett had very nearly been moved to volunteer for guard duty, but only if it involved Miss Tilton. Just thinking about her made Garrett's blood start to bubble. He rolled the window of the Kaiser down a little farther—it was hot enough already.

Miss Cheryl Tilton was the most attractive woman, in an irritating sort of way, he'd ever set eyes on. She was gorgeous; dark and slim like Phyllis Kirk, only a little rounder in strategic places. She had an air, though, or maybe it was more of an attitude, that seemed to say she had men figured out; that she'd never been surprised and never expected to be, and even if she were, she knew already it would be by something she wasn't going to like. Garrett felt a strong desire to wipe that look off her face.

Miss Tilton had said seven words all night: "Thank you," when Garrett had pulled out a chair for her, and "Roast beef sandwich and coffee," when a cop had taken orders for supper. She betrayed not the slightest grief over her employer's death. She had a sexy voice, Garrett decided. But what a cold comfort she must be to a man.

The biggest reaction of the night had come from young Gary Danziger, who cried all the while he gave his testimony. Yes, he had seen the hot-dog man. Yes, he had seen the dead man, only he thought he was asleep. Yes, he knew who killed the dead man.

No, he wouldn't say.

Captain Murphy had the kid's grandfather taken away. He pleaded. He cajoled. He threatened. Gary stood there with his baseball in his glove and cried.

Finally Murphy told the kid it was his duty as an American to speak up. This really turned on the waterworks. Finally, after Murphy had promised the kid that if he wasn't a good American, he'd be sent to a foreign country where there was no baseball, and he'd never see his Mommy or his dog again, Gary revealed the name of the killer.

"It's Mickey Mantle," he sniffed.

8

Gary had heard Mantle's conversation with another man, a man who wasn't a baseball player. They'd talked about a man named Simmons, a man Mickey Mantle didn't like. The man on the radio said Simmons was the dead man. Gary's grandfather had said a red person had killed this Mr. Simmons. Mickey Mantle told the other man that *he* was red. That's how Gary knew. It made him sad, because he liked Mickey Mantle, and now Mickey Mantle was going to hate him.

Garrett did some rapid explaining, including the etymology and use of the term "red ass." All the cops nodded, but Garrett got the feeling that it was very lucky for Mickey that he had been halfway to second base—and in front of thousands of witnesses—when the fatal shots were fired.

As it was, Garrett thought as he crossed from Pelham to the Bronx, the cops still had it on the agenda to talk to Mickey before the Yankees left on their road trip Monday.

Garrett's first stop was Bronx Homicide, where he was briefed by Detective Martin.

"I don't know why the captain is telling all this to a *suspect* . . ." The Negro detective paused and peered at Garrett, waiting for a reaction. Garrett disappointed him; Martin went on, ". . . but here goes. Simmons's brother finally came across with the news that the congressman was at the ball park to pick up evidence of Communists in baseball. Somebody sent him tickets and told him to wait to be approached."

"He was approached, all right," Garrett said. He didn't usually wisecrack in a situation like that, but he wanted the other man to see how little it bothered him to be called a suspect.

"Yeah," Detective Martin said. "Easy to see he was double-crossed."

68

"They have no idea who sent the letter?"

"Nope," Martin consulted a report. "Nope. The brother and the secretary say a second letter was 'withheld by Rex, because of some fool notion he was protecting us from something,' end of quotation. The first letter wasn't signed, the secretary says." Suddenly the detective grinned. "I saw you looking at her last night."

"So?" Garrett asked. "She's worth looking at."

"Damn straight. I understand you've met this bunch before."

"Briefly," Garrett said. "I played ball in Kansas City. The congressman and the ball club would occasionally use each other to get a little publicity.

"Listen," Garrett went on, "this business about Reds in baseball is really going to spoil the commissioner's day. *My* commissioner, I mean. Is there anything concrete you've turned up we should know about?"

Detective Martin was still grinning and showing his white teeth. "Well, Telford and Miss Tilton both say that no names were mentioned but that the letter specifically implied your pal Mickey Mantle was involved somehow."

"Did it ever occur to you," Garrett said through his teeth, "that the whole business was a *trap* for Simmons? That Mantle might have been mentioned in the letter, or hinted at, or whatever the hell he was, specifically to get Simmons interested? Anyone who reads the papers knows how Simmons was after Mickey's tail back in '51 over that draft thing and how Simmons lost out. He'd jump through a hoop if he thought he had a chance to prove something bad about Mickey."

Detective Martin had been perching on Captain Murphy's desk. Now he got up, walked behind it, sat in a creaky swivel chair, and shook his head. "Damn, Garrett, now I owe Vicious a beer."

"What are you talking about?" Garrett demanded.

"The captain bet me you'd spot that right off. He says you have a natural talent for that sort of thing."

"How does he know? He never knew I existed until yesterday."

"Old friend told me about you." Captain Murphy came through the door with a couple of folders in his hand. He growled at Martin to get the hell out of his seat, then took his place behind the desk.

He told Garrett that a pal of his, a former New York cop, was the colonel of military police who had investigated a morphine theft ring at the hospital while Garrett was a patient there. "He says you asked to see him one day and you laid the answer right in his lap."

Garrett shrugged it off. "I had nothing to do, so I spent my time looking at the nurses. I noticed one nurse was a thirty-four C when she made her morning rounds and a thirty-six D in the afternoon. Then, when word went around morphine was missing, it just seemed obvious.

Murphy looked thoughtful. "So that's why that stupid jerk was laughing all the time he was telling me how you 'busted' the case. He says you helped him out a couple of other times, too."

Garrett didn't know what to say. "We just talked. I try to be analytical. I think I might go to law school."

"Just what I need," Murphy sighed. "Another smart lawyer. Look, if it's good enough for my pal, picking your brain is good enough for me. That's why I asked Mr. Ford Frick to make you our baseball contact in this case. I personally know nothing about baseball; you have inside knowledge. I don't know exactly how you can help, or even if you can, but I want you available. This is a hot case, and I'm not ignoring anything. Okay?"

Garrett told him it was okay. "Does this mean I'm not a suspect?"

"No," Murphy told him. "But this does." He held up one of the folders. "Report from the New Jersey State Police. They stopped the killer on the Jersey Turnpike yesterday, but he got away. Disappeared. Left his car and his gun behind—the same gun that killed Simmons, ballistics has already checked it out. He also left bullets in a Jersey trooper. Shot him twice—seems to be a habit of his. Those bullets," Murphy growled, "also match up. So our square-jawed beauty is ready to shoot anybody. For all we know, he's got the whole House of Representatives on the agenda."

"What time was the shooting in Jersey?" Garrett wanted to know.

"A little before six."

Garrett nodded. "That's why I'm in the clear. I was at the stadium being interviewed by you at the time. I guess it clears all the other witnesses, too. Right?"

Murphy rubbed his cheeks. "Well, maybe I was a *little* hasty. There *is* such a thing as a conspiracy, you know." He sighed. He wished the people in the stadium yesterday *were* completely in the clear. Not only was it a big boost to an investigation to get someone—anyone—eliminated from suspicion; clearing the folks at the stadium would mean he could stop worrying about the Vitiello kid. If there was one thing opera needed in this country, it was a good American tenor. No candidate should be wasted; it would be a shame if Murphy had to put one in jail. . . .

But Garrett was saying something.

"What's that?" Murphy wanted to know.

"I said, I don't know anything about the people on this list Martin gave me to look at. I mean, I recognize some from the newspapers, but that's about it."

Murphy was surprised to learn he'd been musing so long—that was a long list. It was Telford Simmons's roster of everyone who had threatened the life of Congressman Rex Harwood Simmons over the past couple of years. There was another list, a much lengthier one, of people Telford and Miss Tilton thought had hated the late congressman. He told Garrett about it.

"Mickey Mantle's on that list," the captain added.

Garrett's handsome face reddened. "Oh, for Christ's sake. Will you lay off Mickey? He didn't have anything to do with this and you know it."

"And *you* know I can't lay off anybody, Garrett. Not in this case or in any homicide."

"I know, dammit, I know." Garrett's face was twisted in a tight frown. "Look, do you plan to talk to Mantle this afternoon?"

"Yes."

"Let me go with you."

Detective Martin made a disgusted noise. "You know that's out of the question, Garrett. Don't let this liaison thing go to your head, you know? This is still official police business."

Garrett ignored him and concentrated on the captain, who had remained silent. "Captain, Mantle is sensitive, and kind of hotheaded. If he thinks he's being persecuted—which God knows he has a right to feel—he'll either clam up or he'll say wild stuff that'll only get him in trouble and won't help your investigation one damn bit. But if I go with you and vouch for you, I can keep him from doing anything foolish, and we'll all be a lot better off."

Martin looked impatient. He was going to tell Garrett nothing doing, but a wave from Captain Murphy cut him off. Murphy brooded about it for a while. His meditations were punctuated by little grunts.

At last he said, "Garrett, do you have a radio in your car?"

"What? Oh, yeah. I do. Why?"

"Never mind. You can come along. I'll go in your car. Martin can follow in the department car."

It was arranged that Garrett would meet the captain back here when he'd finished his report for Mr. Frick. The young man left Bronx Homicide, still not knowing why having a radio in his car suddenly qualified him to go along with the police. He wasn't aware that WQXR was having a program of recordings by Caruso that Captain Vicious Aloysius Murphy didn't want to miss.

9

. . . *Yes, I lost my little darlin' the night they were playin' the bee-yoo-tee-ful Tennessee Waltz* . . .

Damn, Garrett thought as he corrected the last of his typing errors, I'm being haunted by Patti Page. Let me start any sort of routine work, and she springs into my mind in full harmony and hi-fi. Well, it could be worse, he thought.

Johnny Ray, or some of that bebop stuff he couldn't understand.

There were a lot of things he couldn't understand. Like how he got into these things. All of a sudden he was working for the Commissioner of Baseball, helping the police, and playing big brother to Mickey Mantle, who could probably take perfectly good care of himself.

Garrett stacked the pages of his report and left them neatly in a desk drawer. The commissioner was going to take gas Monday when he read it. Garrett could only hope the session with Mantle went okay.

The Rockefeller Plaza offices of Major League Baseball were not idle on Sunday. There were always people standing by to receive results of the games around the leagues and prepare the latest standings and statistics. So Garrett wasn't surprised, as he picked up his hat and prepared to leave, that there was someone walking around outside his office door. He *was* surprised, though, when he opened the door to see it was Tad Simmons who'd been doing the walking.

"Hello, Garrett," Simmons said with a false amiability that set Garrett's teeth on edge. "Finished? I didn't want to interrupt. Shall we go into your office and talk?"

"How'd you get in?"

"I told the guard I had an appointment with you. The police told me you might be here."

"Did they tell you I'm going to meet them again?"

Tad Simmons's foxy face split into a wide grin, a genuine one this time. Garrett didn't like it any better than the old one.

"No, they didn't, but I like it. It'll fit in nicely with what I have in mind."

"I don't know what you have in mind, but I'm just on my way out, so if you'll excuse me—"

"Inside, Garrett. I mean it." The grin was gone from Tad's face, replaced by a look of such menace that Garrett was curious to see what it was all about. He opened the door, waved Tad Simmons to a seat, took off his hat, and reseated himself behind his desk.

"I'm leaving for Missouri this afternoon," Tad told

Garrett. "Jefferson City. The governor is going to appoint me to serve out my brother's term."

"Congratulations," Garrett said.

"He doesn't like me much, the governor doesn't, but he didn't have much choice. The people would have had his neck if he hadn't decided to appoint me to carry on my brother's work."

Simmons paused, seemed to think a comment was called for at this point. Garrett didn't give him one.

Simmons went on. "I want my brother's killer, Garrett."

"Everyone does."

"The Communists don't."

"The police do."

Simmons leaned forward and slammed his open hand down on Garrett's desk. "Don't be so f-f-fucking naive, little boy," he said. "If the Commies can infiltrate the State Department, the New York police shouldn't be much of a challenge."

Garrett was mad at himself for jumping when Simmons smacked the desk. He resolved to stay calm. "I believe," he said, "that Captain Murphy would kick your teeth in for a crack like that."

"Captain Murphy can shove it," said the congressman-to-be. "Now you listen to me, Garrett. You have an in on this investigation. I want to know all about it. I want to know what they find out, and I want to know what they're doing about it. And you're going to tell me."

Garrett raised an eyebrow. "I am?"

"You are. You're going to help me make sure nobody gets in the way of a thorough investigation of my brother's death."

"Mr. Simmons, I saw you and your brother at work in K.C. You put on like you were just a two-bit messenger boy, but it didn't take any great brains to see you ran the show. Your brother may have been able to blame communism for all the bullshit he pulled, but don't you try it; it just doesn't sound right from you. Now, it seems to me that you want to be up to date with the police because you want to know how close they're getting to something you don't want found out.

How does that sound?"

Tad Simmons didn't answer him. Instead he said, "The police showed you my list."

"So?"

"You told them you couldn't help them."

"I couldn't."

"Come off it, Garrett. Jenny Laird's name was on that list."

Garrett started to laugh. "So?"

"Laugh it up, Garrett," Tad Simmons told him. "Laugh while you can. Jenny Laird is the widow of David Laird, the Communist writer and teacher at Columbia."

"Well, I can see why *she* might have wanted to kill your brother. Laird committed a messy suicide in a car-crash fire, didn't he? After your brother got his publisher to cancel his contract, and even Columbia started getting testy? But what's that got to do with me? I never took classes with Laird, never personally met him *or* his wife."

"Jenny Laird is also," Tad Simmons went on, "the cousin of Ann Devore, a Communist student leader—"

"Communist? She circulated a petition supporting the Marshall Plan, for God's sake—"

"—a Communist student leader—I have a list of the organizations she belonged to—with whom you lived for a time in the winter of 1950 and 1951, and who died as the result of an illegal abortion." Simmons looked at Garrett. "Your child, Garrett?"

"Get out of here," Garrett said, rising from his chair. "Get out of here before they have to send you to Congress in a box."

"Think, Garrett. Think of how it will look if I let this all out. What kind of baseball job will you get? What law school would have you? What would it do to your parents to find out their all-American boy is secretly a free-loving, baby-killing Commie?"

"*Get out!*" Garrett practically screamed. "You're a liar, and you stink!"

"Think about it," Simmons said. "I understand your mother isn't exactly well."

Garrett came from behind the desk. Simmons wore his hateful grin, but he kept backing slowly to the door. "My office will be in touch."

Garrett grabbed Tad by the lapels of his jacket and slammed him against the wall. "Listen, you son of a bitch—"

"No, l-l-little boy, y-*you* listen!" Tad stammered. "If you hit me you'd better kill me, because if you don't, I'll use my last breath to bring your whole world down around you. Starting with your parents."

Garrett still had him by the lapels. He trembled with fury.

"Let me go," Simmons commanded.

Garrett let him go.

Tad Simmons tossed his shoulders, straightened his jacket. "Smart move, Garrett. You'll hear from me. And no smart business with the police, or you'll feel like I dropped you from the Washington Monument."

Tad let himself out, closed the door behind him.

It all came back at once, everything he'd gone into baseball to forget. Garrett stood there for a few seconds, then punched the glass out of the door. He buried his face in his bleeding hands and tried to think of a way out.

Chapter Four
Errors

1

Captain Murphy wanted to know what happened to his hand.

Garrett felt the muscles of his face move; he decided his expression was as close to an embarrassed smile as it was going to get and spoke. "I put it through my office door, Captain. Too eager to join you today, I guess."

Murphy grunted. "Did Simmons catch up with you?"

The sun had climbed above the low Bronx skyline. Garrett reached up and pulled down the visor. There were only a few scratches on his hand, but it was still tender.

"Yes, he caught up with me. Right turn here?"

"Just follow Martin." The captain pointed at the car ahead, made a few noises, then adjusted his hat. "Why the hell are you stalling me, Garrett?"

"What?" Garrett demanded, then immediately regretted it. What he really needed was automatic transmission for his mouth.

"Oh," he said. "I'm sorry, I was thinking about something. You want to know what Simmons was after, right?"

"Do you want me to beg you? Come on, Garrett, you're supposed to be helping us on this thing."

"And whose big idea was *that?*" Garrett snapped. "I'm not a cop or anything like one—I'm a *catcher*, for God's sake— and all of a sudden you people come in and take over my life—"

"You want off? It can be arranged."

Vicious Aloysius spoke softly, so softly that Garrett was instantly terrified. He looked at the captain and saw an expression that could have been concern. Garrett, though, read it as pure suspicion.

Okay, wise guy, he told himself. Fix it. The *last* thing you want now is to be out of it.

Garrett sighed. "I'm sorry, Captain. Bad day for me. I didn't get much sleep last night . . ."

Murphy snorted. "Neither did I."

"Okay, and you're used to murders. On top of that, Sunday is my day off. And my parents are worried about me."

"Why?" Murphy wanted to know. "I'm not going to let anything happen to you."

"I know, I know. But they almost lost me once already."

"Yeah, I should have thought of that. Want me to call them or something?"

"No, thanks. But it was nice of you to offer."

"Too much like a note from the teacher, huh?" Both men smiled. "*Now*," Murphy went on, "tell me what Simmons wanted."

"I wish I knew," Garrett lied. "I think he was just trying his new power on for size."

"Yeah, he pulled the same thing on me, too. I think he's one of these clowns who believes the biggest bastard always gets the most done." He mumbled something under his breath. "Listen, Garrett, you'll probably hear from this guy again. If he tries to pump you, I want to hear about it, congressman or no congressman. Okay?"

"Sure," Garrett lied. "There's the stadium."

"Good. Let's hear what your sensitive friend has to say."

2

God bless Caruso, Captain Murphy thought. He'd been the only tolerable thing about the whole afternoon.

For one thing, the visit with Mantle had been a total waste of time. If Mantle was anything but a decent American kid from Oklahoma, Murphy was Richard Tucker, and God knew Murphy was no tenor. Hell, if Mantle knew one goddam thing about the congressman's murder, Murphy was Victoria de los Angeles, and he'd put on a wig and sing *Manon* in front of the whole Bronx Homicide squad.

It wasn't that Mantle hadn't tried to be helpful. When Murphy showed him a drawing the police artist had whipped up, the ball player had studied it carefully before saying it looked like one of the hot-dog vendors, only older. Murphy had sighed, thanked him, and said he hoped he'd make a lot of touchdowns that afternoon. No one had laughed. "It's a joke, goddammit. I'm not *that* ignorant," he'd protested. He got the feeling they didn't believe him.

Garrett hadn't been much of a traveling companion, either. The whole trip over, Garrett had been griping about something or other—the heat, who was going to pay his expenses, stuff like that. Once he'd actually had the nerve to ask why Caruso had to sing so loud. Now they are sitting in the Samuel Tilden rest area, on the New Jersey Turnpike, talking to the manager, and Garrett was still sitting around watching cops work. The captain was beginning to think of Garrett as one of his less brilliant inspirations. He took a sip of the lemonade the waitress had brought.

A New Jersey guy named Johnson was there to keep him company. Johnson had apparently seen the killer. Murphy said, "Let me see the stuff you found in the killer's car."

"It's all at the barracks," the Jersey guy said. "Evidence."

Murphy growled. "I know it's evidence. I wasn't going to steal it." He grumbled. "You got a *list* of the stuff, at least?"

"That I got." He pulled a folded sheet of paper from his pocket. The rest-area manager was forgotten while Captain Murphy, then Detective Martin, looked at the list.

The captain made a face. "Same old crappy—" he began but stopped when Garrett piped up for the first time that afternoon.

"May I see it?" he asked.

The captain nodded; Martin handed the paper to Garrett. The young ball player looked it over for a few seconds, then handed it back to Detective Martin and was silent.

"The toll ticket," Garrett said at last.

Captain Murphy made another face. "Don't bother me with that now, Garrett. I already *told* you the NYPD would pick up your expenses for this trip."

"Not mine, Captain. His."

"Whose?"

"The killer's. Mr. Hot Dog. Look at the list. The gun, some untraceable old clothes, some junk that undoubtedly belongs to the guy he stole the car from, and a toll ticket from where he got on the turnpike, just past the George Washington Bridge."

"So?"

Garrett let the captain hang while he asked a passing waitress for another Coke. She smiled at him and said, "Sure, handsome."

The manager, whose name was Niffin, said, "How many times I got to tell you, Natalie?" The waitress snorted and walked off.

Garrett went on. "So a couple of things. The first is only a possibility if your man overlooked something in his plan."

"I'm waiting," Murphy told him. Amateurs, he said to himself.

"Okay. The theory is that the killer had a spare car waiting here for him; he got here (a little more rushed than he would have liked, what with the state troopers chasing him), switched cars as planned, and beat it."

"That's the theory."

"Okay. So the killer provided himself with an extra car. I heard Martin say the New York cops have found a chain of stolen cars abandoned across the Bronx. So another one here, stolen or not, isn't too hard to swallow. But this is a toll road. You get on, you get your toll ticket, and you don't pay until you leave the turnpike. You hand your card to the toll taker, and he sees how far you've traveled, then tells you how much money to pay. And if you lose your card, you have to pay for the entire length of the turnpike."

Natalie arrived with the Coke. She smiled saucily at Garrett and flounced off. All the men at the table stopped and watched her flounce.

"Amazing," Garrett said. He sipped his Coke. "How did people ever eat before air conditioning? Where was I?"

"Paying for the entire length of the turnpike," the captain reminded him.

Garrett nodded. "I don't think that happens too often, do you? And if it happened yesterday, one of the toll takers would probably remember it. How many can there be who worked the right shift yesterday? A couple hundred? A thousand? Between New York and New Jersey authorities, you ought to be able to get to everybody within a couple of days. Hell, you could almost do it over the phone."

Murphy grinned. "All right, Garrett, nice thinking. Jeez, if we just know what *exit* he got off at, it will at least give us a place to start."

Detective Martin's brown face wore a scowl. He shook his head and ran his hand over his tightly curled hair. "No good, Garrett; it won't work."

"Why not?" Captain Murphy demanded. He was just starting to feel a little hopeful.

"Because the car the killer had waiting here must have also had a toll ticket in it. He drove it onto the turnpike at one time or another—he had to get a toll ticket then, too. All he had to do was leave it in the car when he left it here."

Now it was Garrett's turn to nod. "I thought of that. But then how did he get off the road *that* time without paying for the whole road? If he drove off, he's got to be short one ticket, no matter how you look at it."

"Maybe he walked off."

"Not yesterday, he didn't," Johnson broke in. "He shot my partner—we had this place sealed off. He didn't get to the fence, and he didn't hitchhike, either. We even had surveillance planes."

"On the day he left the car, then," Martin said. "He walked off the turnpike or caught a ride. Then he had a car all set, with a toll ticket and everything."

Garrett watched his soda fizz as he twirled his glass.

"I said it was only a possibility. I suppose you could put out word that you want to talk to anyone who picked up a hitchhiker answering our boy's description lately.

"But there's another possibility. And I like this one—it means we don't have to worry about that other toll ticket at all."

3

Garrett finished his Coke quickly and picked up on his argument. He didn't want Murphy to accuse him of being mysterious just for fun, though Garrett had to admit to himself there was a certain amount of that feeling in him.

"Mr. Niffin," Garrett said.

The manager jumped. He was a stocky guy with hairy arms and not much forehead—wavy brown hair and bushy eyebrows had taken up most of the space originally allotted for it. He had a habit of working his tongue around the inside of his mouth.

"Who, me?" the manager asked. He worked his tongue.

"How far are we from the exit north of here?"

"Seven, eight miles."

"And the one south?"

"Twelve, thirteen. The exits are bunched up pretty tight up here near the city. Farther south they spread out."

"Even so, it's kind of tough on the people who work here, isn't it? I mean, they have to drive a stretch of twenty miles on this road and that much off it just to go to and from work. Not to mention tolls."

Niffin raised his eyebrows until they practically merged with his hairline. He wanted to know what the hell Garrett was talking about.

"Seems pretty obvious to me," Garrett said. He was getting tired of all the quizzical looks. "This restaurant is on the southbound side of a divided highway. You just can't get to it heading north. That means if you want to get here, you have to drive on a county road to the previous exit onto the turnpike and down to where we are now. Then, when you're through with work, you have to drive south for another twelve or thirteen miles to get *off* the turnpike before you have to drive on county roads again to get back to wherever you started."

"No, you don't," Niffin insisted. He worked his tongue again.

"Why not?" Garrett wanted to know.

"Because the restaurant here backs right up to the county road. You use the back door to come in or go out, and there you are. There's a little path—high fence all around, of course—and you go through that, and you're out on the county road."

Captain Murphy wheeled on Johnson. It looked as if Vicious Aloysius was about to live up to his nickname. "That wasn't in the report."

"We checked it," Johnson said defensively. He grabbed a copy of his report. "'The fence and area immediately adjoining were inspected,'" he quoted. "That's part of the fenced-in area."

Murphy groaned. "If Garrett's right, he could have been through here and out before you even came into the building."

Johnson's teeth were tight. "We asked the people in that goddam kitchen if they'd seen anything. That's in the goddam report. They all said no."

Garrett sighed. "Officer Johnson, what would they have seen if they *did* see the Hot Dog man? They would have seen a man in restaurant white walking fast through the kitchen of a restaurant at the dinner hour. While shifts were changing, and people were busy with their own work."

Johnson looked sick. Garrett was touched to see how fast cops closed ranks; Captain Murphy slapped the Jersey trooper on the back and told him to forget it.

"But maybe," the captain added, "we ought to go talk to the kitchen help again."

After one look at the kitchen, Garrett would have to steel himself the next time he wanted a restaurant meal. There was a nauseous smell of cooking old and new, and grease, and cleanser, and sweat. Miserable-looking men stood over sinks and pots, stirring and straining. Garrett saw the corner of a bright green rectangle break the surface of water in a huge cauldron. It horrified him until he realized it was only a block of frozen broccoli being cooked.

Utensils banged; running water screamed. The ceiling lights were frequently obscured by great gauzy clouds of steam that rose from cooking and dishwashing. People were shouting orders and shouting that they hadn't heard the original shouting.

And the heat was unbearable. Standing near the cake oven was enough to give someone a sunburn. Already Garrett could feel drops of sweat starting to run on his brow.

"Jesus," Captain Murphy said. "I'm surprised they notice anything in here. It's like living in a headache."

They were into evening by now, so it was the night-shift personnel they talked to.

The colored cook's name was Levi Barlett. He was small, with quick gestures, and he smiled during his interview like a man who didn't have a care in the world.

"Nah, I didn't see nothin'," he said in response to a question from Detective Martin. "Least not till the po-lice come in and raise such a ruckus. Then I saw plenty." Barlett turned around, got a bag of salt from a cabinet, and began filling a salt shaker.

"We know about that part," Martin said. "What about before that?"

"Nothin', man. Wasn't nothin' to see, as far as I could tell you. Besides, I was havin' a conversation with Lillian." Barlett slyly stroked a graying hairline mustache.

"Who's Lillian?" Captain Murphy wanted to know. "A waitress?"

Barlett laughed; the other cook, a grizzled old guy who reminded Garrett of Poopdeck Pappy, piped up. "It's me, goddammit. Harry Lillian. And we didn't have no conversation. He was talking to me. It's bad enough I got to work with niggers; I ain't about to go having conversations with them."

Vicious Aloysius pushed his hat back on his head and growled. "Is that a fact? Well get this, Lillian. When Detective Martin asks you a question, you're gonna answer him, and you're gonna say 'yes sir' and 'no sir.' All right?"

"You think I got no respect for the Law?" The old man was indignant. "I'm a goddam good American." He turned to Martin. "You go ahead, sonny. You're representing the Law; that means it don't matter if you're a nigger. Ask away."

Levi Barlett was laughing. "Lil, you are too much." He nudged Detective Martin. "Ain't he too much?"

Martin conceded Lillian was too much, waited for the hilarity to die down, and asked his questions. Harry Lillian may not talk to Negroes, Garrett thought, but he sure did listen to them. The old man's replies were the same as Barlett's; if anything, he was even more certain than his colored colleague. "So I tell you again, sonny, I didn't see nothing then, and I don't see nothing now, except a dumb nigger who's gonna set fire to himself if he don't stop laughing and pay attention to his work."

Levi Barlett jumped away from the stove, where a gas flame had indeed started the cloth of his sleeve smoldering. He ran water over it and started laughing again as he wrang it out. "Thanks, Lil," he said.

Lillian ignored him. Instead he had a suggestion for the cops. "Why don't you talk to the dummy?" He pointed at the dishwasher across the way.

"Yeah, that's a good idea," Levi Barlett said. "He didn't leave the kitchen to see what the ruckus was about. He's a very conscientious boy."

Lillian smiled for the first time. "Yeah, but he's always got his head in the clouds. Steam, you know? He comes in, sticks his head over the sink, and that's it for him until quitting time. Don't even take time for a cigarette or nothing. I never seen him breathe nothing but steam."

"Maybe he got him a bad cold," Barlett put in. "Hey, dummy!" he shouted. "Why don't you throw some Vapo-Rub in the water? Maybe do you some good."

The figure over the sink raised a rubber-gloved hand and waved. The official contingent walked over to him, leaving the two cooks laughing together.

Garrett had already heard, from the manager Niffin, that the dishwasher's name was Joey Hart, and that though he was a good worker, talking to him was like pulling teeth.

When they pulled Joey out of his cloud, it struck Garrett what an unfortunate simile that was, because Joey didn't have any teeth, and his face had collapsed on itself to become a mass of lines radiating from the small circle that was his mouth.

Actually Garrett suspected that more than teeth were involved. He'd known a fellow in the hospital who'd looked like Joey—the guy had been separated from his outfit and had wandered around the Korean countryside in the dead of winter, not finding his way back to anything American until his hands, feet, and part of his face were frozen. He'd lost feet, fingers, and most of his lower jaw before Garrett had met him. Something like that had doubtless happened to the dishwasher.

The questioning seemed to last forever. The dishwasher was cooperative enough when he understood the questions, but it was hard to make much out of his answers. His voice was a scratchy whisper that was hard to hear over the din, and his deformity made it difficult for him to shape some words.

With a gentleness and patience that surprised Garrett, Captain Murphy got it established that the dishwasher hadn't seen anything more than any of the other employees.

"Well, Joey," the captain said. "Did you notice anything unusual at all?"

"Unusual?" Joey pushed back some wet spikes of hair from his forehead and looked at Captain Murphy. He had eyes the color of cornflowers, round, bright eyes that looked incapable of guile.

"You know, Joey. Something that doesn't happen every day."

"Oh," Joey said. "Yeah. There was something." Garrett put Joey's age around fifty (possibly less—his condition made it hard to tell), but Joey was acting like a kid.

"What happened, Joey?" Captain Murphy said it carefully, as if he were afraid to break something. "What happened that was unusual?"

"Johnny dropped a tray! A whole tray of dirty dishes!

And the police came. Everybody joked later and said I should be happy I didn't have to wash them, but I felt sorry for Johnny—I think he has to pay for them."

Disappointment was practically audible, even above the noise of the kitchen.

Captain Murphy sighed. "Was there anything else that doesn't happen every day?"

"No, sir," Joey said.

Murphy patted him on the back. "Okay, Joey, you can go back to work now. Thanks. But listen—if you remember anything else—the tiniest little thing—just tell Mr. Niffin, and he'll get in touch with me."

Joey nodded.

"And if you hear someone else has remembered someth—"

"Excuse me, Captain," Joey said. "Do you want to know that the back door slammed and nobody came in?"

Murphy shot a look at Garrett. "Go on, Joey," the captain said.

"That's all. The door slammed—the door that goes to the road—you know about that? That door. It slammed, but nobody came in. It was time to come to work, so I thought somebody would come in. But nobody did."

Garrett couldn't stand it anymore. "Joey, did somebody go *out?*"

The dishwasher scratched his head. "I thought of that, but it couldn't be."

"Why not?"

"Everybody was still here—all the day people, they were still here. I saw them all, later. So nobody went out the back door."

"Nobody who works here, maybe. But couldn't there have been somebody else? Somebody dressed in white, like you are, but who doesn't work here? Couldn't somebody like that have gone out and slammed the door?" My God, Garrett thought, I'm starting to sound like *him.*

Joey shook his head. "Only people who work here are allowed to use that door."

Captain Murphy made a noise in his throat. "Thank

you, Joey. But tell me, why didn't you tell this to the police on Saturday?"

"They didn't ask me."

"Didn't the police talk to you?" Behind Joey, where the captain could see him, Johnson was nodding his head emphatically.

"They talked to me."

"But they didn't ask you—"

"They asked me about what I *saw*. They never said anything about anything I *heard*."

4

Garrett swatted at the buzzing noises that zipped around him in the purple-gray twilight and wondered what it was that had possessed him to come out here.

Here was a small house on a quiet but weedy inlet of Long Island Sound. Lovely to look at, Garrett thought, especially with moonlight shining off the water. He could live without the mosquitoes, though.

He was coming to pay a visit to Jenny Laird. Captain Murphy didn't know he was going; Garrett had gotten the address from one of the police reports. He didn't want to tell Murphy, because the captain would have wanted to know why, and Garrett didn't know that himself.

Someone was singing in the house, a soft, wordless lullaby. It sounded like Ann's voice. Exactly. Garrett wondered (not for the first time) if he really wanted to go through with this.

He was on the front porch before he'd finished wondering, as long as he was there, he figured he might as well knock on the door.

The singing stopped. Garrett heard whispering and rustling inside the house. He found himself hoping that Jenny Laird wouldn't look like her cousin—that might have been too much to take.

When the door opened, he saw that she didn't. Jenny Laird was a petite strawberry blonde, and (as far as Garrett could make out from the light that spilled from the house) she had green eyes. Ann had been taller, and dark.

Still, there were similarities—the shape of the jaw, the clear smooth skin dusted with freckles, and the hot, dancing lights anger brought to the eyes.

Because Jenny Laird was very angry. If her eyes didn't prove it, the shotgun she had aimed at Garrett's face did.

"Get away from my house!" Her voice was something between a whisper and a snarl.

Garrett gulped. "Look, there's no need—"

"Keep your voice down!"

"There's no need for the shotgun," Garrett began again, almost whispering himself this time. "I just want to talk to you."

"About that stupid hate list? I've already spoken to the police. I don't know who killed Rex Simmons, and I don't know why any of you should expect me to care. Now get out of here."

"I'm not a policeman—"

"And another thing. You come up here knocking on my door in the dead of night—just like Gestapo or the NKVD and the rest, and you expect me to—"

"I'm *not* a policeman," Garrett said. He was starting to get irritated. "And it's only a quarter after eight. Now would you please—ahh, to hell with it." He took a quick step forward and pulled the shotgun from her grasp. Even before he finished doing it, he knew what a stupid move it had been, but he got lucky.

Garrett broke the gun and took out the shells. "Jesus," he breathed. "Pumpkin balls. Mrs. Laird, are you insane?" Garrett could feel sweat breaking out in his forehead over what he'd almost put himself in for. A single lump of lead the size of a walnut powered from each barrel. They could make a puree of a man's body.

He shook the cartridges under the woman's nose. "Do you know what these things can *do?* You don't want to know. If you want to kill somebody, kill him. I mean, I've had five bullets hit me, but *these*—

"And why the hell am I whispering?"

He looked at the woman. There were no more angry
flashes in her eyes. Now she was frightened and more than a
little guilty.

"My children are asleep," said Jenny Laird.

"Oh. Then you wouldn't have wanted to awaken them
with any loud noises, would you?"

"I just want to be left alone."

"Yeah." Garrett nodded. "I could do with some of that
myself." He handed her back the shotgun. "I'm leaving now.
I'm taking your ammunition with me. If you've got any more
of these things, for God's sake, get rid of them. Use bird shot.
Or have the gun shop make up rock-salt shells for you. That'll
keep out intruders. Good night."

Garrett turned and headed down the stoop, figuring he
could get to his car and be out of range before this crazy
woman could reload. Jenny Laird spoke before he reached the
bottom.

"I'm sorry," she said.

He looked back over his shoulder at her. She was
smiling. Her smile was very nice; she didn't seem crazy at all.

"Really, I am sorry, Mr. . . ."

"Garrett. Russell Garrett."

The smile was replaced by a puzzled frown. Jenny Laird
tilted her head. "Oh," she said. "You were Ann's . . ."

"Yeah. I was. I wanted to talk to you."

"About my cousin?"

"Mostly."

"Then I really am sorry, Mr. Garrett. Won't you come
in and talk to me now?"

5

"Stop apologizing," Garrett said. He could talk more
normally now; the book-lined study Jenny Laird had brought
him to was away from the children's rooms. "I don't blame
you for being upset. The police have been giving me pains,
too. The shotgun is a little extreme, that's all."

He decided to change the subject. "What sort of articles

do you write?" The room was her office, she'd said. She had to work at home to take care of the children.

She waved a hand. "Oh, all sorts of things. Book reviews, history. There are a lot of magazines. I even write about swimming sometimes—I was quite a swimmer in college. I met David—my husband—at a swimming meet. I still do whenever I can—swim, I mean. Can't swim in this swamp, unfortunately. Still, I've gotten in the habit of keeping my hair short, so I . . ."

She just stopped talking, as though she had a switch that closed her mouth when she started to babble. An embarrassed silence followed, but it only lasted a second, because a baby started to cry in the other room.

"Excuse me," Jenny Laird said and bounced from her chair. Before she had left the room, another voice joined in. Garrett was impressed to hear the two-year-old twins crying in perfect harmony. Patti Page would have been proud of them.

Garrett pulled at his tie, took a sip of coffee (she didn't have anything cold to drink), wiped his forehead with a napkin, and wished he'd never come out here. Not only was he hot, tired, and miserable, but neither he nor his hostess could get the conversation around to what he was supposed to be there to talk about.

He'd found out some things about Jenny Laird. She was thirty years old, from Indianapolis, originally. She'd met and married David Laird eleven years ago, when she was a sophomore at Barnard. She had a son, Mark, who was ten years old, and the twin girls, Dorothy and Alice, who were two. Her husband died a little less than eighteen months ago. Under suspicion of being a Communist.

She'd been through hell since. A distant relative of her husband's had tried to get custody of her children—was still trying, in fact. She had to publish her articles under false names. She was justifiably anxious about unannounced visitors. Garrett was beginning to understand the armament. It didn't have any practical value—she wouldn't be able to take care of her kids if she were in jail—but it was a nice, symbolic doomsday gesture: "If things go wrong, I can always blow something up."

That was a strategy Garrett could sympathize with. All through his adolescence, a baseball career had meant that to him—I can always forget real life and go play baseball. That was exactly what he *had* done, come to think of it. He made a noise in his throat as he suddenly remembered that he had missed his make-or-break session with the stairs today. His hold on baseball seemed to be slipping rapidly away.

He wondered what he could do for his next doomsday gesture. Maybe join the Foreign Legion.

Jenny Laird rejoined him, wearing a tired smile. "I'm sorry about the interruption," she told him. "They're such angels—when they're asleep."

"Twins must be a lot of work."

Jenny's smile got a little less tired. "A whole lot. My son is a big help, especially when I'm working. It's not really fair to him, but Mark never complains."

"I'd like to meet him sometime."

"He'll be sorry he slept through your visit. Especially when he finds out you know Mickey Mantle."

Garrett said nothing. They'd talked about his baseball career, but not the reasons for it. And Garrett, stupidly, was jealous of Mantle. He discovered that he wanted boys to look up to *him*. Or maybe just Jenny Laird's boy.

"Would you like to see the twins?"

"Yes, I would."

Garrett got to his feet and followed his hostess to a bedroom where the twins slept in an oversize crib. Dorothy, Garrett was told, was the one with the thumb stuck in her soft little mouth. Her mother gently removed it. Little Alice gurgled and kicked her legs in her sleep. The soft lamplight in the room picked out highlights in the babies' hair, which was the same shade as their mother's.

Garrett felt a sharp pang of sympathy for David Laird. It was a sin, he thought, for a man to be deprived of seeing his children at times like this . . .

Garrett left the room. Blindly, as if he were running for his life.

Jenny caught up with him in the living room. He was fighting tears. "Are you all right?" she asked.

He rubbed his eyes and laughed. "No." He laughed again. "I'm sorry about this."

"There's no need—" she began.

"Yes, there is. Listen, Jenny—is it okay to call you Jenny?"

"Of course. I'll call you Russ."

"Good. Listen, I don't know how much you know about your cousin and me, but I wasn't the one who left. It's important for you to believe this. She moved out on me. I never knew she was pregnant until I heard she was dead. By then I had dropped out of school. I was in Arizona, trying out with the Yankees. But if I'd known . . . I'd never have let it happen."

"You would have wanted her to have the baby."

"I would have *married* her. I wanted to all along."

Jenny shook her head. She looked very wise. "Annie knew that. That's why she never introduced you to David and me. That's why she left you. That's why she decided not to have the baby."

Garrett said he didn't know what she was talking about.

"Ann and I were very close, Russ, despite the fact that I was six years older than she was. We were more like best friends than cousins.

"I don't have to tell you how stubborn she was, how independent. How devoted she was to liberal causes. How she was going to fix the world."

"No," Garrett said. "You don't. We used to argue a lot about politics. Ann was all heart, without a practical thought in her head."

"But the point is, she was so committed to this sort of work, *nothing* would stop her from doing it."

"I wouldn't have stopped her, for God's sake," Garrett insisted.

"You would have, though, without doing a thing. You were going to go to law school. She said you were going to be a great man, a real success, a boon to society. But Ann could see what was happening. The movie blacklists, the Hiss trial. McCarthy and Simmons and the rest were going to further and further extremes to get headlines.

"Then someone came around asking her questions about my husband. She knew no one was ever 'cleared' in that kind of investigation without a wholesale betrayal of his convictions, and David wasn't the kind of man who'd do that. Ann was the same way. And she'd been active in many of the same organizations David was. When Ed Bristow testified, she knew trouble was coming for all of us. And there she was, living with a man who was not her husband, who didn't believe in the same things she believed in."

"I believed in *her*, goddammit." Garrett was furious.

"Ann knew that, Russ." The woman's voice was soft, crooning, almost as it had been when she sang her lullaby. "And she didn't want you to have to choose between your future and her."

Garrett didn't know whether to laugh or cry. Ann was going to *be* his future. "That's what we used to fight about," he said. "She was so determined to *help* people that she never asked how she could. She was going to help the poor by taking money away from the rich, but she never saw that poor people don't want to abolish wealth, they just want enough to get by on while they hope for a decent shot at someday being rich themselves. And it was the same in this case, wasn't it?"

"I don't know what you mean."

"She was going to save me whether I wanted it or not. And she was going to rid me of the embarrassment of fathering a bastard, whether I wanted her to or not. And she got herself killed by some butcher without even telling . . . even . . ."

Garrett couldn't go on.

"Russ," Jenny said. "Russ," She walked over to him and took his hand. "You told me before there was something I had to believe. There's something you have to believe, too."

Garrett looked at her.

"Ann really suffered over her decision. She wouldn't even talk to *me* about it, though I begged her to. I don't know if it would have made any difference; but—oh, to hell with it. The thing is, she loved you, Russ. That's why she did it."

"I know," Garrett said, "but the fact remains that she ran away with her problem instead of sharing it with me. Or anybody."

Jenny rubbbed the back of her red-gold hair. "Everybody runs away at some time or another. Don't you think so, Russ?"

Garrett didn't answer; Jenny seemed to take it for assent. They were silent for a long time. Finally Garrett said, "You wouldn't happen to have a picture of Annie by any chance, would you? I—I didn't take any with me when I left town."

"I think I do," Jenny said. Her voice was soft. She rose and left the room, returning in a few minutes with an oversize snapshot, the kind you'd take with one of those old accordion cameras. It had been taken at the beach, Oakland Beach in Rye, up in Garrett's home territory, judging by the landscape. Jenny explained that she and her husband had lived there.

There were three figures in the picture. The light-haired woman was obviously Jenny Laird—Garrett noted academically how nicely his hostess's swimsuit showed her trim, healthy figure. The man next to her had to be her late husband.

The third figure was Ann, and after that first glance, it was her face that took all his attention. He allowed himself, for the first time since she'd left him, to forget about the hurt and the anger she'd caused, and he simply missed her. And it was almost more than he could stand.

"Jenny, I'd like to take this with me. I'll have a copy made and bring it back to you."

"All right, Russ. Please be careful with it, though. It's very precious to me. It was my birthday." She gave a sad little laugh. "It was the last time the three of us were together and not scared."

Garrett promised to be careful. Jenny showed him to the door and took both his hands in both of hers. "I'm glad you came here, Russ. . . . That's something I haven't said to a visitor in a long time."

Garrett said he guessed he was glad he'd come, too. And maybe, he told himself, I even mean it.

6

The white girl's name was Lindy, and she seemed taller
than she was because she was so thin. Her skin was pale and
translucent; her hair was almost white. She didn't have a
brain in her head, Gennarro Kennedy reflected, but she was
rather pretty at times. For instance, when she was in the
throes of passion, as she was now.

Kennedy looked down at the enrapt face and smiled.
He'd acquired Lindy quite by accident. Kennedy had once
needed, for a project he'd been working on, the cooperation
of Chicago Ned, who ran various illegal activities in the
Negro community in Kansas City. The negotiations were far
more difficult than Kennedy had anticipated, and it didn't
take long for him to determine why—Chicago Ned was a
bigot. Chicago Ned, despite his own hard-won success, had
been unable to believe a Negro could command respect unless
he carried the same visible trappings of power Ned himself
did—a big gun; a thick roll of money; a white mistress.

Kennedy had always found it easier to humor people
than to educate them. That was how he had made his way
from the Philadelphia slum in which he'd been born to the
position he held now. It was how he managed Mrs. Klimber.
People, all his life, had insisted on believing Gennarro
Kennedy insignificant simply because of the color of his skin.
He had decided early to use that, to manipulate all the fools
who couldn't see him for the man he was.

Chicago Ned had been easy to deal with. Kennedy had
simply gone out and gotten the visible trappings of power.
He'd picked Lindy, who was a hopelessly incompetent
waitress at the time, because she was the whitest woman he'd
ever seen—the type most likely to impress Chicago Ned.
Also, since Kennedy himself was quite black, the contrast
appealed to him esthetically.

In any case, it had worked like a charm; Chicago Ned
cooperated, and the operation was a resounding success.
Then he'd had trouble getting rid of Lindy. She loved him,
she said, which had been, of course, ridiculous. Still,

Kennedy understood that the girl had not known what she really meant. She was excited by him, in awe of him. She, who was so vacant and incompetent, had a desperate need for someone who was completely secure in himself.

So Kennedy had let Lindy set herself up in this apartment at his expense—of course, it was in a section of town where his comings and goings would arouse no comment. It had turned out to be a fortunate arrangement. It gave him a place to go to escape the maternal neuroses of his "employer" and a safe headquarters from which to arrange the more covert portions of his operations.

Besides, in an absent way, he had grown rather fond of Lindy.

Lindy was trying to speak through her moans of pleasure. "Honey . . . please . . . that's enough . . . I—I can't take it anymore . . ."

"Nonsense," Gennarro Kennedy replied. "Relax and enjoy yourself." Kennedy concentrated more on what he was doing, bringing Lindy once more to the heights of passion. Only then did he ease his control over himself and finish it. He rolled over, smiled, and listened to Lindy try to catch her breath. He allowed her a few minutes, then said, "Go take a shower, Lindy. I want to make a phone call."

"Yes, honey," she said. She kissed him on the cheek, rose, and padded to the bathroom. As Kennedy watched her go, he wondered, not for the first time, what it must be like to be brainless and innocent like Lindy. To be so easily contented on the one hand, yet on the other never to know the intellectual ecstasy, the esthetic ecstasy, to know none of the ecstasies except the ones that came from sex.

He sighed. It was unanswerable. His body gleamed like anthracite in the soft lamplight as he reached for the phone.

He told the operator to get him a number in New York and waited while she did so. Finally he heard the phone ringing. It was answered on the second ring.

"Nofsinger," the Negro told the telephone.

"Yes, boss. I been waiting for your call, as instructed." Nofsinger was in charge of Klimber Enterprises' New York "information" office. He reported directly to Kennedy. He was loyal because he was well paid and because Gennarro Kennedy knew every illegal thing Nofsinger had done in the course of his job, and could prove them all.

"What went wrong?" Kennedy asked. His voice was very calm.

Kennedy could hear Nofsinger swallowing on the other end of the line. The two men had never met, but Kennedy had seen pictures of his subordinate, pictures that had shown Nofsinger smiling, fat, and jolly, looking like the neighborhood grocer. Kennedy knew him to be sly, ruthless, and mean.

And stupid. Nofsinger didn't know Kennedy was a Negro; wouldn't have worked for him if he had known. Kennedy wasn't sure who infuriated him more, the pompous whites like Nofsinger—like *all* whites, if you wanted to tell the truth—who thought themselves superior because they lacked pigment in their skin, or the Negroes, typified by Chicago Ned, who let the whites get away with it. Who even believed the idiocy themselves.

Kennedy felt no sympathy for the first, no kinship with the second. He was an outsider; he'd freed himself from their petty concerns. He amused himself by using the position he had created for himself to make the fools—the rich fools, the well-known fools, the powerful fools—put on Punch-and-Judy shows for him. He was the puppet master, Iago in Othello's body. It was a life that suited him admirably. He would make a plan, then convince Mrs. Klimber the idea was hers (although the old woman's senile vaporings were a rich source of ideas in themselves). Kennedy pulled the strings, and the fools jumped.

Every so often, though, a plan went wrong. Gennarro Kennedy did not like it when plans went wrong.

"What went wrong?" Kennedy asked again.

"I don't *know*, boss." Nofsinger's voice was practically a whine. "It was working perfectly. I set up the group, waited for a fanatic, just like you told me, to show up. I let the talk get around to violence, revenge, you know, things like that. The Rosenbergs' getting fried in July was a big help with that part of it, just like you said."

"I know what I said, Nofsinger."

"Yes, sir. Anyway, we got the guy we wanted—a little simple, but devoted to the 'cause'—quiet, except when we were talking about killing somebody. Gave us a name, John Thane, or something like that, but it don't mean nothing. Nobody in a Commie group uses his real name; it's like a tradition."

"Like Lenin," Kennedy said. "Stalin. I know the tradition." The huge black man was growing impatient. "Get on with it, Nofsinger."

"Yes, sir. I went through the whole thing about who should we kill, like we were all figuring it out together— something that would hit at the heart of America, and somebody said the President, and I said naw, that had been done before and had never worked, the workers were still oppressed. I said we needed to do in somebody who *symbolized* America, like a ball player or something.

"That went over real good, just like you said it would. Most of the guys in the group were pale-face nothings that couldn't play baseball if they wanted to. It was one of *them* who beat me to coming up with the idea of killing one of the Yankees because they won all the time, and besides they didn't have any Negroes on their team, which proved . . . Anyway, I've told you all this."

"I know you have, Nofsinger. It's good we review. But let's make it brief; it doesn't pay to keep a line open too long."

"All right, I'll just go over it quickly. Somebody suggested killing Stengel, but I said he was too old, but Thane came back with Mickey Mantle, him being such a big star and all. That went over great—just like you said—and everyone was crazy about the idea. I fixed the lottery about who would get to do it, went to work on Thane, and got him the gun."

"And you left the details up to him?"

"That was the plan," Nofsinger said, "wasn't it?"

That indeed had been the plan. Kennedy sighed inwardly. It had come to him one evening during one of Mrs. Klimber's endless discussion sessions. At one point, when she had for the third time lamented Congressman Rex Harwood

Simmons's lack of progress with his Communists-in-sports investigation, the plan had come to him. He had been wanting to use the bogus People's League for Social Justice for something, anyway. Nofsinger was too bourgeois to fulfill the league's original purpose, in any case. He simply couldn't attract the upper-class New York liberals from show business or academia, especially at a time like this. They had all run for cover, hiding from the McCarthys and the Simmonses. Nofsinger was left with no one but the fanatics, some of whom were probably actually oppressed; therefore useless because powerless.

Very well, Gennarro Kennedy had said to himself, let us use the fanatics. Have them, or rather, the most suitable of them, kill Mickey Mantle, with a gun provided by the PLSJ. And let Nofsinger make sure the gun is traceable to the League. With all the controversy that had followed Mantle's draft exemption, an attempt on his life would provide the imaginative Rex Simmons, perhaps the greatest fool Kennedy had ever known, with enough material to make his committee a resounding success.

The beautiful nature of the plan was revealed in this: no matter what happened, the plan would succeed. If the gunman were captured, so much the better—being a fanatic, he would undoubtedly confess, bringing a rising tide of hatred to the already swollen waters of reactionary fear. If he failed to kill Mantle, Mantle would live to face the ludicrous charges Simmons would undoubtedly have raised—that the attempt had been made to "keep the ball player from talking" or some similar nonsense. If the assassin, or would-be assassin, were to be killed or to get away, the bullets fired would lead to his gun, and the gun would lead to the League.

There was only one way the plan could have failed. Kennedy cursed himself for not having seen it.

"We chose the wrong fanatic, Nofsinger," Kennedy said. He could hear the fat man's sigh of relief when he heard the word *we*. Let him relax, Kennedy told himself. It was his fault, and he'll pay for it, but for now I need him.

"I'm sorry, boss; I don't see how he did it. I don't even know how the congressman came to be at the game."

"I want this Thane, Nofsinger."

"I'm looking, boss," Nofsinger said. "But it's not going to be easy. He must have been wearing a disguise yesterday. All the descriptions say sandy hair, square jaw. Thane hardly had a jaw at all, and his hair was sort of brown. It was our gun he used, though."

"Find him." Kennedy's voice was flat and hard. "If I have to come to New York to do it myself, I'm going to be displeased."

Nofsinger gulped. "Boss, there's something else that's going to make you displeased."

"Yes?"

"I went to consult Bristow about this—you know, our tame Commie, the one we used in the Laird busi—"

"I know who you mean. Was he any help?"

"He wasn't there. He's disappeared."

"Disappeared."

"Yes, sir. Friday afternoon he left his office for a late lunch, and nobody's seen him since. I've talked to his wife, his nurse; nothing."

"That's very interesting, Nofsinger. Do you think it has any connection with the business at hand?"

Nofsinger thought it over for a minute. "Don't see how it could," he said at last. "But it's funny. I thought you ought to know."

"Very good, Nofsinger. I'll speak to you again Tuesday."

He hung up.

"Honey?" asked a timid voice.

Kennedy turned to see Lindy standing in the bathroom doorway, her platinum hair darkened to yellow by water and steam. Behind her, the shower still ran.

"Yes, Lindy?" Kennedy asked.

"Honey, can I come out of the shower now? I'm getting all pruney."

"Yes, Lindy, you may come out now," he said. Lindy thanked him and disappeared back into the bathroom to turn the water off.

Gennarro Kennedy had already forgotten her. He was

thinking that he didn't like to be duped. And he was working on new plans to put things back in their proper order.

7

Garrett's parents were in the living room watching Donald O'Connor wrapping up the *Colgate Comedy Hour.* Garrett's mother doted on Donald O'Connor, so they watched the Colgate show anytime he was the host. Every other week it was Ed Sullivan.

Garrett said hello, went to the kitchen and got his dinner out of the oven, and joined them.

Garrett's father got up and switched to WABD, where it was time for Roscoe Karns in *Rocky King, Inside Detective.* It was just about the only thing on the DuMont Network they ever watched.

"How do you like that picture, Russ?" Mr. Garrett asked.

"Looks great. New picture tube?"

His father laughed. "Nah, turned out not to need one. I just adjusted the antenna. Must have blown off-line in the last big storm."

Garrett's mother sniffed. "The damned fool was up on the roof all afternoon. I had to keep running in and out to tell him how the picture looked. Quite a show for the neighbors."

"You can't argue with results, Florence."

"It *is* a great picture, Mom," Garrett said. "I bet Donald has never looked so good before."

Mrs. Garrett sniffed again. "In *Singing in the Rain* he was in color."

Rocky King was underway, but it was a klinescope of an episode they'd already seen, so they kept talking.

"One of my magazines at the shop says NBC's gonna do a *Colgate Comedy Hour* in color come fall," Mr. Garrett said.

"In the movies?" Mrs. Garrett wanted to know.

"No, TV. They're working on a way to show color and black and white on the same show. If it works they'll start selling color TVs."

"If nobody's got a color TV, how will they know if it works?"

"NBC has got some. For the test. Use your head, Florence."

She stuck her tongue out at him; everybody laughed.

Russ Garrett thought about color TV. That would be great, like dreams. His dreams, anyway, though he did know some people who claimed to dream in black and white. That didn't make much sense to Garrett—people were dreaming before there were movies, or TV, or even photographs. Where did they ever get the *idea* of the black and white when the human race was already in color?

He relaxed and let his mind wander, letting the day slide off his shoulders like a heavy pack. Baseball would look great on color TV, he thought; the color of the crowd, all that green . . .

Which reminded him. "How did the Yankees do today, Dad?"

His father looked surprised. "Weren't you at the game?"

"No, the cops had me out running around with them all day."

Garrett's mother sniffed. His father said, "Get anywhere?" Garrett shook his head.

"Commie bastards," the older man grumbled.

Garrett let it slide. "So how did they do?" he asked again.

His father shrugged. "They won, but I'm starting to get a bad feeling about them."

"They're still in first place."

"They're coasting, son. Taking it easy. They fall into that kind of habit, the National League will whip their tail come October. Lightning can strike the Yanks as easily as anybody else."

Rocky King had wrapped up his case at nine thirty. The elder Garretts went to bed. Russ switched to CBS and watched *Man Behind the Badge*, followed by *The Web*. *The Web* boasted stories about "normal, everyday people who find themselves in situations beyond their control."

"This," he muttered, "is the show for me." When that

was over, he switched to NBC and watched Ralph Bellamy in *Man Against Crime*. It was starting to irritate him how easily these TV guys solved their cases.

Garrett watched the late news and was about halfway through *The Late Show* when he admitted to himself he'd put it off long enough. He was going to think about what had happened today sooner or later; he might as well get it over with.

God, what a mess. All he'd accomplished was to set himself up for big trouble when Captain Murphy found out about his little side trip. That, and reopen a wound he'd thought had healed over.

Garrett took the photograph from his pocket.

He was going to look at the picture. He was going to look at the picture, and he wasn't going to cry. And he wasn't going to hate Annie for being so stubborn, and he wouldn't punish himself for something beyond his control, like the show said. He wouldn't curse his fate for *being* beyond his control.

Sure he wouldn't.

Okay, Garrett, he told himself. Let's take this easy. Turn the picture over. That's it. Look at the beach, the waves, the sky. Don't look at the people yet, especially not at Annie.

Okay. Now look at Jenny. She's a nice lady; she won't hurt you. She's pretty, too. Now look at the man. Take a good look at him. You never met him, never knew him, but he was instrumental in this whole mess. Try to get to know him from the picture. Looks sort of familiar, doesn't he? The light-colored hair, that square jaw. Just like in that police sketch , , ,

Garrett looked again. "No," he said to no one in particular. "Get out of here with this stuff." But the picture refused to change.

Garrett's first impulse was to run for the phone, but he stifled it. Tomorrow. Tomorrow would be plenty of time to call. It would give him a chance to think. Besides, he didn't want to wake the babies.

8

Garrett sat in the telephone booth for ten minutes, holding a dime in his hand and feeling sweat running like a river down his spine. Garrett had always thought he liked summer—now he realized he hated it. It was *baseball* that had been making his summers tolerable all these years. It was an interesting thing to find out. Of course, baseball was a warm-weather game, so you'd think if you loved baseball so much, you'd like the kind of weather it had to be played in. On the other hand . . .

Garrett was doing it again. He was sitting in a phone booth in a New Rochelle gas station, watching the Monday-morning traffic crawling into the city. Delaying his phone call.

He was delaying it, he knew, because he shouldn't be making it in the first place. There were other people to talk to. If he were an idealist, he would tell Vicious Aloysius Murphy about the man in the picture. If he were a pragmatist, he would tell Congressman Simmons the Second, newly appointed this morning.

Instead, he was going to call Jenny Laird, and he didn't know *what* that made him. Noble, maybe. Or a horse's ass.

He left the phone booth, and for a few seconds the sweltering morning air felt cool by comparison. He walked to the soda machine, where he invested a nickel in a bottle of Coke. The Pause That Refreshes, he thought.

The trouble was, he didn't know enough. How could he call up a widow and tell her her husband was a dead ringer—so to speak—for the guy who had murdered the man who'd driven her husband to suicide, and what do you think of that, Jenny old kid?

Garrett couldn't bring himself to do that, but he knew if he told the cops, they could bring themselves to ask her that question without a second thought.

Garrett finished his Coke, placed the empty bottle in the rack, and went back to bake himself in the phone booth some more.

What the hell, Garrett thought. I'll call. What did he have to lose? What if he didn't know enough about the (purportedly) late Professor David Laird to approach his wife about him? Then he'd find out. And the first thing he'd do was tell the (purported) widow to expect him. He had to tell her in person. He picked up the receiver and dropped his dime in the phone.

9

"Let's go out on the rocks," the taller boy said. "The beach is too crowded."

That was not exactly true. There *were* plenty of people at the beach today and plenty more at the amusement park just behind it. But it was still only a Monday morning, and compared to the crowds that had been here yesterday, the beach was practically deserted. What the boy, whose name was Jeff, had meant was that there were too many people around who inhibited him from talking the way he wanted to, or running around as much as he wanted to, or laughing too loud. Jeff was fifteen.

His companion was a year younger and five inches shorter. His name was Larry, and he was waiting impatiently for the "growth spurt" his mother promised him would come along any day now. He was tired of being the shortest one in his crowd; the whole business was making him into a grouch.

"What are we gonna do out on the rocks?" he asked rhetorically. "If the lifeguard sees us, we'll get in trouble, and besides, the breakwater is going to be covered with bird shit." Larry pointed to a spot about halfway down its length. The air above that one spot was so thick with birds, it was hard to see how they avoided colliding. Their creaking, raucous cries could be heard even above the sound of the waves of the incoming tide.

"We could dive off," Jeff suggested. Jeff had seen newsreels of the diving competition from the Olympics in Helsinki last year.

"Uh-uh," Larry told him. "Who knows how deep the water is? We could break our necks."

"Chicken."

"Showoff."

"Okay, okay. We'll jump in feet first. It's just so damn hot here—maybe it'll be cooler out there."

"What about the birds?"

"We won't go out as far as the birds. Come on, Larry."

Larry said, "Oh, all right," and went along.

It *was* cooler out on the breakwater, and the lifeguard hadn't seen them yet. The boys talked about the upcoming school year, and they talked about girls. They both admitted (and this was a true mark of their friendship) that they watched the *Mickey Mouse Club*, even though they were much too old for that, to look at the girls. Jeff liked Annette, but Larry was partial to Darlene.

"I wonder what those birds are interested in so much," Larry said after a while. "Look how long they fly in a circle without even flapping their wings."

Jeff decided he was going to see what it was, bird shit or no bird shit. Larry followed.

Whatever had attracted the birds was stuck down between the rocks. Every so often, as the boys watched, a gull would dive-bomb the spot and fly off with something. Jeff picked his way over the rough surfaces of the boulders as the birds yelled at him in resentment. He looked down.

He saw a blob of pink and greenish white, with the rising tide just starting to lap across it. It was, Jeff realized to his astonishment, a man's face, except a lot of it was . . . the birds had . . . the eyes . . .

Jeff screamed. He threw his arms across his eyes and sobbed and screamed. Larry reached him, looked at the horror amid the rocks, shuddered, and turned to his friend. "Jeff, let's get out of here." Jeff kept screaming.

By now the lifeguard had noticed the boys and was blasting his whistle, ordering them to come off the rocks.

Jeff wouldn't uncover his eyes, wouldn't expose them to the gulls or to a chance he might see that face again. Larry had to lead him to the beach.

10

Nofsinger was speculating on the cleverness of the Rockefellers as he waited for Jenny Laird and her kid to leave the eye doctor's office on East Forty-third Street.

It had really been a sharp move. A few years ago this area here, First Avenue in the high Thirties, low Forties, had been nothing special, a little seedy if you got right down to it. The only notable thing about it was that the Rockefellers happened to own it. Okay. Then the United Nations comes along, a chance for a bunch of foreigners to park on our doorstep and tell us how to run the world we'd just almost single-handedly saved the ass of. And the UN is looking for a place to stay, instead of having to rent office space like an insurance company or something.

Then the Rockefellers step in. Sure, they say, we got some land by the East River with nothing but a few old tenements and stuff on it. Here, go ahead, take it, I can use the tax deduction. And the gooks and geeks and the top-hatted cookie-pushers all say gee, thanks, and raise money to build the fancy blue glass affair Nofsinger would now be seeing if he would deign to look over his left shoulder.

Nofsinger didn't need to see the building to appreciate the Rockefellers' ingenuity. Trust them to see a way to make some good old-fashioned American capitalist money out of this liberal world government crap. Because when the UN took the Rockefellers' generous gift, and people from all over the world started coming to this particular neighborhood, the real estate values of the whole area went through the roof. *And the Rockefellers still owned most of it.*

Nofsinger chuckled. He loved people who made money out of nothing that way. He couldn't do it himself, but he appreciated a sharp deal the way other people could appreciate a fine painting. It was almost enough to make Nofsinger glad that cable from the boss had been waiting for him when he arrived at the office. For some reason Mr. Kennedy had decided that the Laird woman should be followed, starting today, and that Nofsinger himself should do the following.

Nofsinger was reluctant to leave the nice, air-conditioned office Klimber Enterprises had taken for him in a brand-new building on Park Avenue, but orders from Kennedy had to be followed. He'd gotten to the Laird woman's place on the Island just in time to tail her and her son back to Manhattan. He'd watched her bring some stuff to *Coronet* magazine (she was a writer—Nofsinger knew that from when he'd done a job on her husband), then take her kid to the ophthalmologist or whatever he was.

Nofsinger was fanning himself with a sweat-stained fedora when his subjects left the office. To his surprise, she headed directly across the street to the UN. Hastily Nofsinger replaced his hat and followed.

Despite his bulk Nofsinger had the knack of not being noticed unless he wanted to be. It was easy to get close enough to catch the name of the guy she was meeting. It figured she would be meeting a guy—cute widow, still young, what the hell, right?

"Hello, Russ," Nofsinger heard the woman's bright voice say. She turned to her son. "Mark, this is Mr. Garrett."

Russ Garrett. Okay. Now he had something besides the doctor to put in his report. Time to move on, watch them from a distance. No sense in making himself too obvious.

11

Mark was a good-looking, intelligent kid whose eyes managed to look clear and bright even through the lenses of his hornrims.

"Mom says you play for the Yankees, Mr. Garrett." The kid looked up at Garrett through narrowed eyes. There was caution in his voice that verged on suspicion.

Garrett smiled. "No, your mother was giving me a promotion. I played for the Kansas City Blues. Sort of the junior Yankees. If a player is good enough there, he gets to go to New York."

"Do you really know Mickey Mantle?"

"Good friend of mine. We played together in Kansas City."

Garrett could feel himself rise a notch or two in the boy's estimation.

"How come they call the team the Blues?" Mark asked. "If they called it the Junior Yankees, everybody would be proud of them."

"Well," Garrett said, "Kansas City is in Missouri, and Missouri is in the South—at least, it's more like the South than it is like the North—and you couldn't have a team called the Yankees in the South, could you?"

Mark said he guessed not. "Do you go to the Yankee games a lot, Mr. Garrett?" Garrett told him he did. "Gee," Mark said, "do you think I could go with you once and meet the players? I wouldn't bother them at all, except maybe ask for their auto—"

His mother grabbed him firmly by the shoulder. "Mark!" she scolded. "What happened to your manners?"

She started to apologize, but Garrett grinned and waved it aside. "I might be able to arrange it, Mark. If your mother says it's okay."

Mark immediately turned to his mother, but before he could ask if it was okay, she told him she'd think about it. The boy, seeing his best plan was to keep his mother happy, subsided. "Can I go look at the flags?" Mark was trying to memorize the flags of all the United Nations. There was a breeze today, although it was a hot, wet one off the East River, so this was a good day for it.

"Yes, Mark, go look at the flags. Mr. Garrett and I will be on that bench."

They took a seat. "Your call was a pleasant surprise," Jenny Laird said.

Jenny Laird smiled at herself as she remembered how she'd tried to sound calm on the phone while changing two diapers at the same time (the twins did *everything* together). Then how she'd lied and said it was the day she had planned for a trip to Manhattan anyway, and called Mrs. Perkins to see if she could watch the twins and the doctor to change Mark's appointment.

She'd taken extra care with her appearance, too. She was wearing her nicest daytime dress, the navy blue one with the nautical collar. She had a white straw hat, sort of an *H.M.S. Pinafore* kind of thing, white shoes, and nice white gloves—lord, she hadn't worn gloves since before . . . she hadn't worn them in a long time. Lipstick and round red earrings (they set off her hair nicely) gave the ensemble a touch of color. A dash of powder, and she was ready to go.

It occurred to Jenny Laird to wonder why she was going through all this schoolgirl nonsense to meet a man she had seen for the first time last night, at the other end of her shotgun. She couldn't think of an answer. She only knew she wanted to make a good impression today on Mr. Russell Garrett, and that desire felt *good*. It had been so long since she'd cared this much about anything. She'd been all seized up inside, like a typewriter with all its keys jammed together. Maybe with Rex Harwood Simmons dead, she could stop being The Woman Who Wasn't Ashamed of Her Husband and just let herself be herself for a change.

She smiled and asked Garrett if he'd been waiting long.

"Not too long," Garrett replied. "I got here early and took the tour." He looked over at Mark, who was studying the flag of the Byelorussian Soviet Socialist Republic.

"How did you like it? Isn't this a wonderful place? Inspiring, I mean, in a practical sort of way. A permanent headquarters devoted to peace. I—" Jenny noticed that Garrett wasn't responding. He was, in fact, looking at his shoes.

"What's the matter?" she asked.

Garrett looked up and gestured at the General Assembly Hall, the completed part of the complex. "Look at that thing. If they wanted a headquarters devoted to world peace, why the hell did they build a place that looks like the roof is about to cave in?"

"Gloomy today, aren't you?" Jenney said. Garrett didn't respond. She tried again. "What were they talking about in there today? Is it World War Three or something?"

Garrett took a deep breath. "Not today, at least. I don't know. Something France should be doing in Morocco or something like that."

"Oh."

Two more minutes of silence. The Circle Line ferry cruised by. Some African diplomats passed them. They seemed to be enjoying the weather. Jenny could feel her gloves getting damper by the second. She took them off.

At last she said, "*God damn it!*" A couple of people turned around to look at her, but Jenny didn't notice. "Russ Garrett, what is the matter with you?"

Garrett made a sour face and reached into his jacket pocket. "I want you to take a look at this, Jenny," he said.

She took the folded piece of grayish paper from him and opened it. It was a photostat of a sketch of a man's face.

"So?" Jenny said. She didn't know what he was up to, but she knew she didn't like it.

"Look familiar?"

"Should it?"

"Look again."

Jenny looked. "Is this supposed to be David?" She was getting impatient with all this. "Is that it? Because that's the only reason I can think of that you'd expect me to recognize this thing. Is this supposed to be my husband?"

Garrett's eyes looked deeply into hers—Jenny could see he was as unhappy about this as she was. She wanted to look away but decided not to. Foolish or not, this was something important.

"It's *supposed* to be," Garrett said, "a composite sketch drawn from witnesses' descriptions of the man who shot Congressman Rex Harwood Simmons to death Saturday afternoon."

"What are you getting at?" Jenny was surprised to hear her voice so calm. She did not feel calm.

"Jenny, *could* this be a picture of your husband?"

Jenny couldn't stand it. She looked down at the white gloves she was holding and felt soiled, betrayed. He was no better than the police. He was worse. He was doing this out of—of *curiosity*. He had used his relationship with poor, dead Ann; he had even used her son to win her confidence. Then to put her through this! She was sick. She almost wished she had her shotgun.

"You are insane. My husband is *dead*." She gave the

young man beside her a look of bewilderment and fear.

Garrett looked at the sky. "God, I hate this," he said, then held her eyes again. "Jenny, how can you be sure of that? I have a friend who works for the AP, and this morning after I called you, I got to look at the files. The stories all said your husband's body was burned beyond recognition in his car at the bottom of a cliff up in the Catskills. That he mailed you a letter telling you he was sorry."

Jenny felt her hands forming claws, checked herself and made fists instead. "I *know* all this, damn you, I lived through it! Why are you raking it all up?"

"The picture you gave me last night, Jenny," Garrett said. He removed the photo from a pocket, held it close to the police drawing. "He looks just *like* him, Jenny."

"He does *not!*"

"He looks enough like your husband for me to have spotted the resemblance in a picture I hardly noticed he was in. Okay; you were his wife, and you knew him better than anybody—you can see the differences where other people see only the resemblances. But it's *too close*. The resemblance is too goddam close to ignore." Garrett pulled at a cheek, twisting his handsome face into an ugliness Jenny found more appropriate to his actions. He went on. "Look, Jenny, you have to help me on this. I need you to—"

Jenny laughed, a loud, wild, slightly hysterical noise. "You want me to *help* you! You mean you can actually sit here and tell me you want me to help *you*? You must be crazy. Mark!" Jenny stood and started looking around for her son.

Garrett grabbed her wrist, not gently, and pulled her back down to the bench. "*Shut up and listen, goddammit!*" Garrett was shaking and talking through clenched teeth. It was the first time she'd seen him angry, and she was surprised to learn how frightening his anger was.

She rubbed her wrist and listened.

Garrett had stopped shaking, but his voice still ripped small, ragged holes in the humid summer air. "Your husband's life was ruined by Rex Simmons and his stupid witch-hunts. Simmons was shot to death by a man whom all witnesses describe as your husband's double. And when I check into the circumstances of your husband's *suicide*, the only thing that says it's really him that's dead is the note he sent. Whatever was left in the car was burned beyond recognition."

Hot tears scalded Jenny's eyes, but she wouldn't wipe them away. She couldn't move. She was frozen by the horror of the situation and the loathing she felt for the man beside her.

"Look, Jenny," Garrett said. His voice was gentle now. He was trying to reason with her. God, she hated him. "That could have been *anybody* in that car. Your husband may have been alive all this time, planning revenge." Garrett took a breath. "Is he, Jenny?"

"You make me sick," Jenny Laird said.

"I'm trying to help you. I don't care if you believe that or not, but it's true. Because the police are going to wonder the same things. And they're going to find out. And if they decide he *is* alive, I have this awful feeling they're going to assume you've known about it all along. And I'm in the middle of this, in trouble myself. And I can't do anything to help either of us until I know exactly how things stand."

He took her wrist again, tenderly this time. "Please tell me, Jenny."

She pulled her hand away as though she knew Garrett not only had but *was* some sort of loathsome disease.

"*Liar!*" she screamed so loudly that even Nofsinger could hear her. The fat man had been watching the whole business from a safe distance. Some sort of lovers' tiff, no doubt. He listened; the woman might say something useful while she was still being loud.

"You disgust me, all of you!" she said. "It's not enough you hounded him to death; you can't leave him alone even after his ashes are scattered!" She looked like she was getting warmed up for a long, loud speech, and Nofsinger was afraid she would draw a crowd. He'd have to make himself scarce. It was easy to see what had happened. The boyfriend, this Garrett guy, had found out she was a Commie. Commies always cried and cut up rough when things went against them.

Nothing to worry about this time, though. The Laird babe took her kid and stalked off, leaving this Garrett looking miserable. It was Nofsinger's cue to follow. All probably a load of horseshit, anyway. As he closed in on his quarry, Nofsinger heard the kid asking when Mr. Garrett was going to take him to the ball game, and kids usually had pretty good instincts about that sort of thing.

12

Captain Murphy was waiting in Garrett's office. He was reading Garrett's copy of the *Sporting News* and humming something dramatic, from an opera, no doubt.

Garrett was more surprised that he had actually recognized the music than he was at the captain's presence. Somehow he'd been expecting him, or if not the captain himself, than Detective Martin or some other cop.

"That's the music from *Flash Gordon*," Garrett said. "I saw all twelve episodes at the Capitol Theatre in Port Chester when I was a kid."

Murphy looked disgusted. "That," he growled, "is the 'Ride of the Valkerie,' by Vogner."

"Who?"

"Wagner. Only pronounced *Vogner*. You're a barbarian, Garrett. Ah, screw it. How are you doing?"

Garrett made a face. "Not bad. How are you, Captain?"

"Tired, Garrett. Tired. I was up in your home territory today."

"Port Chester?"

"Rye," Murphy replied. "Couple kids found a body on the beach. Stuffed between the rocks of the breakwater like a beer can."

"Why did they call you out on a Westchester homicide?" Garrett asked, though he thought he could probably guess the answer.

"Because some Rye cops read the papers, and they remember what they read. So when they got this guy identified—from fingerprints, by the way; sea gulls had made hamburger of his face—they figured they ought to call me."

"Who was it?"

"Ever hear of a guy named David Laird? . . . Garrett, what's wrong?"

Garrett didn't want to know what his face looked like just then, what combination of surprise and guilt. Instead he said, "Somebody found David Laird's body? *Today?* He's supposed—I mean, I thought he killed himself three, four years ago. Didn't he?"

Murphy grunted, pushed back his hat, and looked surprised. "He's dead as far as *I* know. What in hell gave you the idea it was *his* body?"

Garrett shook his head as though to dismiss the whole business.

"You *do* know who he is, then," Murphy demanded. Garrett could hardly deny it.

"Good," the captain went on. "The body was his dentist's."

Garrett let out a slow breath. Things were starting to come together now. He remembered, he hoped irrelevantly, that that was how the A-bomb worked, two big chunks of uranium coming together. When that happened, you hung a sign on the door that said Gone Fission. With an effort Garrett dismissed the image from his mind. "Bristow," he said.

Murphy raised his eyebrows. "You know a lot about Laird, don't you? Even his dentist's name."

"It was a big story at the time, you know, and I was sort of a Columbia alumnus. So of course I followed it. One of Simmons's early triumphs."

"Yeah. I know all about Dr. Edward Bristow. I got it all rehashed for me this afternoon. God knows what good it's going to do anybody. I even know he wasn't actually even a dentist—"

"Periodontist," Garrett volunteered and was immediately sorry.

"A gum doctor," Murphy countered. "I even saw some pictures of him the way he was before the birds got at him. You'd never figure him for a Communist—crew cut and big smile he had—but you never know, I guess.

"Anyway, he and this David Laird were great friends, belonged to all the liberal organizations—ban the bomb, world government, that kind of thing. Used to go to demonstrations and stuff—they got arrested once; that's where Bristow's fingerprints came from—no big deal, lots of good citizens do that kind of thing. Then Simmons came along with his committee, investigating some of the organizations the two of them belonged to."

"And there was Bristow," Garrett added, "sitting in the witness chair, telling the congressman how they were constantly in touch with Joe Stalin and how they were going to take over the country. Laird, especially. Of course, Dr. Bristow had seen the error of his ways and was telling all about his former comrades to make up for the damge he had done to his country. Laird and lots of other witnesses came on to refute Bristow, but the public and the papers seemed to think he was telling the truth."

"Whereas you," Murphy said, "think he was merely throwing his friends to the wolves to keep from having a bite taken out of his own ass."

"Don't you?"

The captain shrugged. "I won't say it's not possible. One of the Rye cops was resurrecting some old rumors to the effect that Bristow was queer for little boys and that Simmons used that as leverage to fix the testimony."

Garrett snorted.

"But they had to be resurrected for me, Garrett. That means they were dead, you understand? Keep them that way. Bristow left a family."

"So did Laird."

Murphy raised his brows again and looked at Garrett, then went on. "Bristow left his office Friday afternoon and wasn't seen again, as far as anyone knows, until the body was found this afternoon."

There were several seconds of silence.

"So I thought I'd come over here and tell you about it. We *are* supposed to be working together on this thing."

Garrett opened his mouth, closed it, opened it again. "Captain, can I ask you a stupid question?"

"I wouldn't be surprised," said Vicious Aloysius.

Garrett's hand stole toward his jacket pocket. "What makes you think," Garrett said, "that Bristow's death ties up with Congressman Simmons's murder? I mean, he ties up with Laird, certainly, but Laird is dead."

Murphy leaped to his feet with a roar of rage that fluttered the letters and statistics sheets on Garrett's desk. "All right, Garrett," he roared, "that does it!"

Garrett backed away as though he were afraid the captain would bite him.

"I can't believe," Murphy roared on, "that you have the balls to sit there all coy when *one of my men saw you this afternoon holding hands at the United Nations with David Laird's widow!*"

"Now wait a minute," Garrett began.

"Wait, my ass. You start talking, boy, and I mean right *now!* Or the next thing you know you'll be playing ball on the Sing Sing team."

"I was going to tell you, but I wanted to make sure I wasn't making an idiot of myself."

"You don't know how close you are," Murphy told him, "to making a *statistic* of yourself. He wasn't even tailing *you*—just happened to pass by. Maybe I *should* have you followed. You better talk."

So Garrett took out the pictures and told the captain what he thought, and after a few minutes Captain Al (Vicious Aloysius) Murphy was calmer, but no happier.

"No," he said flatly. "No zombies allowed. I refuse to consider the idea that this son of a bitch is alive and killing the people who screwed him over before."

Garrett told him he didn't really mean it.

"No, goddammit, I guess I don't. But if he *is* alive, Garrett, I, for one, will never forgive you." He adjusted his hat. "Come on," he said.

"Where are we going?" Garrett wanted to know.

"Bronx Homicide. I want to get a statement from you before you grow hair all over and start howling at the moon."

13

Four people sat at a card table under an elaborate crystal chandelier in an otherwise-empty ballroom. Voices, when there were voices, echoed strangely off the distant walls and the high ceiling.

Congressman-designate Telford Simmons took a wooden tile from his tray and placed it on the board. "SMITHY," he said. "A place where a b-b-blacksmith works," he added in case anyone had any doubts. No one seemed to, so he went ahead and added his score. "Fourteen points on a double-word score—twenty-eight."

Scrabble, they called it. Stupid game, a big fad a few months ago. Somebody was making a fortune off it.

Tad was winning; that was the only consolation. The rest of it was simply beneath his dignity. Here he was, on the way home from his brother's funeral, the new congressman from one of only a handful of Republican districts anywhere near Kansas City, paying a courtesy call on a favored constituent, and what happens? He gets dragooned (along with Cheryl) into a game of *Scrabble*, for God's sake, with a senile old woman and her colored assistant. Tad didn't like it one bit.

Granted, Mrs. Klimber had been a big help to his brother and stood to be just as important to Tad's own ambitions. Granted, the old lady had to be humored. But only within reason. This would be the last time something like this would happen.

Because Tad Simmons was in the driver's seat now. His brother's death gave Tad a sort of political holiness—no one had better mess with *him*. The governor had seen that; that was why his seat in Congress waited only approval of the full body. Hell, even the local *Democrats* had seen it. Alive, Tad's brother Rex had been a nuisance to the remains of the old Tom Prendergast machine. Dead, he threatened to smash it. Tad almost smiled. Rex would have been proud of him.

The only cloud in Tad Simmons's blue sky was the investigation of his brother's death. That had damn well better turn out right—it had damn well better be a Communist who'd done the foul deed instead of, say, a jealous husband. There could be plenty of those around, too. Of course, Cheryl had pretty much distracted Rex from that sort of thing, especially over the last year or so, but Tad still worried. It was the not knowing that got to him. Why the hell hadn't Garrett reported to him yet? It had been two whole days. Hadn't the cops found anything?

But someone was talking to him. "Excuse me, Mrs. Klimber?" he said. "I was, ah, planning my next move."

"No wonder you're beating us so badly, Telford," the old woman said. "I was just saying that you made quite a score with one little letter."

Tad nodded and growled. The game went on.

Cheryl Tilton would have taken more notice of her employer's discomfiture, and enjoyed it more, if she hadn't been so fascinated by Mrs. Klimber. Cheryl took great pride in herself as a woman—it offended her to think Zenith Klimber fell into the same category.

Cheryl found her intolerable. Her build was so broad it reminded Cheryl of the front third of a hippopotamus. She had the wide mouth and the broad nose of a hippo, too, and her smile, which was frequent, showed huge, white, symmetrical teeth, manufactured, no doubt, by some dentist who wanted to complete the picture.

Mrs. Klimber constantly ate chocolate-covered cherries, the kind with liqueur centers. She consumed about a box an hour. Everyone thinks the old woman's crazy ideas come from senility, Cheryl reflected. Maybe she was just continually looped on cherry liqueur.

None of which would have been so bad if she didn't keep talking about her son all the time. Her Late Son. Even now as Mrs. Klimber was pushing a chocolate-covered cherry into her maw and reaching out her massive hand to make her word (BOOTY), she commenced a story about Her Late Son and how quick he had been to learn to walk.

It seemed to Cheryl that the old woman always directed these stories to her exclusively, as though the old monster were trying to make some kind of perverted match between Cheryl and Her Late Son.

Mrs. Klimber had even given Cheryl a set of keys to the mansion Her Late Son and his intended bride had planned to move into when he came home from the Philippines. Of course, he had never come home, and the intended bride had eventually married someone else and moved to Oregon. And if you ever wanted to see real insanity in Mrs. Klimber— shouting, and crying, and hippopotamus-size fury—all you had to do was remind her of what Her Late Son's beloved had done.

The mansion was across the river, in Kansas, in Mission Hills, where practically all the area's wealthiest (except Mrs. Klimber) lived. Out of curiosity Cheryl had gone there once and had a look around. On the outside it could have been the twin of the building she was now in—an enormous mound of Victorian gingerbread. Inside, though, it was as modern and stark as this one was traditional and elegant. Cheryl had learned that Mrs. Klimber had furnished it all herself. Cheryl didn't even want to think about what that might mean.

It was Gennarro Kennedy's turn. Building off the T in BOOTY, Kennedy made the word THANE.

"Gennarro," Mrs. Klimber chided, "I'm sure you could have made a much better move than that. You've only eight points with that word. Go ahead, take it back and try again. We'll all let you, won't we?" She was very fond of Gennarro. He was so helpful. And he'd been in the army with Her Late Son.

That was another thing about Mrs. Klimber that made Cheryl's spine crawl. That wheedling, conniving, coquettish little-girl voice coming from that grotesque body.

It didn't seem to bother the Negro. "Thank you, Mrs. Klimber," he said, "but it pleases me to make that word." Then he smiled and gestured to Cheryl that it was her turn.

Gennarro Kennedy was *very* pleased with the word he'd made. He was glad the opportunity had come up. THANE—a Scottish nobleman. Something like a Laird. Something, unless he missed his guess, *quite* like a Laird.

He'd speculated on the words Sunday, instructed

Nofsinger this morning to begin surveillance of David Laird's widow. If Nofsinger hadn't been so ignorant, he might have made the connection himself months ago, when a man calling himself Thane became the most likely candidate to become an assassin.

But, Kennedy had to admit, that was not entirely fair. If Dr. Bristow, who was an important figure from the Laird case, hadn't been missing, Kennedy, too, might have failed to make the Thane-Laird association. But he *had* made the connection, and acted on it, and it had already borne fruit. The Laird woman was involved in this case. He'd had a report from Nofsinger that she'd met that very afternoon— not with a boyfriend, as Nofsinger had originally supposed— but with the man who'd found Rex Simmons's body, who was also a friend of Mickey Mantle's. Who was also, according to the report Kennedy's agents had assembled, assisting the police. And who was also, Kennedy knew, *supposed* to be Tad Simmons's tame information source.

Kennedy smiled. It would be interesting to see the young Simmons's reaction to that piece of news; Kennedy would have to tell him, but not just yet.

Things were just getting interesting. Kennedy had assessments to make before he acted. It was a challenge, and he loved it. Even now, as he plotted a new word for the Scrabble board, he was making plans for the next round of the bigger game.

14

David Laird sat at the table in the cottage that was located between the ocean and the oil refinery and read the newspapers. He hadn't bought the newspapers—he didn't want anyone to see him reading or buying something to read.

Instead, he took the newspapers from gutters or garbage cans he passed on his way. Sometimes the newspapers were stained with other garbage that made them smell, but David Laird didn't notice, any more than he noticed the perpetual stench of the refinery.

There were some interesting stories in today's papers.

Bristow's body had been found; two boys had found it. Good. Laird had been afraid that it might have come loose and washed out to sea. That would have been safer, of course, to have Bristow just disappear, as the drifter had disappeared, without a trace. But Laird was glad the body had been found. "Brutally tortured before being shot," the paper said. Laird laughed.

It was that drifter, that nameless old man, really, who had put David Laird on the road he still traveled, the one that was now nearing its end.

That's trite, he thought. I used to take points off essays for phrases like that.

Besides, it's a lie, Laird thought. The old drunkard was a prop, the merest accident of fate, a cipher that suddenly became important in an equation on a different part of the page.

It had happened at precisely the right moment. Laird's book contracts had been canceled; his public reputation was destroyed; his best friend had betrayed him; he was about to go to jail because of that betrayal; he had done something that could hurt Jenny terribly; and he had just learned he was a sick, sick man.

Laird could see himself now, the way he was then, filled with hatred and despair, sitting at his desk in the home Jenny had since had to sell. Composing suicide notes. But it had been all too much to face, even in a suicide note. He had needed air. He decided to go for a drive. He reached a decision on that drive. Somehow they would pay. Everyone, but especially Bristow and the Honorable Rex Harwood Simmons—a coward and a maniac, who had combined to destroy his life.

Violence was not yet part of Laird's plan. He didn't even *have* a plan. He'd think about one as soon as he stopped driving, he'd decided, then discovered he couldn't wait to stop driving. He stopped his car outside an all-night diner, intending to buy a cup of coffee.

That's where the drifter came in. The man loomed out of a doorway and asked for a nickel. There were scabs on his face, and he smelled like something a distillery had flushed into a sewer. With impatience and disgust Laird pushed him away.

The drifter staggered backward and fell, and never got up. It wasn't that he had fallen especially hard or hit his head or anything like that. It was just that somewhere between the shove and the landing, the drunkard's abused body had ceased to function anymore.

Laird didn't realize it at first. He'd apologized to the corpse, offered him a dollar, tried to help him to his feet.

Then awareness seeped in, and David Laird felt a flash of fear—they'd be after him for *murder* now. But that was followed by a much stronger surge of inspiration. *He* would die. The drifter would vanish—no one would look for *him*— and David Laird would be free.

He did everything in the white heat of that moment. He had an old envelope in his glove compartment and a three-cent stamp in his wallet. He tore a page from his journal and wrote a "suicide" note to Jenny, which he immediately mailed.

He stuffed the dead man into the car and drove upstate to a dangerous mountain road, stopping along the way to pick up a discarded beer bottle. He stripped the corpse and switched his clothes for the drifter's bug-infested rags.

He got his gas siphon from the trunk and filled the beer bottle again and again, dousing the body and the inside of the car.

And realized he had no matches. Laird sat down and almost wept in frustration. He couldn't turn back. And he couldn't just hope the car would burst into flames when he pushed it over the cliff.

Then he had an idea. He tore a rag off what he was wearing and soaked it in gasoline. He started the car motor and revved the engine, wedging the drifter's leg so that his foot kept pressing on the accelerator.

Laird opened the hood and laid the gasoline-soaked rag on the radiator as the engine heated up. It was risky—Laird knew that even if it *did* light, he was gasoline-soaked now, too, from his work inside the car. He didn't care. He just wanted this over with.

Seconds went by, then minutes. Nothing. Laird got a blanket from the car and wedged it down between the radiator and the grill, giving the heat nowhere to go. After a few minutes the rag burst into flame, and seconds after that David Laird pushed his car and his whole life down the face of the cliff in flames.

It wasn't until days later that it began to dawn on David Laird what he had done to himself. To cut himself off from his children, and from Jenny. To leave them to face everything alone. To run out on Ann, just when—what had gotten into him?

But even as his mind formed the question, he knew the answer.

What had gotten into him was the *fear*, the constant fear, the diseased fear that the witch-hunters exploited, preyed on, and (Laird now knew) felt themselves. He had become, he realized, as brutal and inhuman as they were. Because he had yielded to the fear.

They had made him an animal; very well, he would stalk them. He was safe; they thought he was dead. His time, while not unlimited, was ample. He could take months to find the weak spot, to make his revenge perfect.

As he had. David Laird could almost smile just thinking about it. He remembered discussing with his classes Machiavelli's famous quote about revenge being a dish best eaten cold. It was true. It was true.

Laird's pains were back, but not so bad that they kept him from thinking, from remembering. He stacked up the newspapers, turned off the light, and lay on his cot.

He remembered the time he had spent just getting ready to *start*—the new documents, the surgery, the long drudgery of working at odd jobs to raise the money to buy these things. It didn't matter. It had bought him time, and it had made him resourceful, and it had allowed him the perfect disguise.

So he had begun. He studied Congressman Rex Harwood Simmons, and a single, badly disposed of piece of paper had put him onto Mrs. Klimber. From there it had been a trivial step to Gennarro Kennedy, the Negro whom she used to pass along her orders. Putting himself close to

Kennedy (physically, that is—the time for infiltration was yet to come) yielded the merest glimpse of a photograph of a fat, jolly-looking man, but the glimpse had been enough for him to recognize the face of the man who had been the harbinger of all his troubles. The fat man had claimed to be a reporter and had first started stirring up Laird's associates and neighbors with questions.

That was the weak link. The fat man, who had called himself Norton, was a front for Kennedy, who was a front for Klimber, who was behind Rex Simmons. A direct line but far enough removed for Laird to move in safety. Laird returned to New York and found his man in two weeks, fronting a supposed liberal organization.

Laird had, in fact, felt safe enough to exhibit a little bravado. He'd called himself Thane. Just to give his enemies a fighting chance.

Which had been more than they'd given him. He began setting the trap for the congressman, using the name of Mickey Mantle as bait. It had been easy.

"Brutally tortured," the newspaper had said. Laird snorted. Bristow had gotten off easily. Laird's conscience was clear, at least on that score. He still felt bad about Jenny. He missed her. Perhaps, now that his work was over, he'd get a chance to see her. Before it was too late.

David Laird tried to rest. The pains in his head, more frequent now, were too severe to let him sleep.

Chapter Five
Road Trip

1

Exactly one week later, on Tuesday, September first, 1953, Russ Garrett was fastening his seat belt as the TWA Constellation that carried him made its final approach to Kansas City.

Detective Martin had the next seat, but the two men weren't traveling together—not officially, at least. Martin was going to confer with the Kansas City police and with the local office of the FBI about their end of the increasingly futile Rex Simmons investigation.

Garrett, on the other hand, was supposed to be using the trip to K.C. to check on employment opportunities with American Association ball teams for his veterans. And he probably would do some of that.

But his real reason was to talk to Hal Keating. Hal used to work for the Yankees. He was the scout who had originally signed Garrett to a pro baseball contract. Now he was a Kansas City businessman, exploring the possibility of bringing major-league ball there. Hal had a Silver Star for OSS work during World War II, and he combined common sense with an open mind. He was a good friend.

Garrett wanted to see Hal Keating to discuss the possibility that he, Garrett, was losing his mind. He also figured he would play out at least one scene of the farce that had him spying on the police for Tad Simmons. All he'd be able to tell the new congressman was "no progress." Garrett was not about to go to Simmons with his David Laird idea. He'd been laughed at about that enough already.

Well, Garrett thought, maybe "no progress" wasn't entirely fair. Things had happened during the past week. The New York Yankees had traveled to Detroit, Cleveland, and Chicago, winning four games and losing three. The rest of the road trip would take them to St. Louis, Philadelphia, and Boston before they returned home.

During the past week Garrett had discovered Detective Martin's first name to be Cornelius. They continued to use last names.

The Westchester Medical Examiner's office had finally finished the report on the remains of Bristow, Edward P. The hardest part had been sorting out the damage that had been done by the birds, the tides, and the rocks from that inflicted by the killer. They decided that the bruises about the abdomen—the small, black ones—had been the result of deliberate blows. The two bullet holes at the base of the left side of the neck were obviously the killer's work, while the sea gulls and wave action were equally obviously the cause of the lighter bruises and the missing flesh. Bristow's fractured jaw was up for grabs, with the killer a slight favorite.

The FBI (though they hadn't taken the case away from the NYPD, much to Captain Murphy's disappointment) had been conducting their own investigations, and while they wouldn't come out and *say* they were positive no known Communist group or individual had killed Congressman Rex Harwood Simmons, they *would* stake J. Edgar Hoover's mother on the conclusion that Moscow hadn't ordered them to do it. All the law-enforcement people Garrett knew were inclined to believe this. As Captain Murphy had put it, "When Hoover lets the Russians off the hook, they've *got* to be innocent. Hell, the FBI's still trying to pin the Bonus Army Riots on them."

Still, there was some evidence linking the shootings to a liberal (or worse) organization. Some time ago, about the beginning of July, in fact, a man who gave his name as Norton had walked into a Greenwich Village precinct house and reported his .22-caliber target pistol as stolen. He'd given the serial number, and it was the same gun that had shot Congressman Simmons and Officer Olsen of the New Jersey State Police. Further investigation had indicated that this Norton (who police said was middle-aged and heavyset) was the same Norton who was chairman of the People's League for Social Justice, a leftist group. Norton had not been found since the routine investigation had turned up the connection. The police were still looking.

Garrett's ears felt the pressure as the plane descended. He swallowed, then swallowed again. The way, he thought, he'd been swallowing his opinions all week.

If only the ballistics people had been able to *prove* Bristow had been shot with the same gun as the other two, Murphy would have had to take Garrett's theory seriously. Unfortunately, the bullets they'd dug out of the periodontist, though obviously .22s, were too beat up from contact with ribs and hipbones to be of any use as evidence.

Jenny Laird, on the other hand, had been taking Garrett very seriously. She'd taken him so seriously, in fact, that she refused to have anything whatever to do with him. His letters brought no replies; his phone calls were clicked off before he could finish saying hello. Except once. Jenny hadn't been home, and her son, Mark, had answered the phone. Garrett had identified himself, and Mark had proceeded to ream Garrett out for making his Mom cry. "I thought you were supposed to be *nice*," the boy had said, contempt oozing from his voice. "You can forget about your old baseball game." Then the kid had hung up on him.

That had happened yesterday morning. Garrett, by now, was happy for a chance to get out of town.

He looked out the window of the plane and watched the big propeller shimmering in the sunlight. Through the shimmer he could see Kansas City—the home, he reminded himself not quite bitterly, of his greatest baseball triumphs.

2

Unlike LaGuardia Airport, which was safely tucked away in suburban Queens, or the new Idlewild, which was so far removed from Manhattan it might as well be out in the country, Kansas City's airport was smack in the middle of the city itself. You could land, walk away from the airport, and find yourself in the heart of town in minutes.

Detective Martin had shown some qualms about the plane's swooping down past the city's tallest buildings. "Might as well use Broadway for a damn landing strip," he'd said. He was upset that Garrett hadn't warned him.

Hal Keating met them at the airport. He was a tall, thin man with a florid face, gray hair, and bushy black eyebrows that swept exuberantly out from his head like crow's wings. His voice was a musical baritone and, even dressed casually in a seersucker jacket, dark blue sport shirt, and white slacks, he seemed to carry with him an almost formal elegance.

Keating introduced himself to Detective Martin, pumping the Negro's hand so vigorously that some people passing through the airport stopped to look.

Martin looked around and grinned. "You could be breaking a social taboo or two, Mr. Keating. People are giving you the old hairy eyeball."

"Fuck 'em," Keating said, loudly and heartily. "When I know you better, I'll kiss you." The three men laughed.

Keating turned to Garrett and embraced him. "Rags, my boy, it's great to see you! How are the old legs?"

Garrett hadn't warned him. "Hanging by a thread, Hal. But at least I've still got them."

Keating punched him on the arm. "Don't give me that crap. You think I don't have my spies out? I know you're working out at the stadium, trying to get back to play again."

"And?" Garrett was no longer grinning.

"And? And stick to it, you touchy bastard!"

"I thought you were going to tell me how crazy I am, like everybody else."

Keating paused in the middle of lighting a long black cigar. "I figure," he said around puffs, "you already *know* how crazy you are. The odds are against you—so what? The odds are against anything. The only way to change the odds is to go out and work your ass off to make things come out the way you want. Now let's get your bags and head on out to the hotel." Garrett and Martin had booked rooms at the La Salle, the same hotel Garrett used to stay at when he was with the Blues. It was more nostalgia than anything else; he could have stayed at a better hotel, like the one where Hal was staying, but since this was a baseball errand, he decided to bunk at the place the ball players favored.

Martin protested that he should go and check in with the local police first, but Keating offered to drive him there after he checked in, so they decided to do it that way.

Outside the air-conditioned lobby, the temperature was 101 degrees. Garrett remarked that the contrast was like walking into a brick wall.

"You get used to it," Keating told him. "What the hell, Rags, you used to play ball in weather like this, remember? Of course, it's my hometown, and I don't mind it—"

As they crossed the street, a hot, heavy wind swept down on them from the north. Detective Martin made a face. "What in the name of God is that *smell?*" he demanded.

Garrett laughed. "I'm sorry, Martin. Something else I should have warned you about. Remember how I said Kansas City offers the best prime rib you'll ever taste?"

"The airport's not the only thing convenient to the center of town," Keating explained. "A cow'll come in on a barge or a train in the morning, be on somebody's plate by tonight. Stockyards don't smell pretty, but by God, with the slaughterhouse working twenty-four hours a day, we get some fresh meat."

Martin was still wincing. "How can you stand to put food in your mouth with that smell in your *nose?*"

"You only notice it when the wind is right." They got in the car—Keating drove a new Cadillac. "You've got to impress people when you're trying to buy a ball club. Besides, I keep running back and forth to St. Louis so much, trying to talk Veeck into selling me the Browns, I want something that won't give me a pain in the ass from just sitting in it."

After they'd dropped Martin at police headquarters, Keating said he felt like driving so he'd get Garrett reacquainted with some of the sights in town.

The first sight was Keating's own factory, to the south of the city. He made parts for radar. "Actually, it's my partner's invention—some kind of circuit. I had the army contracts from my OSS days. Rags, my boy, I'm cleaning up. The Klimber Company keeps offering to buy us out, but to hell with them. Maybe after I get the ball club—"

"How are your odds on that?"

"I don't know," Keating admitted. "Veeck wants to keep the club and move it himself, but the owners won't let him. They still hate him for that publicity stunt when he sent that midget up to bat. So he's gonna have to sell it, either to me or to these guys in Baltimore. Maybe Mrs. Klimber. I hear she's after it, too. But it would be unnatural for a woman to own a ball club. And it would be stupid to put a team in Baltimore—the Washington Senators or them would be out of business in ten years. So who knows?"

Garrett said something encouraging and went back to looking out the windows. In the two years he'd been away, the town had grown. One of the things Garrett liked most about Kansas City was its general air of confidence and enthusiasm. Rodgers and Hammerstein were dead wrong in the eyes of the locals. There was a general attitude that the city's best days were ahead of it. With a million people living in the city and the surrounding area, K.C. was nothing like a small town—except, Garrett told himself, to a blasé New Yorker. Still, there was that small-town air of civic pride and boosterism Garrett found refreshing.

"Sinclair Lewis," he murmured, "was a horse's ass."

"What?" Keating asked.

"Oh, nothing," Garrett said. "I see a lot of air force uniforms around town."

"Yeah, hadn't you heard? The Central Air Defense Command has put a big combat group here. That's to distract the Russians' attention and make them attack *us* instead of Chicago. Still, it's good for business—the General Motors plant is making Thunderstreaks for them to fly at the same time they're turning out Pontiacs for them to drive."

Keating was garrulous, Garrett quiet. They took the whole tour. Kit Carson's house; Union Station, that great

marble monument to the railroad empire building. Garrett
wondered if the bullet holes from Pretty Boy Floyd's Kansas
City Massacre in 1933 remained in the marble. Keating
assured him they did.

They drove in silence for a while. Finally Keating said,
"All right, kid. Ready to tell me what's on your mind?"

Garrett sighed and said he supposed so, and they went
back to the older man's hotel to talk it over.

3

". . . and that's it," Garrett concluded. "What do you
think?"

Hal Keating rubbed an eyebrow and puffed at his cigar.
One thing he thought for sure, his young pal Garrett had
gotten himself into one hell of a mess.

Keating liked Garrett, liked him as a ball player ever
since he'd first scouted him back in high school (Hal had been
living in the New York area then), and liked him as a person
for just as long. Garrett had always shown the makings of a
good man. Guts, honesty, a disinclination to believe too
much bullshit.

But now look at him. Keating stabbed his cigar in the
direction of a chair. "Sit," he commanded. "You make me
nervous walking around like that."

Garrett sat.

Keating leaned back against the pillows of his hotel bed.
"You want to know what I think? Okay, I'll tell you. Now,
this David Laird. I have to admit the autopsy on Bristow was
suggestive. Punched in the solar plexus, like the hot-dog
vendor. Shot twice in the neck with a twenty-two like Rex
Simmons himself. It looks almost like a dress rehearsal for the
Simmons kill."

"Just what I thought. The witnesses' descriptions fit him
perfectly. And who else had a grudge against Bristow *and*
Simmons?"

"David Laird's wife."

Garrett started to say something, swallowed it, rubbed
the back of his head, got up, and began to pace again. "No,"

he said after he'd paced fiften yards or so. "It's ridiculous."

"Maybe so," Keating replied, "but the cops are going to find it a whole lot less ridiculous than the idea of somebody they're already perfectly satisfied is dead coming back to kill off his enemies. If you weren't so muddled trying to keep ahead of your last lie to the cops, you'd realize that if they had one tiny shred of evidence she hired the muscle to do this stuff, she'd be in a cell so fast it would make your eyes water."

Speaking of water reminded Keating he was thirsty. He called room service to send up some beer.

He kept his eyes on his young friend while he made the call. It didn't take long for the dawn to break over Garrett's face. It was sinking in that the police weren't being completely open with him any more than he was with them.

"Suppose," Garrett said after the beer arrived, "that Jenny Laird isn't behind this, though—and if you knew her, Hal, you'd see how impossible that was. Who then?"

"Look, I don't know," Keating said again. "When you think about this a little, you'll see how nice it would be for all concerned if your dead man *was* the killer."

"What do you mean?"

"You'll work it out for yourself. That's my point, Rags. You can't count on the cops to bail you out. Tad Simmons has cut you off from that. And Simmons'll discard you like a used Dixie cup as soon as he's done with you. Listen, I'll help you as much as I can, but I can't really do much."

Garrett finished his beer in one long swallow. "I guess I've known that all along, Hal, and just didn't want to face it. I'll grab a taxi back to my hotel." He picked up his hat and began to leave.

"I'll drive you back. Rags, you've got to do it yourself. You've got to accumulate power and knowledge to get out of this hole you've dug.

"But there's something else bothering me."

Garrett wiped his brow. "What's bothering you?"

"What you were telling me about this Bristow guy. How it's a toss-up about whether his jaw was busted by the killer or by the waves."

"Yeah?" Garrett said.

"Say it was the killer. If, as it looks, he used Bristow as a dress rehearsal for things he was going to do later, about now I'd start looking for a corpse with a broken jaw."

4

I should have done this sooner, Garrett thought.

He'd just finished his report to Congressman-designate Telford Simmons in the congressman's office.

It was an idea Garrett had come up with after his talk with Hal Keating that afternoon. Stir things up a little. So far Garrett himself had been on the receiving end of all the grief. It was time to spread it around a little.

So he'd phoned Tad's office (speaking to the secretary, Cheryl, who sounded even sexier than he'd remembered) and had been asked to come right in. Ordered, in fact.

He came in, was ushered into the presence of the newly crowned public servant, greeted curtly, and commanded to speak. Cheryl sat quietly behind him, taking notes.

Garrett had nodded quietly and filled in the background of the investigation. Then he started talking about David Laird. He made the best case he could for Laird as the killer; so good, in fact, he wished Captain Murphy could have been there to hear it. This time, Garrett felt, even *he* might have believed it.

Now he was watching the way Tad Simmons reacted to the theory. The reaction was very interesting.

Because Tad was taking this all wrong. He should be jumping for joy at the possibility that David Laird was the one who killed his brother. For one thing, he had David Laird branded a Communist in the eyes of the world. For another, to fake a death and come back for revenge was more than a little devious. And the Simmons family loved devious Communist plots. They'd climbed to power on them. Tad should be ordering a press conference right now.

Instead he was chewing Garrett out.

"What the hell is this c-c-*crap*, Garrett? Is this some sort of game to throw me off the t-t-t . . ." Tad must be really upset, Garrett thought. He wondered if he'd ever get the word out.

"*Track!*" Tad said at last, the word practically exploding from him.

Garrett pretended to be hurt. "Thanks a lot, Congressman. I'm trying to do my best for you. This is how it looks to me, that's all. I'm supposed to keep you informed, and that's what I'm doing."

Garrett took a breath and looked around the room. There were a lot of small, square light patches in the paint, as though a lot of framed pictures had been removed. Photos of big brother, Garrett figured. He risked a wink at Cheryl and went on. "If it's any consolation, the New York police don't like it, either. And now that I think of it, didn't you blackmail—"

Simmons's eyes narrowed in his foxy face. He found his voice. "Watch that kind of talk, Garrett."

"Excuse me. You *persuaded* me to help you out on this because you were afraid of that very thing—the police not following up the Communist angle." Garrett shrugged. "I don't know if I'm right or not, but I figured you ought to know. I certainly didn't expect to get my head bitten off."

"Don't worry about your head, Garrett. At least not yet." Tad had calmed down now and was no longer stuttering. "But keep this Laird business under your hat. Until we have more evidence, that is. Cheryl, I think you can rip up your notes from this meeting."

A knowing smile passed over Cheryl's wide mouth. "Yes, Congressman. May I go now? My phone is ringing." Simmons dismissed her with a wave of his hand.

He made Garrett hang around a few more minutes for a combined intimidation session and pep talk, but the young ball player could tell his heart wasn't in it. Tad Simmons was worried.

Garrett wondered why the man had been so upset by news that should have made him happy. He could see a couple of possibilities. Maybe Tad didn't want people sniffing around a trail that seemed to lead to David Laird because Tad knew Laird wasn't dead; perhaps Tad was in on the disappearance somehow and didn't want the news to get out. That didn't seem likely, but it was possible.

Or maybe it bothered Tad because if Laird was alive, he might have spent the two years accumulating proof that he'd never been a Communist or anything like one; proof that the Simmons brothers had framed him like a Norman Rockwell cover for the *Saturday Evening Post*. It would be a lot more convenient, in that case, for Laird to stay dead, or at least alive and unfound.

Of course, if Laird insisted on continuing to kill people, that wasn't going to be so easy. Garrett could understand how the congressman-to-be could be made nervous by a thing like that.

Garrett only hoped now that Simmons would be so nervous, he'd stay off his back.

Simmons was finished talking. Garrett forced himself to smile and shake the offered hand before he left the office.

5

Cheryl was sorry she'd answered the phone. She sat at her desk with the phone at her ear, cooing assent to statements she wasn't listening to, thinking about things.

"Yes, Mrs. Klimber," she cooed to the phone.

Mrs. Klimber was one of the things Cheryl was thinking about. Apparently Rex's death had affected the old woman deeply—she probably felt she had created Rex, and she didn't know if her—power, toy, whatever it was—was safe in Tad's hands.

Cheryl was getting tired of reassuring her. "Yes, Mrs. Klimber," she cooed again.

Just then Russ Garrett emerged from Tad's office with a smug expression—it wasn't *quite* a grin—on his handsome young face. He waved and mouthed "Good-bye," but Cheryl had a sudden inspiration and held up a hand for him to wait a minute. He seemed surprised but complied.

"Dinner this evening, Mrs. Klimber? And Scrabble after, too? Oh, I'm sure the congressman would love to attend, but I can't make it." She picked up a pencil and started playing with it, tapping first the point, then the eraser on the blotter.

Since Rex's death, Cheryl had temporarily abandoned her plan to seek other employment. She wanted to see if things would improve with Tad in the position of power. So far, they hadn't. Cheryl came to two decisions—one, she was leaving if things didn't get better soon; and two, even if she didn't, her relationship with Tad would be strictly business from here on in. *Office* business, that was. She'd actually decided the second one some time ago—she didn't know if Tad had figured it out yet. The transition period had been so busy, the question hadn't come up. All the animosities that had been forgotten in the shock of the murder were starting to reappear. Tad was making noises like a caveman again.

Cheryl would make it clear for him. She'd offer her own little Declaration of Independence.

"No, Mrs. Klimber, I have a previous engagement for this evening. Bring him along? No, I'm afraid I can't."

Mrs. Klimber wanted to know why; Cheryl held the pencil across her lips and gave Russ Garrett a sloe-eyed smile. "Because it's a working engagement, Mrs. Klimber. At least for him it is. No. He's a baseball executive, and they're expecting him at the ball game this evening. He's taking me along." Cheryl had heard Garrett tell Tad his ostensible reason for being in Kansas City. "Excuse me? Oh, please hold the line a minute, Mrs. Klimber. I think that must be the White House calling about the President's visit." Cheryl was proud of the lie—it was well known that Eisenhower was coming to Kansas City in October to address the Future Farmers of America. She punched a button to put the old woman on hold, then turned to her visitor. "Will you rescue me, Mr. Garrett? I know this is probably a terrible imposition—"

"I'll rescue you, but only if you call me Russ. I would have asked you myself if I'd thought of it."

His face got more smug. Cheryl smiled; there was lots of time to take care of that. "Thanks, Russ," she said.

"It does seem a shame, though," he said.

"What do you mean?"

"Well, back East we're always hearing about Mrs. Klimber, reclusive business genius and all that. And here I of all people have a chance to meet her, and I can't do it because I have to go to a baseball game."

Cheryl looked at him. He *was* attractive. He probably thought he was up to something. Cheryl decided she could stand Mrs. Klimber's company long enough to find out what it was.

"Well, don't worry about that," she told Garrett. "Mrs. Klimber never gives up. Her next suggestion will be drinks this afternoon at The Homestead."

Garrett said it sounded good to him. Cheryl popped a button and told Mrs. Klimber, "Hello, again. Mrs. Eisenhower sends her regards. This afternoon? Wait one second, I'll ask him."

Garrett was nodding, laughing silently. "We'd be delighted. Five o'clock? That will be fine. No, no need to send your chauffeur. We'll drive out."

She said thank you and good-bye and rose to tell Tad she was leaving. That would be the start of the fun. This was going to be an interesting evening.

6

This, Garrett decided, was turning out to be an interesting evening.

Beside him, Cheryl Tilton sat dressed in tight blue slacks and a low-cut white blouse with a loose ruffle around the collar, leaning against his arm at appropriate moments and pretending to be interested in the game.

She wore low-heeled canvas pumps, too, with no socks or stockings. She'd changed into all this when she'd stopped at her place on the way home from Mrs. Klimber's. Garrett had wondered why she'd insisted on doing that, but now he was glad she had. Cheryl looked almost girlish. She looked friendlier. She looked, in fact, fabulous. Garrett sat next to her and acted as if he didn't notice she was only pretending. He told her about baseball exactly as if she wasn't going to drive him nuts leaning her cleavage up against his arm like that.

Vic Power came to bat.

"Now look at this guy," Garrett told her. "If he's not playing for the Yankees next year, they really *are* prejudiced."

"He made an out the last time," Cheryl said.

Garrett laughed. "Even the greatest make outs most of the time, Cheryl. Power is batting .353. That's terrific in any league, but it still means they get him out something like fourteen out of every twenty times he comes to bat. But look at his swing; look at that concentration. And when the Blues are in the field, take a look at him on defense. The Yankees are going to have to bring this guy up, or some other colored player, or they'll prove what people have been saying all along." Power lined a double to left field, and Garrett said, "See?"

Garrett found something pleasant, adolescent about the whole evening, right down to wondering how far past a goodnight kiss she would go.

He seemed to have Mrs. Klimber's blessing, if that meant anything. Garrett was still trying to figure out the meaning (if any) of what went on at the old woman's mansion this afternoon.

It was called The Homestead, not, Garrett discovered, for any reason of history or architecture. One of the previous owners had liked the name and had slapped it on the Kansas City Castle Dracula he lived in. Mrs. Klimber and Her Late Husband had never found any reason to change it.

As she ushered him and Cheryl onto the veranda on the shady side of the house, Mrs. Klimber told him the family history. The woman's problem, he decided, was that everybody she cared about was Late. All she had now were people like Cheryl and her right-hand man, a big Negro, to play up to her. It occurred to Garrett to wonder if a certain amount of Mrs. Klimber's eccentricity was put on in order to make her attendants dance for her amusement. He never did decide.

Garrett recognized Gennarro Kennedy the minute he laid eyes on him when the chauffeur wheeled a portable bar out to where they were sitting. He asked what they would have; Mrs. Klimber and Cheryl wanted sherry. "And you, Mr. Garrett?"

"Bourbon and soda," Garrett told him. "Didn't you play football? I remember your name. Colgate? Right after the war."

Garrett hadn't been around many servants, but he didn't think servants were supposed to smile the way Gennarro Kennedy was smiling now. "Briefly," Kennedy said. "Between stints in the army."

"Gennarro was in the service with My Late Son," the old woman announced. "He got the little monster that killed him." Garrett sipped his drink and listened to the talk about Her Late Son. It turned out that one of Her Late Son's dreams had always been to bring major-league baseball to Kansas City.

"I intend to make his dream come true," she said. "Russ, Cheryl tells me you're very important to the baseball people." Her voice had taken on a wheedling tone. "If you just tell people—I'm sure you know the right ones to tell—that I'm willing to buy Blues Stadium from the Yankees, and any team that wants to come to a city where they'll be appreciated, why, I'd be very grateful to you. I wouldn't forget it." Then she folded her flipperlike hands over her stomach, and so help him, fluttered her eyelashes at him.

Garrett was taken aback, but not so much that he didn't see his opportunity to quench the flickering curiosity that had sprung up in Cheryl Tilton's eyes when he'd first mentioned his desire to see Mrs. Klimber.

"As a matter of fact, that is part of the reason for my trip. This is a complicated situation, and the commissioner wants me to speak to as many of the people involved as possible."

Garrett took a glance at Cheryl just in time to see her nod her head to douse the fires of curiosity. A few seconds later, though, something that looked like mischief was blazing in their place. "Speaking of complicated situations," Cheryl said, "Russ has a chilling theory about poor Rex. He thinks David Laird killed him!"

Mrs. Klimber gasped. "I knew it was a Communist!"

She insisted that Garrett tell her all about it, but Gennarro
Kennedy interrupted, offering a second round of drinks. This
gave Garrett a chance to look at his watch and say, my
goodness it's time to go and his theory was nothing really,
he'd come back sometime and tell her about it. Mrs. Klimber,
to Garrett's surprise, thought that was a *wonderful* idea, and
he should come back soon. "You do remind me so of My Late
Son," she said. "Doesn't he remind you of Junior, Gennarro?"

Kennedy declined to offer a comment.

Mrs. Klimber told Garrett, "I'm *so* glad dear Cheryl
found you." She turned and offered a pendulous cheek dusty
with powder. Garrett followed "dear Cheryl's" lead and
brushed it lightly with his lips. Mrs. Klimber squirmed in
delight.

Back in the car Cheryl announced her intention of
stopping at her place to change.

"Sure," he replied. "We've got plenty of time." Garrett
watched her drive. She was a good driver, both hands on the
wheel, eyes on the road, no sudden, unsettling turns. He had
the feeling that driving was the only part of her life she
treated that way.

After a while Garrett said, "Would you mind, Cheryl,
explaining to me what the hell the big idea was back there?"

"What big idea?" Cheryl asked the windshield of her car.
It was a bright blue Hudson Hornet, and it seemed to
demand a more adventurous driver.

"The big idea," Garrett replied, "of telling Mrs. Klimber
about David Laird."

Cheryl just laughed. A low laugh, slightly nasty.

Garrett offered to take a guess. "I think you're mad at
your boss about something and you're using this to tweak
him. You saw how he reacted to my theory this afternoon,
and you know that Mrs. Klimber is his most important
supporter, so you just figured you'd put a bug in her ear, let
her plague him about it, then you can watch the congressman
wiggle. Sometimes I don't think you're such a nice lady,
Cheryl."

She laughed again, a little nastier. "I can be," she said,

"*very* nice, Mr. Garrett." She pulled the car to the curb. "Here we are. Wait here—I'll be just a minute."

It took her three minutes; Garrett was impressed. She'd hopped back in the car and driven them to the ball game.

7

The game ended with the Blues beating St. Paul 4 to 3.

"Pretty good game," Garrett said later. Moths were dancing in the headlight beams of all the cars around them as they tried to leave the parking lot.

Cheryl honked her horn at the other drivers. "It certainly ended better than the last baseball game I went to." She honked again.

"Don't honk," Garrett told her. "You'll only make them mad. Or they'll think you're celebrating and join in. It will all clear up in a second."

Cheryl turned, glared at him, and hit the horn again. Then she smiled. "Okay. I'll be good. Are you hungry?"

"I could eat four hours' production from the slaughterhouse. Barbecued." He thought about it for a second. "Yes, definitely barbecued. I've been in Kansas City almost twelve hours and I haven't had barbecue yet."

"Well," Cheryl said. "We'll have to fix that, won't we? Where do you want to go?"

"Arthur Bryant's is the best place. If you want to go there." Arthur Bryant's was in the Negro neighborhood. Garrett would have run a gauntlet to get at the barbecued beef there, but Cheryl might get nervous.

"Why shouldn't I want to? I go there often; they know me. Besides, I've got a big strong baseball player to protect me, haven't I?"

"Oh," Garrett said. "Absolutely." She had a way of making all her come-on lines sound as if no one had ever used them before.

Arthur Bryant's was crowded, as it was every night. Garrett and Cheryl went through the line, getting an order of beef, one of ribs, some greens, and peas and rice. They were going to share everything.

They found a spot and ate. It was every bit as good as Garrett had remembered it.

"I wish we could get this in New York," Garrett said, waving a denuded rib as punctuation. "I still can't believe anything tastes this good."

Cheryl was doing an expert job on a rib of her own, teeth and lips and fingers perfectly coordinated.

I never thought, Garrett mumbled, I'd ever be jealous of a spare rib.

Cheryl put the bone daintily on her plate and said, "Don't worry, there are plenty of things in New York I'd trade good barbecue for. Or in Washington. I can't wait until fall and the session starts again."

So they talked about Washington for a while. Some Blues came in, going for their after-game meal, recognized Garrett and came over to say hello. They were delighted to meet Cheryl; then, in that unsuave way men develop in the army or on ball teams and similar all-male situations, they gave Garrett sly winks and nudged each other and made suggestive gestures.

Eventually Garrett stopped laughing long enough to tell them to get lost. He apologized to Cheryl, who said she didn't mind. "They probably meant it as a compliment." They left the restaurant.

Cheryl drove west, toward the river, and the State of Kansas. "Where are we going?" Garrett asked.

"Mission Hills," Cheryl said. "I want you to see something."

Gravel crunched under the Hudson's tires as Cheryl drove off Ward Parkway and up to the big oak doors of a mansion that could have been built from the same set of blueprints as The Homestead.

Cheryl might have been reading Garrett's mind. "This one doesn't have a name," she said.

She used her key and opened the door.

"I don't know why you bother with an apartment in town when you've got a place like this," Garrett said.

"Very funny. Come on inside."

Garrett stepped in as Cheryl hit a switch by the door.

Lights came on, accompanied by a whoosh of air conditioning.

Garrett wanted to rub his eyes. It was hard to believe this inside and that outside belonged to the same house. From what Garrett could see, a mad family of modernist interior decorators had been turned loose in here and told not to miss a thing.

The whole place was chrome and glass and white wood, in abstract shapes or unorthodox ones. There was a round chair, for example, and a glass-and-metal coffee table in the shape of an arrowhead. Someone had put a spiral staircase in the room, and poked a hole in the ceiling to give it some place to go.

Cheryl was talking. "Isn't this wild? This was what the Late Junior Klimber was supposed to come home to. Mrs. Klimber keeps it in perfect repair. She spends a *fortune* on it, has people in to clean once a week. What do you think of it?"

"You first," Garrett said.

"I like it," Cheryl said.

Garrett looked around the room again and decided it figured. It was like her: dangerous, somehow threatening, yet very seductive. There was drama in the glinting angles of aluminum and the muted pastels of the walls and carpet. The lamps were all cones and cylinders that erupted from unexpected places in the walls, casting hard-edged shadows and illuminating the room only by reflected glow.

"I like it to look at," Garrett said at last. "This is not a place for living. Is the whole house like this?"

Cheryl nodded. "Pretty much. The beds are normal."

Garrett let that go. Cheryl suggested they sit down and talk for a while. "You're not likely to find a cooler place—the air conditioning is wonderful."

They sat on a sofa that was white wood with black velvet cushions. "So," Cheryl said. "What's a nice guy like Russ Garrett doing in a spot like this?"

Garrett was still trying to decide on an answer when Cheryl said a rude word.

"What's the matter?"

"Look," she said. She pointed a red nail at a small orange spot on the frilly collar of her blouse.

"Oh," Garrett said. "That's too bad. It hardly shows, though."

Cheryl ignored him. "I'd better go run some cold water on this before the stain sets. If it isn't too late. *Damn*—I just got this when I was in New York—do you see what I mean about trading barbecues and Kansas City?"

She excused herself and dashed up the spiral staircase. Garrett got up and started looking the room over in more detail. He was especially interested in what might be behind some free-standing screens at the far side of the room. It turned out to be bookshelves, which made sense to Garrett—it would be hard to make bookshelves look futuristic.

The books themselves were something else again. It was all science fiction; many of the volumes were bound pulp magazines. Garrett had the impression of being under assault by the emphatic adjectives that made up the titles: *Amazing, Astounding, Unknown, Startling, Bizarre, Thrilling*. Apparently Junior Klimber had been a science-fiction fan, saving his dimes and buying this stuff the way Garrett had hoarded *Doc Savage* and *The Shadow* and *Operator No. 5*. Maybe his mother had nagged him about wasting his time on junk; maybe that was why, after he went away, and after she was afraid she'd be losing him to a wife, she'd had the magazines bound and given Junior this science-fiction house to keep them in.

There were books here, too, all of which seemed to be published by small publishing companies with names nearly as strange as those of the magazines. Garrett checked a couple of volumes at random and made another discovery—Mrs. Klimber had been keeping the library up to date. God alone knew why.

There was even something from *this* year—*The Demolished Man*, by someone named Alfred Bester. He looked at the first couple of paragraphs, got hooked, and read the best part of three chapters before a starburst clock with no numbers on it on the wall above bonged midnight and made him realize Cheryl had not returned.

He started to call up the staircase to her, stopped himself, decided that was stupid, and went ahead and yelled.

No answer. He called again. There was silence except for the quiet hissing of the air conditioning.

Garrett climbed the spiral staircase, sorry for the noise his feet made on the white-enameled metal steps but not knowing exactly why.

He found himself in a little alcove at the top, a little square of space that opened onto the second-floor corridor. The corridor was dark except for the light from the alcove itself and for a little slice of light gleaming around a not-quite-closed door at the end of the hallway.

"Cheryl?"

Garrett walked down the hallway, consciously stifling the desire to creep silently. He walked to the doorway, stood outside, and tried again. "Cheryl?" He told himself she was probably asleep, that she'd rinsed the blouse, lay down to wait while it dried, and dozed off.

No answer.

Garrett took a breath and pushed open the door. He took another as he looked inside.

Cheryl was leaning against the frame of the room's other door, the one that led to the bathroom. She was wearing her slacks, bra, and a knowing smile. One lovely arm rested on her head, the other on her hip, just below where the slacks started. She was a sinuous, seductive arrangement in pink and black and white.

"Hello, Russ," she said. "I was wondering how long it would take you to come looking for me."

"Yeah. I . . . um . . . got involved in a book and didn't realize how long you'd been gone."

"I think I've just been insulted."

"How come there are brand-new science-fiction books downstairs?"

"Mrs. Klimber was going to donate her son's collection to the U. of K., but they didn't want it—not serious-enough literature or something. One day she's going to make them take it, and when that happens, the Junior Klimber Science Fiction Collection is going to be complete." Cheryl pouted and crossed her arms under her breasts, deepening the shadow between them.

Garrett noticed. He also noticed that Cheryl was aware
he had.

"Now I *know* it!" Cheryl said in mock anger. "I *am* being
insulted."

"No," Garrett said.

"Yes," Cheryl insisted.

"Maybe," Garrett suggested, "I can make it up to you."

"I doubt it."

"I can try," Garrett said. "Come here."

She came to him. Slowly, brazenly. With a smile on her
lips that was both skeptical and challenging. Garrett was
going to wipe that smile off her face if it killed him.

8

They'd fallen asleep with the lamp on. Garrett woke up
to a feathery touch on his thigh and the sound of the clock
downstairs telling the otherwise-silent house that it was half
past three.

"You were hurt," Cheryl said, tracing his scar with her
finger.

"A Communist shot me," Garrett told her. "In Korea."

"I never thought a bullet wound would look like that."

"That's not a bullet wound. That's where they operated
to put the bone back together." He reached down to move her
hand. "That dent in the flesh—that's the bullet hole."

"Both legs," she said. "Poor Russ." She leaned and
kissed the scar, then moved, still kissing.

"You'd better watch that stuff," Garrett warned her.

"I'm not worried," she said. "You're not bad, for a
child."

"You're pretty decent yourself, for an old lady."

Garrett didn't smile. All the bantering didn't hide the
fact that "not bad" was all it had been. Oh, she'd responded
all right, but it had been all physical, just as she would have
sneezed if he'd rubbed her nose. He'd never gotten close to
where that smile lived. Hadn't caught sight of the real Cheryl
Tilton, assuming there was one.

Cheryl stopped what she was doing. "I'll be right back,"

she said. She patted Garrett on the chest and strode gracefully to the bathroom.

Garrett watched her, then closed his eyes again. He opened them to another feathery touch, this time at his throat. It wasn't the same touch as last time—this one was ice cold.

"Don't move, Russ," Cheryl cooed. "This is Junior Klimber's razor. It's very sharp. You'd think he would use an electric razor, wouldn't you? But he didn't."

Garrett tried not to swallow. Every time he swallowed he felt the edge of the razor take just the tiniest bite into his skin.

"This isn't necessary, Cheryl," he said. "I shaved this morning in New York."

"I don't plan to cut your *whiskers*," Cheryl said. "Your throat, I think. Or something else."

Garrett could feel himself starting to sweat.

"I can—don't *move*, Russ! I told you that already. You make me nervous when you move." Her voice dropped back into the soft coo. "I can get away with it, too. You followed me here; got me to let you inside; forced yourself on me. There's evidence of that, isn't there? Then you went to sleep, and I tried to sneak away, and you woke up and tried to stop me. I ran into the bathroom, grabbed the razor to protect myself . . . I guess it had better be your throat, after all."

"What," Garrett asked slowly, "is the big idea behind all of this?"

"Why should I tell you? It will give you something else to think about."

Something rang false in Garrett's mind. "Okay, Cheryl. Not funny. Put it away."

"I'm not joking, Russ." Garrett looked at her face. The woman would have made a hell of a poker player. He was sure Cheryl was playing some sort of sick game with him. He couldn't believe this woman would pass up the chance to tell him why he was about to die.

It also crossed Garrett's mind that that particular line of reasoning might be something cooked up in a desperate portion of his brain to let him go out with a tiny shred of dignity.

"I'm going to count to five," Garrett said. "You'd better cut my throat by the time I'm finished, or I'm going to take that thing away from you and carve my initials in you. One."

Cheryl only smiled at him.

"Two. Three." Garrett could feel himself starting to tremble. He wished he'd said he was going to count to three. "Four. Five."

Cheryl was pulling her hand away from his throat even as Garrett's left hand was catching hold of her wrist. "Let go of it," he said. She didn't; he twisted her wrist, hard. Cheryl yelped and let go. The razor fell over the edge of the bed onto the floor.

The wrestling match finished with them sitting up in the center of the bed, facing each other. Cheryl was laughing, loud, joyful laughter. "That was exciting! God, that was good!"

"Stop it!" Garrett commanded. Cheryl kept laughing. "You crazy bitch, stop it!" Garrett hit her, openhanded, once, very hard. Cheryl rocked to the side. Her black hair flew. She lay there a second, then with her arms pushed herself back to sitting position.

Garrett was still taking in the fact that he had hit a woman for the first time in his life. He looked at Cheryl.

Her mouth was open in surprise. She was holding her hand to the red mark on her face. Her lovely naked body trembled as breath rasped in and out of her.

Garrett started to speak, to say something that would make sense of the whole business, but the look in Cheryl's eyes stopped him.

"Now, Russ," she said reaching for him. "Right now. You win. I'm yours. Only right now, *please?*"

"Lie down," Garrett told her.

At last he had found the real Cheryl Tilton. What she liked was power. Political. Physical. Sexual. It made no difference who *had* it—Cheryl just liked to be around it and to see it used.

Garrett was still angry enough over the little razor charade to use all of his now. And Cheryl cooperated all the way. The challenging smile was gone for now. Now was the time for gasps and whimpers.

They moved together now like parts of an engine barely under control, shuddering and groaning, oiled with sweat, and at last finishing the job in a stroke of frozen power. All that was lacking was a cloud of steam.

They fell apart, instantly reached for each other, and lay panting in each other's arms.

Over the sound of their breath, Garrett heard the faint chimes of the clock downstairs. He counted them, then started to laugh.

"What?" Cheryl asked wearily. "What is it?"

"Five o'clock lightning," Garrett told her. "This Yankee just got hit with some five o'clock lightning."

"Mmmm," Cheryl said. "That's nice," then pillowed her head on Garrett's chest and went to sleep.

9

Garrett stepped out of the shower, dried himself, then started to put on the clean clothes he'd spread on the bed. There was a knock on the hotel-room door.

"Who is it?"

"It's me. Martin. Let me in, Garrett, all right?"

"Sure, just a second." Garrett finished buttoning his trousers, then let the detective in.

Martin looked sour. "When did you finally get back here?"

"About an hour ago," Garrett told him.

"Jesus, Garrett, it's four thirty in the afternoon!"

"I didn't see any punch clock downstairs. When was I put on the payroll?"

"All right, all right." Martin raised a hand. "If you want to know, I was worried about you. Vicious would tan my black hide if I let anything terrible happen to you out here."

"I'm touched."

Martin wagged a finger at him. Garrett put on his socks. "I had a date last night," the ball player said.

"How was it?" Martin was still sour.

Garrett grinned. "Amazing," he said. "Astounding. Unknown. Startling. Bizarre. Thrilling."

"Well, I'm glad *you* had a good time."

"What do you mean?"

"You got a million phone calls last night. Went on till past two o'clock in the morning. I could hear it through the walls. After the plane trip I didn't think anything could keep me awake, but that did the trick."

"Yeah, there was a note for me when I came in. Some woman, apparently. Never left a message, except on her last call; said she would try again today—meaning tonight, I guess—the day clerk didn't have any other messages."

"You gonna be here tonight?"

"Later on. I'm meeting Hal Keating for dinner at the Plaza, then making a duty call on the ball game. We were going to hit a few spots, but we can drink back here just as easily." Garrett stood at the mirror and knotted his tie. "You're welcome to come along if you like."

"No, some big shot in the police department here is having me over to dinner at his place to show what a liberal he is. Talk about astonishing and bizarre and all that crap. I tell you . . ."

Garrett wasn't listening. "I wonder who could have been trying to call me," he mused.

"Break any hearts when you were here the last time?" Martin asked him.

"No," Garrett said. "That was a time when I was . . . Let me put it this way: the only broken heart I had anything to do with in Kansas City was my own, and I brought that with me."

The phone rang. "Speak of the devil," Martin said. Garrett picked up the receiver. "Hello?"

"Mr. Garrett?" a sweet voice asked him. The note the clerk had given him said a woman had called, not a little girl. Garrett decided he'd said that only because little girls don't stay up that late. You certainly couldn't tell by the voice.

"I'm Russ Garrett. Were you trying to call me yesterday?"

"Yes, I was," the voice said. "I know—"

"Wait a minute, you haven't told me who you are yet." Unconsciously Garrett had put a hearty, avuncular tone in his voice, just as he would have if it had actually been a little girl he'd been speaking to.

There was a pause at the other end of the line, then the voice came back. "That—that doesn't matter. I know something about Congressman Simmons." Another pause. "The way he died, I mean."

"That's interesting," Garrett said. He tried to get Martin's attention by waving, but the detective was involved in a magazine. Probably didn't want to look as if he was horning in on Garrett's business. Garrett picked up a cuff link from the bureau and threw it at him. Martin looked up, saw Garrett's frantic waving, and joined him at the phone.

"That's *very* interesting," Garrett said again. "But why tell me?"

"Well . . . because." Pause. "I have to tell *some*body."

Martin grabbed Garrett's arm. His handsome brown face went through comical contortions as he mouthed the words "Keep her talking." Garrett nodded, and Martin sprinted from the room.

"You really should be telling this to the police," Garrett told the phone.

"I don't like the police. I'll tell you, and you can tell the police."

"How did you even know who I am or that I'm in town?"

No pause this time. It was almost as if she was waiting for the question. "I saw you," the little-girl voice went on. "At Blues Stadium. You were with a lady with dark hair. I remember you from when you played with the Blues. And it was in the news that you were there when Congressman Simmons was shot. I know something about that, but I was afraid to tell the police. So I thought I would tell you."

That made sense, sort of. Garrett used it to stall a little more. "Are you the little redhead who used to hang around the hotel and get autographs from all the ball players?"

"No. I just remembered you."

Garrett was running out of things to say. "What is it you want to tell me?"

"No," said the voice. "I—I want money first. I have to go to Chicago."

"Okay. Hell, it costs less than ten bucks to go to Chicago from here. What's your address; I'll mail it to you."

"No, I want to go there to *live*." The girl sounded as if she thought Garrett's wisecrack had been the most natural of misunderstandings. "I need five hundred dollars."

"Where am I going to get five hundred dollars?"

"I don't know. I bet you can get it if you really want to know what's going on."

"Your faith in me is wonderful."

"What?"

"Never mind. Okay. Suppose I can get the money. Then what?"

"At midnight you bring the money to a place called Barney's Tavern. Do you know where that is?"

Garrett said no; she gave him the address. Down by the river, in the oldest part of town, lost in the maze of warehouses and small factories between the airport and the slaughterhouse. Not one of Kansas City's showcase neighborhoods.

"You go to Barney's, at midnight, and you sit at a table facing the front window. I'll come by and tap on it three times with a key. Then you come out. Okay?"

"How do I—" Too late. A few minutes later Martin returned.

"Any luck?" Garrett asked.

"Luck? What the hell is that?" Martin collapsed in a chair and made a face. "I love it how easily they trace telephone calls in the movies."

Garrett wanted to know what he did now.

"You go meet her, what do you think?"

"You don't think this is just a crank call, then."

"Why the hell should people be calling *you* with crank calls?" Martin had another sour look on his face. "Before I came back here I spoke to the local cops. If it makes you feel any better, Garrett, they feel the same way you do."

"I don't know what I feel," Garrett protested. "I just wanted to find out what you think."

"I think you can't afford not to talk to her—I mean, *I*

can't afford not to have you do it." Martin laughed. "What the hell; maybe you'll pick this dame up and get laid again."

"Droll," Garrett said. "Only if she's as young as she sounds and I pick her up, the cops will pick *me* up. I can see it now: BASEBALL EXECUTIVE ARRESTED ON MORALS CHARGE."

Martin shrugged it off. "So what?"

"There's another thing," Garrett said, suddenly serious. "This could be a setup. I mean, I may have unknowingly offended someone, and this could be their charming way of getting me to a spot where they can work off their grievances."

"I thought of that. Don't worry, Garrett. You just go ahead and meet the lady. I'll be right behind you."

10

Lindy felt very happy. She walked down the street toward Barney's Tavern humming a merry little tune. She was being useful—it was a good feeling. In all the time since she'd become Gennarro's girl friend, this was the first time he'd ever asked her to help him; the first time he'd ever asked her for *anything*, actually.

Okay, it wasn't much, just to talk to some man on the phone, then meet him and bring him to the place where Gennarro and he would talk. Still, Lindy had done a good job so far—she'd had to stop a few times so Gennarro could whisper to her what she was supposed to say next, but when she finished the call, he had kissed her and told her he was proud of her. Lindy wanted to keep doing a good job.

It was about one minute past midnight when she got to Barney's Tavern. She looked in the window to see if the Garrett guy was there. There were more colored men than white men in the place, so he was easy to spot. Gennarro had given her a good description. Lindy took out her keys and tapped three times on the window.

Garrett, inside the bar, swallowed the rest of the beer he'd been drinking and hastened outside. He was a little overdressed for the area, but not too much—he and Hal

Keating had eaten at a not-too-fancy place in the Plaza, downtown.

Kansas City was really proud of the Plaza. Built in the thirties, the hollow squares of stores and buildings were the nation's first shopping center, the forerunner of the ones that were popping up all over the country now.

They could use one around here, Garrett thought as he stepped back into the fetid air. The heat, humidity, and smell from the slaughterhouse made it something slimy and tangible, and it felt as if you had to push it aside to walk.

The girl was a small platinum blond, but Garrett looked in her eyes and decided he was safe from any possible morals charge. There was a lot of experience in those eyes.

And, he was surprised to see, a certain cheerful friendliness.

"Hello, Mr. Garrett," she said. "I'm glad you came."

"Hello. Can you tell me your name now?"

She nodded. "It's Lindy." Garrett waited; the girl looked at him, wondering what he wanted. "Lindy," she said again.

"I was just wondering if you had a last name."

"You're funny," she said with a giggle. "Come on, let's go somewhere we can talk, okay?" She took him by the arm and started to pull him.

Garrett went along, but before he did he took a glance across the street, where Detective Cornelius Martin waited in the darkened interior of Hal Keating's car. He saw the tiny flame of a cigarette lighter flicker on and off. Garrett felt better.

11

Garrett had expected any number of things, but not this. "What the hell are we doing *here?*" he asked Lindy.

"Oh. A friend of mine is a foreman here. On the night shift."

She had led him to the employees' entrance of the slaughterhouse. If he leaned back a little, Garrett could see around the corner of the building to the stockyards that stretched out toward Genessee Street, a sea of dehorned heads and spotted backs of cattle waiting for their date with a sledgehammer. Every now and then a frightened bellow would cut through the background sound of melancholy mooing, as if one of the animals had realized what was going on.

Garrett didn't like the place. The building itself was a rickety-looking affair of unfinished wood, maybe as high as a three-story building, all ramps and conveyors and blood channels. Hand-painted signs, crudely lettered in white paint on pieces of wood that looked as if they had fallen off the building somewhere, told the stock handlers where to take the new arrivals. Similar signs along the side of the building where Garrett and Lindy now stood designated areas for "DEAD" and "CRIPS," sunken pens for animals that had been damaged in transit. Garrett wondered how frequently someone came along and put the crips out of their misery.

He began to regret his steak dinner.

The scene was bathed in a pale phosphorescence, a combination of moonlight and bare electric bulbs strung on wires. It gave the whole place an unhealthy look.

The light was better inside, but not much. Bellows were a lot more common in there; they had entered the building where the butchering process began. In spite of himself Garrett watched in fascination as hammers rose and fell like metronomes and killed or stunned cows slid down a ramp, where other men would cut their throats and hook them on conveyors to drain.

Lindy showed him a door. "You go inside and wait a second. I want to tell my friend I'm here." Garrett entered.

Lindy saw the door close behind him and smiled. Gennarro would be proud of her—he'd be here any minute to talk to nice Mr. Garrett.

12

Chicago Ned could still swing a hammer. His muscles were a little sore, maybe, because he was out of practice, but Chicago Ned could still split a cow's skull like a jeweler could split a diamond. He could see some of the regular employees here looking at him, wondering how a man could just walk in off the street, ignoring the union, and do a job better than any of them. The answer was he'd spread a lot of Gennarro Kennedy's money around to union people to let him and a few of the boys in the plant tonight. The answer to the second part was that they had stockyards in Chicago, too, and Chicago Ned had built up some muscles and picked up some skill working in them.

He watched little Blondie close the door of the foreman's office behind this guy from New York (the foreman had been sent to the movies, too). That was his signal to show this Garrett how good he was with the hammer.

Chicago Ned bashed one last cow, lit a cigarette, put the hammer over his shoulder, and signaled the boys to follow him.

13

Garrett sat before a pinewood desk in the windowless cubicle that passed for an office, dividing his attention between a girlie calendar on the wall and an article in *Meat Processor* magazine about compressed air guns that would shoot a bolt into a cow's head, killing it more humanely, efficiently, and economically.

He wondered what the hell was going on, where the woman had gone. This was starting to look more and more like a trap—okay, he'd been ordered to play along, and he had. He wished he knew where Martin was.

The door opened; Garrett started to get up. He froze midway when he saw the men with the sledgehammers come in.

They were Negroes, various shades. All muscular. All solemn. Garrett began to feel like the guest of honor at a New Orleans funeral.

Garrett's mind scrabbled for something he could do. There was a paperweight on the desk, but it was one of those water-filled things with St. Anthony trapped in a blizzard inside it. Not much of a weapon.

The head man was a light-skinned fellow with a reddish

tinge to his hair and mustache. He held a sledgehammer like he knew what to do with it. Garrett noted that there was blood on the hammer already.

"Come ohn, boy," the boss crooned. "This is gonna be just as easy as you let it be. I know what I'm doing—you won't feel a thing."

Garrett was silent.

"Just sit in the chair and close your eyes, and it all be over in a second." He took a deep drag on the cigarette in his mouth.

Garrett swallowed. There was something hypnotic about the voice, but not quite hypnotic enough for Garrett to offer himself up like a head of cattle. The paperweight wasn't much, but it would have to do. Slowly Garrett reached behind himself for it.

Still crooning, the man with the hammer came closer.

14

Detective Cornelius Martin watched Garrett and the girl enter the slaughterhouse, cursing the Kansas City Police Department the whole time. They wouldn't listen to him. They were so busy trying to convince him they weren't prejudiced, they hadn't heard a word he'd said about needing some help tonight on a tail. And he hadn't felt, considering their attitude, like spilling the whole story to get their attention. So he left the party, met Garrett, and followed through on his own. Up until Garrett had gone inside, that is. What did he do now?

He was still trying to decide five minutes later when the girl left the building. Without Garrett. Martin waited until she reached the sidewalk and stayed there before he started his serious thinking.

It was getting to be obvious the girl wasn't going to move. A lookout? Martin didn't believe it. Maybe she was waiting for a lift.

It didn't matter; Martin had to get inside. He could handle the girl if he had to.

He didn't have to. She took no notice of him, that he

could tell. She might have nodded at him, or even smiled, but Martin wouldn't have sworn to it. He was preoccupied.

He pulled his gun as soon as he entered. God only knew what he'd be up against in here. He found the one thing he never would have guessed. Solitude.

Martin was alone in what he took to be the main killing room of the slaughterhouse. Blood, more or less fresh, gleamed stickily in the glare of bare electric bulbs. Freshly killed cattle had been abandoned at various stages of the process. It was unsettling; more upsetting, in its way, than if cattle were being killed at full working capacity. There was something . . . Martin didn't know; something *unholy* about the whole business.

He circled the big room, listening, holding his breath. At last he came to a door with voices behind it, one of them Garrett's.

Martin pulled back his leg and kicked in the door. He could see Garrett across the room, on the other side of a bunch of ugly men with sledgehammers. One had his hammer raised over Garrett.

That was the one he shot. The man crumpled. Garrett ducked the hammer as it fell. "Thank God!" he said. Martin thought he sounded sincere enough for both of them.

"All right," the New York detective said. It sounded stupid to him, like a movie. But there weren't any Negro detectives in movies, and he couldn't think of anything better to say.

"All right," he said again. "Just stay put. Garrett, you come over here and get behind me."

"Bet your ass," Garrett told him and complied.

"You all right?" Martin asked

"Tell you later," Garrett told him. "Let's get the hell out of here."

Chicago Ned's boys were standing quietly at attention, but one at the back was starting to fidget. "Brother," he said, "let's stop talking and *all* us get out. This place gone catch fire!"

15

That, Garrett saw, was not exactly accurate—the place *had* caught fire. Chicago Ned's cigarette had landed neatly on the magazine Garrett had dropped when the boys came into the room. From there the flames had apparently spread to the varnish on the foreman's desk and then to the wood. As the thugs fled past him and Martin, heedless of Martin's gun, Garrett could see the wood darken and the flames climb. Above the desk the ceiling was beginning to char.

Garrett shook himself out of it; Martin still seemed to be mesmerized. Garrett grabbed his arm. "Come on," he said.

Martin shook his hand off, pointed with the gun to the man lying on the floor. "What about him?"

"What about him, for Christ's sake? Let's go!"

"Bullshit! We can't leave him here to burn!"

"You shot him! He's probably already dead!" The flames had stopped crackling; now they were making a low, level roar.

Martin didn't say anything else. He bent forward and went to Chicago Ned. Garrett shook his head, cursed under his breath, and followed.

The fire was hot—it hurt to breathe the air at that end of the room. The mustache had been singed off Chicago Ned's face on the side near the fire. The skin was blistering from the heat.

Martin and Garrett each grabbed one of the gangster's feet and dragged Chicago Ned the length of that long office to the doorway and through.

A bullet whistled past Garrett's head. His initial reaction was to be more hurt than afraid. Those ungrateful bastards. He almost wished Martin had gunned them all down. Garrett hit the floor, heard the thud of Martin's body a fraction of a second later.

"You hit?" Garrett said.

Martin shook his head. "Uh uh. Shit." More shots rang out. Martin peeked out from his shelter alongside the door frame and returned fire.

Fire. Garrett had almost forgotten about the blazing monster behind him. He guessed it was difficult to be scared to death of more than one thing at a time.

Garrett stayed low and pulled Chicago Ned to him as Martin fired again. "Ha!" the detective said. "Got the son of a bitch in the kneecap."

Garrett wiped his hands on his jacket. "Yeah," he said. "You're a hell of a shot, all right. You killed *this* guy, too."

"Wish I'd known that a minute ago; I wouldn't have tried to save him."

Garrett had had about enough. He slammed his hand to the floor. The wood was hot to the touch. "Goddammit, Martin!" he exploded. "Let's stop proving to each other how brave we are and figure out how the hell we get out of this!"

Martin fired another shot. "I'm working on it. You think I—" Another bullet whipped through the doorway. "You think I want to die like this? Listen, Garrett—"

Garrett shook his head; the crackling was too loud for him to hear. Sweat poured off both men now. Garrett could almost feel his own face starting to blister.

He leaned close to Martin. The detective took a deep breath, coughed, cursed, and yelled. *"I've only got one bullet left, so you better think of something almighty fast!"*

Sure, Garrett thought, just like that. What he had to do was give his playmates something to think about. Anything. Garrett couldn't get his brain to work. This goddamn fire. He coughed—he couldn't take much more than another minute or so of it. He was getting to the point where he'd just as soon face the bullets as let the fire eat its way down the slaughter chute of this office and get him. He had to get away.

Finally it came to him. Screw it, let *their* mothers worry. Garrett leaned close to Martin. "Give me your jacket!"

The detective looked at him. "Come on, goddammit!" Garrett demanded. Martin gave it to him. Garrett shed his own jacket and proceeded to wad the two garments into tight balls. He took a deep breath from the air as near the doorway as he dared, broke a piece of molding off the wall, and walked back toward the fire. He tried to stay out of line of the

162

doorway—the thugs were still shooting at them—but it was difficult because the room itself was so narrow.

Luckily Garrett didn't have to go far to reach the flames.

As soon as he did, he forced the piece of molding into the wad that was the detective's jacket and held it in the fire like a pyromaniac toasting a giant marshmallow. When the jacket was blazing, he sprinted toward the door of the office, holding his homemade torch like a lacrosse stick. Trying not to worry about bullets, he whipped the stick forward, shooting the blazing cloth into the slaughterhouse.

Garrett didn't wait to see where it landed; he was back to the flames with his own jacket, repeating the whole business.

Garrett risked a peek around the door frame. He saw that his plan had begun to work—at least one of the jackets had landed on bare wood or sawdust, and the new flames were beginning to spread. Chicago Ned's boys had to find new positions if they wanted to keep shooting at all.

"Let's go!" Garrett shouted, and the two men sprinted for freedom between two walls of flame.

16

Lindy was supposed to return to Barney's Tavern, get a cab, and go straight home, where Gennarro would meet her later. She decided it would be nice, though, to wait outside. Then they could go home together after Gennarro finished talking to Mr. Garrett. She was sure Gennarro wouldn't mind. It was a nice night, all the stars were out, and it was kind of peaceful here, despite the smell. Lindy'd grown up on a dairy farm, and ten thousand cows didn't smell a thousand times worse than ten cows. Besides, she liked the noise they made. It was kind of musical. Lindy laughed.

Then, suddenly, it wasn't musical. The cows went quiet for a second, then started to make nervous, crying noises. And there were sounds from inside. Sharp cracks, like balloons popping, only louder, and something that smelled like . . .

Lindy sniffed the air with her little nose. Fire! And Gennarro was inside! Lindy didn't even want to think what the popping noises might be; she ran back to the door of the slaughterhouse to see what had happened to her man.

17

Gennarro Kennedy sat quietly in one of Mrs. Klimber's limousines up the road from the slaughterhouse, deciding exactly how he was going to punish Lindy for disobeying orders. It was obvious now that little blond idiot was not going to leave the premises until he, Kennedy, did. And since he, Kennedy, was not in the building, she would stand there for a long time.

He would have to go to her and take her away; there was no way around it. That displeased him. Kennedy did not want to be seen *in propria persona* in the vicinity of the slaughterhouse tonight by *anybody*, Lindy included. He would have been content to drive up when Garrett was inside and Lindy gone and wait for Chicago Ned to come out to collect the remainder of that night's money, secure in the knowledge that by then the inquisitive Mr. Garrett, or, rather, pieces of him, would be turning into sludge and soap along with parts of various substandard cows in the lye vat.

He had been angry when he'd arrived to see Lindy standing at the entrance. He was coldly furious now to see her still there. How to punish her was the question.

He didn't like the idea of hitting her; the bruises would mar her esthetically. He would simply, he decided, make it clear to her how disappointed he was and withhold approval or affection from her until he could be sure she'd learned her lesson.

Gennarro Kennedy closed his eyes and nodded his head, sealing the decision, when he first heard the gunshots. Even at this distance they were unmistakable. The cattle had heard them, too, and seemed to be on the edge of panic. He'd better drive up now and get Lindy out of there before they decided to stampede.

Then, just as he put the Cadillac in gear, he saw Lindy run back inside, and for the first time since his childhood, Gennarro Kennedy didn't know what to do.

18

Garrett's plan had worked too damned well. His spreading the fire had scattered the hoodlums all right—they'd all run out through the doorway he'd entered the building by. They'd been held up momentarily by the girl who'd led Garrett into the trap in the first place. Then they threw her roughly to the bloody floor. One of them said, "Out of my way, bitch," before he trampled her. She lay there, stunned.

Garrett watched this all happen while he and Martin made for that exit themselves. Then he watched as the fire he'd started circled around behind her and closed the exit off.

Martin had him by the arm. "This way!" he said, pointing back over his shoulder. "We'll go down the ramp!"

"The what?"

"The ramp! The way the cows get in!"

It sounded good to Garrett—that ramp had cost a few thousand or a few million animal lives—now let it save a few human ones. "We've got to get the girl first!"

He didn't wait to see if Martin agreed; he just went. Garrett got an arm under her shoulders and led her as fast as he could to the ramp. Martin had already climbed it and was waiting for Garrett to hand the girl up to him.

She didn't want to go.

"*Where is he?*" she screamed. "*I can't leave him here! Help me find him!*"

"*Who?*" Garrett demanded.

"*Where is he! You were talking to him!*"

The place was an inferno now. Huge hunks of flaming wood were crashing loose from walls and ceilings. Lindy continued to struggle.

Martin's voice cut in, rasping above the roar of the flames. "*Garrett, for Christ's SAKE!*"

Garrett looked where the detective was pointing. The ramp had started to char.

"Stop it!" Garrett ordered the girl. "We've got no more time for this, goddammit, stop!"

She didn't; for the second time in two nights, Garrett

found himself hitting a woman across the face. Lindy didn't fall, but she stopped struggling and looked at him. Her eyes were wide with shock, and unless Garrett was mistaken, hurt. Of all things.

Garrett didn't take time to figure it out. He grabbed the girl before she could recover and handed her up to Martin. Then he scrambled up the woodwork himself. His legs trembled just a little. No real trouble, so far.

The ramp was foul with droppings and blood. Footing was practically impossible. They half-ran, half-slid down the ramp to the holding pen. There was a crash behind them as the part of the ramp inside the building collapsed.

Cornelius Martin had complained about the air of the stockyards, but now he took huge, grateful lungfuls of it. Paroled from hell. All they had to do now was get clear of the building before it collapsed, too. He ran to the gate of the holding pen and tried to figure, in the dark, how the latch opened. He didn't have to open the latch. A mass of terrified, stampeding cattle broke down the wall.

19

It was a living picture of panic: cattle running desperately in any direction there was room to run. They were a deadly, mindless force, an avalanche of living flesh, set off by the noise of the guns and the flashing of the flames that licked the roof and walls of the slaughterhouse.

Garrett knew he had to stay on his feet; he heard someone screaming it again and again over the thunder (there was no other word) of hoofbeats. He was amazed to realize he was the one doing the screaming.

He was equally amazed to realize he had the girl. She was no trouble now because she was, quite literally, too scared to move. They stood together in the midst of the stampede like two sticks in a river, with shoulders or rumps bumping them from side to side. Garrett thanked God for whoever had removed the horns.

Suddenly there was a gap in the rush. Pulling the girl behind him, Garrett sprinted past the "CRIPS" pen to take shelter among the dead. He pushed Lindy down between two carcasses and looked up over the rim of the pit.

He was looking for Martin. He hadn't seen him since the wall had caved in on him and he'd disappeared in a forest of hoofed legs. Garrett cursed.

It was maddening to look out over the backs of the cattle and see safety on the other side of a fence less than twenty-five yards away; a fence that before long rubberneckers would line up to look over. Garrett saw cars stopping on the street beyond the fence. Garrett saw flashing red lights, too. Someone had called the fire department. Now if they could only get to the building.

The girl was standing beside him now, her eyes as wide as one of the cows'. Suddenly Garrett heard his name called in a horrible voice. He looked.

It was Martin. The detective was badly hurt. He was dragging himself along with one arm along the rim of the "CRIPS" pen. His lips were red with blood, and a good portion of his forehead had been scraped aside by a sharp hoof.

"Don't move!" Garrett ordered the girl. Then he forced himself to leave the safety of the "DEAD" pit and help Martin. He got there just in time to pull Martin out of the way of more charging cattle. He dragged him in among the dead and tried to make him comfortable.

All this time the girl had been looking over the rim, frightened but fascinated, the way a child watches a thunderstorm from the safety of a house.

Then she screamed something, one or two words, and clambered out of the pit. She tried to run for the fence and safety. She didn't get five yards. She went down before a wave of cattle like a stalk of wheat before a scythe. Somehow she seemed to get under and among their legs and was rolled over and over, like a snowball. Then they left her behind, and she lay on the dirt, pathetic in her red dress, her platinum hair falling down to cover her face.

There were no more waves of cattle, just a few angry stragglers. Garrett learned later the fire department had kept them at bay with hoses. They put the fire out, too.

Garrett left the pit and made his way to where the firemen were working on the building itself. He told a rescue-squad driver there was a man hurt and took him to Martin. Then he slipped away.

There was nothing more he could do. And Garrett had something to think about. Lots of things. Like what was the meaning of this whole evening. Why should the girl be part of a setup where five Negroes tried to kill him with sledgehammers? Why try to kill him at all?

And the girl, Lindy. What the hell had it been she was trying to say as she ran to her death? "Tomorrow?" "Too narrow?" It was an irritating little question. The kind that would bother him for a long time.

20

Garrett coughed up blackness. It was hard to believe just two lungs could hold all that soot. He took another sip of scalding-hot tea and pulled the blanket closer around him.

The blanket was thin and light, but very warm. He took a look at the label to see what it was made of. Acrilan. One of those new miracle fibers. It figured.

Garrett was back at Mrs. Klimber's Tomorrowland mansion in Mission Hills with Cheryl Tilton. Cheryl was making phone calls; Garrett listened and threw in suggestions as they occurred to him.

". . . So Mr. Martin is in serious but stable condition—is that what I should tell the congressman?"

Garrett smiled at the smooth way Cheryl slipped in a reminder of her employer's title. That had been on his mind from the minute he'd staggered away from the carnage at the slaughterhouse. He'd needed a safe place to stay, he needed food, a bath, new clothes. But most of all he needed some facts. Cheryl was the one to get them.

He'd been astonished at how easily Cheryl had agreed to help him; she hadn't asked a single question. Garrett reflected ruefully that his caveman act from the night before still carried some magic in this woman's eyes. She was scary.

But efficient. Cheryl got further details from the hospi-

168

tal. Detective Martin had a broken arm, three broken ribs, a punctured lung, a dislocated hip, and assorted burns, bruises, and lacerations. Garrett had gotten away with just the last three and considered himself lucky.

"Find out when he can be moved," Garrett told Cheryl.

"Just a second, please." Cheryl covered the mouthpiece. "What did you say?"

"When can I get Martin back to New York?"

Cheryl uncovered the phone and asked. "Thank you. Yes, thank you very much. Yes, I'll tell him." She hung up. "Not for at least a week, they say," she told Garrett.

"Damn," the young man said. He got off the sofa and walked to the phone, which was kept in an aluminum box, and called Hal Keating.

"Russ!" Keating said when he heard Garrett's voice. "Are you all right? Goddamnit, I've been worried sick about you. You were supposed to call me as soon as you were through, remember? What the hell did you do, stop to watch the fire at the slaughterhouse?"

Garrett made a noise that started as a laugh and ended with a cough. "You might say that, Hal."

"Well, how'd it go?"

"Badly. Hal, I need help, fast. Martin's hurt; in the hospital. He should be watched. You use security men at your plant?"

"Sure. The best. Picked them and checked them out myself."

"Can you spare some? Twenty-four-hour guard on Martin's room until he's well enough to get back to New York?"

"Well, yeah, I guess I could. But what's wrong with the police?"

"I don't trust the police."

"Come on, Russ. I know this town. The cops aren't perfect here, but they aren't anywhere. Kansas City's force is pretty damn good."

"I don't care. It only takes one. Martin tried to get them in on this; they wouldn't come. And the whole thing was a setup. So I don't trust them. I trust you. Will you take care of it right away?"

"All right, Russ, take it easy. I said you should get more aggressive, but don't go overboard. Yeah, I'll do it right now."

"Thanks. Call me back as soon as you do, all right?" Garrett gave him the number. Keating said he would and hung up.

Garrett looked at Cheryl. "If your boss was in on this, I'll have his head. I don't care what it takes, I'm going to pin this on him. If he did it. If Martin dies . . ."

"What about me?" Cheryl asked. She led Garrett back to the sofa.

"What about you? It goes for you, too, Cheryl. You play the power games, too. I'll be watching you."

She put her hand on his chest under the blanket.

"You're upset," Cheryl said.

Garrett looked at her. "I've been lied to, sledgehammered, burned, stampeded. I've seen a friend hurt and a young girl smashed to applesauce. I'm hiding from cops and killers, naked, having crossed a state line, in the company of a woman who pulled a razor on me the night before. Yes, I am upset. Fucking good and."

"I'll make you feel better," Cheryl said. She kissed him on the cheek.

"No time," Garrett told her. "As soon as Hal Keating calls back, I'm going to tell him to check me out of the hotel and bring me my clothes. I'm getting out of Kansas City. I've got to get back to New York. I've got friends in New York."

"What are you going to do?"

Garrett smiled at her. It would be an interesting experiment to tell her—he would return to New York, go about his business, and if nobody killed him or the people he wanted to talk to, then Cheryl was just a lovely girl who happened to like power and slightly offbeat sex.

And who brought out the same things in him, Garrett realized, half-ashamed. He was seriously tempted to tell her, but good sense won out. He just kept smiling until she gave up.

Garrett was going back on the trail of David Laird.
Nothing had started to happen in this case until Garrett had
started tossing Laird's name around. Garrett had to keep
pushing it. It all meant too much to somebody. He had to
keep pushing it until it broke.
Or he did.

21

Gennarro Kennedy sat in the dark in Lindy's apartment,
smoking cigarettes and thinking.

She was dead. His little, empty-headed Lindy, who had
loved him so much, was dead. And dead for those very
reasons—because she was stupid, and because she loved him.

If she had followed orders she would be alive now.
Somehow Kennedy could find no comfort in the fact. She
had waited for him because she wanted to be with him; she
had gone back inside the burning building because she
thought he was in there, in danger.

And she died because she saw him in the crowd of
spectators, safe on the other side of the fence, and had called
his name in relief and had, unthinkingly, run to him. To her
death.

Poor, foolish, devoted, gentle, loving Lindy.

Kennedy decided he would wait a while before he looked
for a new woman. A good long while.

He lit another cigarette, and his thoughts turned to Mr.
Russell Andrew Garrett of New York City.

Kennedy reminded himself that the object of the exercise
tonight had been to kill Garrett. It was the right move.
Garrett was onto Laird; that road could have led back to
Kennedy himself. So it was a good idea for Garrett to
disappear. It had been prudent.

Now it was imperative. Kennedy recognized something
in himelf that he thought had died. Hatred. Russell Andrew
Garrett had earned the hatred of Gennarro Kennedy. He
would regret it.

Garrett was going to die. He would be killed by
Kennedy. Personally. For damaging the plans Kennedy had

made. For being the cause of Lindy's death. For thwarting Kennedy.

But he'd do more than die. He would be used to repair the plans he'd been trying to destroy. Kennedy toyed with the idea of letting Garrett have his head, letting him go ahead and find David Laird, that other monkey wrench in his beautiful works, then killing them both together.

Kennedy crushed out his cigarette, lit another. The match light revealed a scowl on his face.

It wouldn't work. Garrett might find out too much on the way to Laird, things he might pass along, to the further inconvenience of Gennarro Kennedy. Garrett apparently had friends. Even Negro friends, it seemed—witness the man in the hospital. He also had police friends and baseball friends . . .

Kennedy began to smile. Garrett's baseball friends. Exactly. A diversion. Something to keep their minds off David Laird.

Alone in the darkness Gennarro Kennedy started to chuckle.

Yes, perfect. A diversion, and something for Garrett to puzzle over right to the moment Kennedy killed him. Something that would take the case in an entirely new direction and leave Kennedy free to deal with Laird, wherever he might be, at his leisure.

Kennedy looked at his idea from all angles, cherished it; loved it, most of all for its symmetry. *In my end is my beginning*, he thought.

He would go back to the start, back to the idea that had inadvertently done in Rex Simmons, and this time do it right. It would be done right because he would do it himself. There could be no failure with no underlings to knock the plan off kilter.

For the second time Gennarro Kennedy began to plot the assassination of Mickey Mantle.

Chapter Six

Curveball

1

"Oh, lord, Russ," Jenny Laird said. "I'm glad to see you."

Garrett was astonished, more surprised than he'd been when she pulled the shotgun on him. Jenny Laird had been far from Garrett's greatest fan when he'd left for Kansas City; now she looked almost as glad to see him as his mother had been.

It was his second warm welcome in a row; he didn't know which one had been more surprising.

It was Thursday, September 3. Garrett had arrived in New York from Kansas City early yesterday, gone immediately to Port Chester, and slept something over sixteen hours, fourteen of which had been nightmares.

First thing this morning he'd gone to Bronx Homicide to fill Murphy in. Garrett figured it would be an unparalleled chance for Vicious Aloysius to live up to his nickname, but the captain passed it up.

Instead, Murphy expressed concern over Martin (whose injuries he'd already heard about from the Kansas City police), and over Garrett, who assured him he was all right. Murphy told Garrett there had been no progress in the investigation.

"Zero. Nothing. Except maybe one stupid little development you'll be interested in. Unless you really *have* stirred something up with this David Laird crap—and the violence out there means something."

"They were out to kill me, Captain," Garrett told him. "The girl was killed. Martin almost bought a ranch, too—so to speak—though Hal Keating told me on the phone this morning the doctors say he's going to be all right. I'm not saying it *has* to be somebody I met out in Kansas City, you know. I haven't exactly been keeping my ideas secret."

Murphy looked disgusted. "I know you haven't. That was inconsiderate, Garrett."

"Oh, gee, well, I'm sorry."

"Yeah, right. Look, I started checking into this Laird business as soon as you told me about it. I didn't believe it, but it was part of my job."

"Did you find anything? Why the hell didn't you tell me?"

"I don't have to check with you every time I fart, do I? I thought your idea was stupid, and I didn't want you to go off half-cocked. I would have been better off whistling jigs to a milestone." Murphy suddenly smiled. "My mother used to say that."

Garrett carefully stifled any remarks he might have wanted to make about Murphy's mother. After a few seconds, very quietly, he asked, "Did you find anything on Laird?"

Murphy kept smiling for a while, then said, "What? Oh, no. Not yet."

Garrett was faintly encouraged. "You're going to keep looking, then?"

"I'd be a sap if I stopped, wouldn't I? With one of my men in the hospital and people getting killed? I swear, Garrett, you were touted to me as some kind of egghead, but I'm beginning to have my doubts."

Garrett frowned. "Two points. One, you damn well weren't touted by *me* about my being an egghead; and two, you asked for me, I didn't volunteer. I would just as soon have passed."

"Hmph. Wouldn't we all." Murphy loosened his tie. "I

just keep telling myself it's going to be winter someday, and I'll wish it was hot again. At least the opera's going in the winter.

"But the *worst* thing about your shooting off your mouth," the captain went on as though they'd never left the subject, "is the bind that puts me in now."

Garrett wanted to know what he meant.

"You say somebody's trying to kill you," Murphy said. "Okay, what if someone is? It could be Laird. It could be somebody trying to protect Laird. It could be somebody who wants to get a shot at Laird first. Or—and this is my personal opinion—it could be somebody who wants us to spend our time jerking off over Laird, someone who knows he is dead, to keep us from following up lines of investigation that will lead to *him*. Sort of a red herring. Like all that Communist bullshit."

Murphy paused to take a breath. Garrett thought it over. That argument was one he hadn't thought of; Garrett was beginning to suspect the captain deserved his reputation.

"Killing me is quite a distance to go for a smoke screen, isn't it?" he asked.

"Yeah," Murphy replied. "And Kansas City is quite a distance to find you, 'cause how'd he know you'd be there to set you up? But Christ, Garrett, look at this whole business from Simmons's murder on—the whole thing smacks of somebody who thinks big and has a long reach."

"You were talking about the spot I put you in," Garrett said.

"Right. The spot. It's like this: no matter which of those possibilities is right, I *still* can't launch a full-scale investigation of Laird's possible whereabouts. And liveabouts—I can't even go heavy on if he's alive."

"Because my odds are better," Garrett put in, nodding, "if whoever tried to kill me thinks . . ."

"Right; that I don't believe you."

Garrett stood up. "I wouldn't worry about that, Captain. It didn't seem to discourage him in K.C."

"I know," Murphy growled, "and I don't like it one damned bit."

"They find out who the leader of the sledgehammer gang was?"

"Yeah, but no big thanks to you and Martin. They managed to make him by part of one fingerprint, which was all they had left. The rest was pretty well barbecued. I understand Kansas City is famous for that."

Garrett said nothing.

"Guy's name was Edward Williams, known in K.C. as Chicago Ned. Hit the Midwest, moved around. Illinois, Indiana, St. Louis, Omaha, Kansas City. Yellow sheet so long you could keep it on a roll, like toilet paper. Strictly hired muscle. A contractor. Somebody'd approach him to rough up somebody else; he'd either do it himself or hire help. So the cops out there are rounding up his usual pals, but you and Martin managed to kill the one guy who could have told you anything. Not that *anybody's* going to talk."

"My heart is breaking," Garrett said.

"Yeah, well, the cops out there might have a little leverage if they'd had a witness who'd hung around to identify people."

"I thought about that, Captain. And I wouldn't recognize anybody. All I could see was the man with the hammer. I was trying very hard not to wet my pants. I didn't want to be killed."

Murphy looked at Garrett, then laughed and slapped him on the back. "Nobody does, Garrett, nobody does. I remember the first time somebody got the drop on me. One of Frank Nitti's boys—I had just stumbled across a truck loaded with enough Canadian booze to fill the Met to the third balcony. He had a gun like an artillery piece. I was lucky enough to have another cop come by and rescue me. And I *did* wet my pants." He laughed again.

"Oh," he went on. "Speaking of being killed, that little development I mentioned: I heard from your friends up at Yankee Stadium."

"What's up?"

"Your friend Mickey Mantle got a death threat a couple of days ago."

2

"I got a photostat of it right here," the captain said. "Want to see it?"

Garrett said, "Sure." Murphy opened a folder on his desk and got it out. Garrett took the slick, dirty-gray paper and read it.

The photostat showed an envelope and a letter, typewritten, badly. The envelope was addressed simply to MICKEY MANTLE, YANKEE STADIUM, Bronx, New York, and bore a Boston, Massachusetts, postmark and a three-cent stamp.

The message itself began "HELLO . . MICKEY," and warned Mantle not to play against the Red Sox in the series beginning next Monday, September 7. "Don't show you face in Boston again, or you're baseball career will come to and end with a 32 . . . ," the letter said. "This ain't no joke if you think it is." It was signed, "yours untruly, a loyal RED SOX fan."

There was a postscript, but that was the gist of it.

"What do you think?" the captain asked.

Garrett shrugged. "Typical," he said.

The captain looked surprised. "I agree," he said. "But where the hell do you get to be such an expert on threatening letters?"

Garrett grinned. "I've seen a few. Emotions run pretty high over baseball, Captain. Sometimes even high enough for somebody to make an opera over. But that wasn't what I was thinking. To me, it seemed typical of Red Sox fans. We're natural enemies, Yankee fans and Red Sox fans. We got Babe Ruth from them, and they never got over it. The last time the Yankees lost the pennant, Boston beat them out and they *still* couldn't make it to the World Series."

"When was that?"

"Nineteen forty-eight."

"Jesus," the captain said. "I can see where they might get homicidal."

"Or want to be," Garrett added. "A letter like this comes

through the commissioner's office every so often. First one I know of directed at Mickey, though. How's he taking it?"

"He ain't turning cartwheels over it, but he ain't running for cover, either. Hell, I'd be upset myself if I got one of these things, but it looks pretty much like another stupid crank."

"Not as stupid as he pretends to be," Garrett said.

Murphy scratched his cheekbone and looked at Garrett. "Go on," he said.

"He makes plenty of mistakes in the letter," the younger man said, "but they're so inconsistent. Look at this one sentence— 'Don't show you face in Boston again or you're baseball career will come to and end with a 32.'

"I don't believe it. He wants to say the word *your* twice and gets it wrong both times, in two different ways. I would think a mistake like this would be consistent, wouldn't you? 'You face' followed by 'you're career' doesn't add up. Especially since later on he says *'Ive* got a good gang' and so on. Sure, it's illiterate to leave the apostrophe out, but it would be even more illiterate and lots more natural to say *'I* got a good gang.' I know people with diplomas who say 'I got.' I think the writer is pulling our leg a little."

"Maybe you got—excuse me. Maybe *you've* got a brain after all, Garrett. That is also typical of threatening letters. The idiots who write them pretend to be even stupider than they are, figuring the police will go after an illiterate instead of a smart person like they are. Which always fails. Like I said. Stupid cranks." Murphy narrowed his eyes. "Unless you don't happen to agree with me."

"No, it looks like crank work to me. It's just that when you pulled it out, I thought it had something to do with the congressman's murder."

"Nah. I just wanted you to see it because the kid is a friend of yours. Anyway, we've passed it along to the Boston cops. They'll do what they have to to protect him."

"Right. I'll tell our security people at Mr. Frick's office, if the Yankees haven't told them already. If it's okay with you, that is."

"Sure," Murphy said. Garrett got his hat from the rack

and put it on. When he had his hand on the door, the captain said, "What are you going to do now, Garrett?"

"Keep on looking for Laird, I guess."

Murphy laughed again. "I figured that's what you were going to say. Can I stop you?"

"I doubt it. They've already tried to kill me over it, whoever they are. What have I got to lose? Besides, I might do some good."

"The terrible thing about this whole situation is that you just might, goddammit." Captain Murphy took a breath and planted his fists on the desk. "Okay, Garrett, here's the way it's going to be. My office is going to get a phone call from you every two hours when you're away from your home or office. If I don't hear from you, I'll call out the cavalry. A two-hour-old trail can't be too hard to follow; might even catch up with you in time to save your fool life."

Garrett felt embarrassed. He felt like a teenager who had to be home a half-hour earlier than all the rest of the kids. "Captain," he said, "I don't really think that's going to be necessary . . ."

Murphy wasn't having any. "Just do it, starting two hours from the time you walk out that door."

"What happens if I forget?" Garrett wanted to know.

"If you forget, a squad of cops shows up at your office, or your home, or Yankee Stadium, or wherever the hell you're supposed to be, and starts looking for you. It'll make for a lot of embarrassing questions when you finally turn up."

Garrett cocked his head. "You're really serious about this, aren't you? Never mind, I can see you are. Okay, Captain, you win." Garrett looked at his watch. "I make it twenty-five after eleven. You will hear from me at, to make it neat, one thirty and every two hours after that. Do I have to speak to you personally, or should I talk to anyone who answers the phone?"

"Anybody who answers," the captain told him. "I've got better things to do than to wait around here all day for the phone to ring."

3

Traffic had been bad into Queens, so the two hours were almost up when Garrett arrived at Jenny Laird's cottage. Her warm welcome solved a problem for him; he had wondered how he was going to induce her to let him use the phone. As it was, he just asked. Jenny looked puzzled but said of course, go right ahead. Garrett got the operator on the line and placed a call to Captain Murphy—collect.

"What was all that?" Jenny asked when he was through.

"I had some trouble out in Kansas City; Captain Murphy is worried."

Jenny bit her lip. Garrett noticed how nice her lips were, even now, with no lipstick on them. She was dressed casually, in a blouse and slacks, and looked much too young to be the mother of three.

"I'm worried, too, Russ," she said.

"What's the matter?"

"I think I'm being—I think someone is following me. Not all the time, but often."

"Oh," Garrett said. "It's probably the police. Or maybe the FBI. I'm sorry to bring this up, but there's still evidence pointing to your husband, you know."

She shook her head. "It's not the police. Russ, sit down. You're the only person I can bring myself to tell about this. I . . . I don't have any evidence or anything . . ."

She led him to the same chair he had sat in the week before. "It's not the police," she said again. She sat down.

"Russ, I'm sorry. I was unforgivably horrible to you. And it wasn't because your idea about David's being alive was so outlandish; it was because it *wasn't*. It was too much for me to face; I loved my husband. It hurt too much to lose him. I don't want to think of him—no, no, that's not right." She was getting flustered, talking rapidly. "I *hated* the idea of his being alive and doing mean things; he never hurt anyone when I knew him. He—I mean the idea of David's coming back after all this time, but not coming to *me*, coming to . . . kill people, getting revenge on them, was too much for me to

180

face. That's why I shut you out. You were trying to make me face it.

"But now I have to face it."

"Why?" Garrett asked. His voice was very soft.

Tears came to Jenny Laird's eyes, big ones that welled up and spilled down her cheeks almost before Garrett could be aware of them.

Jenny sniffled some words.

"I'm sorry, what was that?"

"*I've seen him!*" Jenny practically screamed it. "*I've seen my husband! David is the one who's been following me!*"

4

Garrett pulled his Kaiser into the parking lot of the Samuel Tilden rest area, switched off the ignition, and turned to the woman beside him. "Okay," he said. "This is where you saw him first, right?"

Jenny seemed pale and nervous. She bit her lip. "No, this is where I *felt* him—I had an uncanny feeling he was around." She shuddered. "I'd been thinking over what you'd said, and . . . Oh, damn it, I just can't say it without sounding stupid!"

"Don't worry about how you sound. Just tell me."

"I don't even think I understand it myself, now, but at the time—this was last Monday—the uncertainty of it was driving me crazy. I was snapping at the children, driving them crazy, too, I guess.

"Somehow I became convinced that if I saw some of the places the killer was supposed to have been, I could be sure if it was David."

"So you came here." Garrett swatted at a fly that had buzzed lazily into the car.

"But not right away," Jenny said. "I agonized over it for hours. The only other place I could have gone was Yankee Stadium, but the Yankees weren't playing, so I didn't have any way to get inside to where the man was seen."

Garrett grinned. "It's easy enough if you know how. You'd have to hop a fence or two, that's all."

Jenny smiled in return, and a touch of color came into her face for the first time that afternoon. "I was wearing a skirt that day."

"This was your best choice, then," Garrett deadpanned.

"I'm glad my brain was working for something," Jenny said. "I was beginning to wonder. Because all along, totally apart from all the things I was thinking about David, I've also had the feeling I was being *watched*."

"What do you mean?"

"I don't *know*, that's the maddening part. Things like seeing the identical car both on Long Island and in Manhattan, when I'd go in to drop off an article or talk to an editor. But that wasn't something positive—I never saw any cars that continued from day to day, and I looked. Mostly, it was all feelings."

Garrett didn't tell her that it would only make sense for someone on a long-term shadowing job to change cars daily. "Go on," he told her.

"Between my indecision and having to find a baby-sitter for the kids, it was evening by the time I got here. I sat where I could see into the kitchen when a waitress brought something out, and I ordered a meal. I didn't eat much of it."

"The food's not too good in these places, anyway. All that frozen stuff."

"I probably wouldn't have tasted anything even if I did eat it. I just sat there looking around, and suddenly I was aware of David."

"Aware *how?*" Garrett had had trouble understanding this part the first time.

Jenny held out her hands, helpless. "I was *surrounded* by him. I'd hear a voice no, that's not right. I'd suddenly find myself thinking *that was David's voice*, but I'd look around me and no one would be there. No one who could be David, I mean. Or I'd jump and be *sure* I'd just seen him walk by. I must have seemed like a crazy person. By the time I left I was trembling so badly I could hardly walk."

Jenny took Garrett by the wrist. He was surprised at the strength in her small hand.

"Then the next day I saw him. On Madison Avenue, in

the Fifties. I had to take a bus to my next appointment, and I was looking across the street to see how many people were waiting at the bus stop. To try to guess how long I'd have to wait. Do you do that?"

"Sure," Garrett told her. "It'd be good news if you saw a big crowd; that would mean there had been a long time since the last bus and the next one would be along any minute."

"Exactly," Jenny said. "And in this case there was a big crowd. I looked down the street, and the bus was already coming, so I started to hurry across."

"And that's where you saw him."

She took a deep breath and closed her eyes before she answered. "Yes," she said. "*Yes!* And nothing anyone says could ever make me believe it wasn't!"

"Relax," Garrett told her. "It's just that this is important; we have to get the facts straight. He was standing there, waiting for a bus."

Jenny sounded miserable. "Like I told you before, Russ, he was standing there. I don't think he was waiting for a bus. It would be ludicrous. I can't have seen my dead husband waiting on the curb of Madison Avenue, waiting for a bus I was running to catch."

"Okay, I'm sorry. I don't really think he was waiting for a bus, either."

Jenny looked at him. She was still miserable with doubt, confusion, and fear, but there was a tiny spark of happiness in her eyes at the thought he might believe her.

"What do you think he was doing, Russ?"

"Waiting for you. It's the only thing that makes sense. If it really was him, and he's the one who's been following you, it only stands to reason he'd wait somewhere he could see the entrance of the building you'd gone into and pick you up again when you left."

Jenny put both her hands on top of her head in a little-girl gesture that said, "Why didn't *I* think of that?"

"Of *course*," she breathed. "It has to be that."

Garrett scratched his chin. "You didn't get a really close look at him, though, dammit. It was across most of the avenue, and at an angle."

"It wasn't a close look, but it was a good look. Besides, he saw me, too. I know he did. Our eyes met. I—I couldn't be mistaken about that, Russ. I couldn't. The first time I was sure I loved him was when our eyes met that way across the grass . . ." Jenny's voice trailed off, replaced by soft sobbing.

Garrett figured the best thing to do was ignore it. He told Jenny he wished he knew *why* her husband would do something like this.

Jenny's voice was almost a whisper. "I'm afraid of him, Russ. He looks the same, but he must have changed inside. He shouldn't be *toying* with me this way. I *know* him, Russ, or I did. Even if he did kill the congressman, he would have gotten a message to me some way."

Jenny closed her eyes and leaned back against Garrett's green leather upholstery. "Maybe he hates me now."

Garrett frowned. It was a possibility he'd thought of; he hadn't wanted to share it with Jenny.

"Maybe he thinks I've betrayed him in some way. If you're right, then he killed Simmons, he killed Ed Bristow, and who knows who's next? I've sent the children away. I leave the lights on and the radio going all night. You know, Russ, I didn't tell you this before, but right after I saw David, when he looked at me, then ran away into the crowd, I forgot all about my next appointment. I got a taxi to the baseball offices in Rockefeller Center, to tell you about it. They told me you were out of town. It was hell until you got back—I was afraid to talk to anyone. If I don't find out what's behind this, I'm going to go insane."

Garrett patted her shoulder. "We won't let that happen."

"I'm not joking."

"I didn't think you were," Garrett told her. "Let's go inside and see what we can find out."

5

They'd deliberately waited until after six so that conditions would be as close as possible to what they had been when Jenny had become "aware" of her husband's supposed presence. Garrett had spent the time telling Jenny what had

gone on in Kansas City and making, with increasing irritation, his calls to Captain Murphy's office before driving to
New Jersey.

Garrett had tried to devote some of the afternoon to
thinking of some brilliant way to flush Laird (or whoever was
behind all this) from hiding, but the only plan he'd been able
to come up with was to ask people questions.

Niffin, the manager with hair of one sort or another
where his forehead was supposed to be, remembered Garrett
from his previous visit, and what was even better, remembered him as some kind of cop. Garrett let him go on
remembering that way. Niffin gave him the run of the place.
He didn't even ask what Jenny was doing there. Garrett
figured he took her for a policewoman.

Garrett still had the photograph Jenny had given him.
He showed it to the staff one by one, starting with Niffin,
and asked them if they remembered seeing anyone like that
recently. The reactions of the waitresses were summed up by
a blue-haired veteran of a million orders: "I notice tips. Who's
got time to look at faces?"

Garrett renewed his acquaintance with the kitchen staff.
The kitchen didn't seem as bad to him this time; his
experience in Kansas City had hardened him to hellish
scenes. Harry Lillian, the old cook, was working next to a
heavyset woman at the stoves. Garrett learned it was Levi
Barlett's night off. Not having the colored cook around
seemed to bother the old man. He was grumpy and un-
cooperative; said he was tired of answering questions. Garrett
finally got him to look at the picture; Lillian took a look,
squinted, and declared he didn't recognize nobody. They
tried the woman cook, just to be polite. She declared it looked
like her son-in-law's cousin, except her son-in-law's cousin
had a harelip, and wasn't it a shame, a nice-looking boy like
that.

Joey Hart, the dishwasher, kept his head in the steam—
he might have been embarrassed to show his deformed face in
the presence of a lady, or it might have been he was shy in
front of women, face or no face. Finally Garrett practically
pulled him out by the neck and made him look at the picture.

He took one look and shook his head while rasping out a
sound that was probably no. Garrett saw Jenny flinch when
she saw the puckered wound that passed for Joey's mouth.
He should have warned her. Garrett decided the cook's
distant relative was lucky to have gotten off with only a
harelip.

"No luck at all," Jenny said as they left the building.

Garrett shrugged. "So we keep trying," he said.

Jenny wanted to know where they were going now.

"I'm taking you home. Nothing else we can do today."
They walked to the car. Garrett started the engine, put the
Hydra-Matic in drive, and took off. "Did *you* notice anything
in there?"

"What do you mean?"

"Were you aware of any more strange sensations?"

Jenny looked straight ahead at the pool of brightness
Garrett's lights made on the road. "Don't make fun of me,
Russ."

"I'm not," he protested. "I wouldn't. Look, all I meant
was, that other time you were noticing things without
realizing what they were. Your unconscious—subconscious—
intuition—whatever you want to call it—put them together
into a certainty that your husband was around. I was just
wondering if anything like that had happened this time."

Jenny shook her head. "I'm so mixed up, I'm not even
sure what I felt. My mind was filled with David, but it was
before we got there. It's been filled with him since the first
time I came here. So I just don't know."

Most of the rest of the ride passed in silence. At one
point, when they'd just gone through the tunnel from
Manhattan to Queens, Jenny said, "Russ, that poor dishwasher. What was wrong with him?"

Garrett told her his guess about frostbite.

"Can't they do anything for him?"

"I suppose somebody somewhere can fix that up, at least
so it looks okay, but how's he supposed to afford it on a
dishwasher's salary?"

"That's the sort of thing that would have outraged my
husband, that a man should have to go through life like that

because he was poor. David worked to get some sort of health insurance in this country, and they called him a traitor." Jenny Laird paused as if sorting through an especially rich selection of things she could say next. Finally she said, "I read in a book once where someone said, 'There's no justice and little mercy in this world.' I remember being angry, thinking that was the worst kind of lie. Now I don't know."

Garrett didn't know, either, so he kept his mouth shut until he pulled up at Jenny's cottage. When Jenny started to open the door, Garrett was struck with a flash of intuition of his own.

"Stay put," he told her. He took the car keys out of the ignition and handed them to her. "Let's swap; my car keys for your house keys. Stay in the car; keep the door locked. Have you got a watch?"

"No. What's this all about?"

"Nothing," Garrett said, "I'm being silly. Humor me, okay? All right. The dashboard clock keeps terrible time, but you can count ten minutes on it. If I'm not back by then, slide over to the driver's seat and go get the nearest cops. Will you do that?"

"What's the matter?"

"Nothing. I'm just getting nervous in my old age. I'm going to check out the house, make sure it's okay, before you go inside. I'll be back way before ten minutes are up. Okay?"

Jenny nodded. He left the car, then signaled through the window for her to lock the door. She pushed the button and sat back to wait for him while she tried to decide just what sort of nightmare she had stumbled into.

It didn't take long for Jenny to begin to doubt Garrett's words about the accuracy of the clock. Hours passed in the time it took the luminous dial to show three minutes gone by.

The night was crowded with noise. Funny she'd never noticed before how loud the frogs were, how strange and insistent the crickets seemed. She didn't like it out here in the car alone. She couldn't see past the windows of the car because of the utter darkness of the night. The moon and stars were covered with clouds. The only sounds she could hear were strange cries, all of which had some meaning for the creatures who made them but absolutely none for her. Jenny shuddered. It was all too perfect a symbol of what her whole life had become.

Seven minutes. That clock *had* to be wrong. Where was he? Jenny began to tap her nails against the steering wheel. She could stand that for about thirty seconds. She cursed and folded her arms across her chest. Something had happened to him. Jenny had to find out.

She unlocked the car door and began to push it open. It went about six inches and stopped. Jenny looked up, saw a man's hand pressed against the window, and screamed. She slammed the door and started fumbling with the keys.

The man was pounding on the window. Jenny held her breath, trying vainly to control her trembling. She just couldn't get the key into the ignition. The pounding continued.

Then the man said, "Hey!" Russ Garrett's voice. Jenny looked up and saw the concern on his face even in the darkness. Jenny was overcome with embarrassment and residual fear. She looked helplessly through the window at the young man. Then she unlocked the door, jumped from the car, and fell sobbing into his arms.

Garrett made soothing noises and led her to the house. "I'm sorry," he said. "I didn't know you were so upset. I never should have left you alone."

"I just couldn't—"

"Shh, it's okay." Garrett took her inside and sat her in a comfortable chair. "Is there anything I can get you? A glass of water or something?"

Jenny looked at him and nodded. Garrett said okay and went to the kitchen.

This is a good man, Jenny thought. I'm a fool, and I'm a coward, and he still doesn't get angry. She couldn't have taken it if he'd gotten angry, and he'd seen that. Not many men would have.

Garrett came back with the water. Jenny took it, sipped some. "Better now?" Garrett asked. Jenny nodded.

"Good," he said. He looked at his watch and made a face. "Time to call the warden. Can I use the phone again?"

"Sure." Jenny smiled in spite of herself. "We're practically partners in this by now." Garrett laughed and picked up the receiver.

Jenny said, "Russ, wait."

Garrett turned and looked at her. He put the receiver down.

Jenny was starting to panic again. She was afraid of saying what she wanted to say but even more afraid not to.

She compromised on a whisper. "Russ, don't leave me tonight. I need you here."

Garrett picked the phone back up, dialed 0 and made his call. When the connection was made, she heard him say, "Yeah, Garrett. Tell Murphy or whoever I'm in for the night. No more calls until morning." He put the phone down. "Okay, Jenny?" he asked.

Jenny could feel her fears starting to slip from her. "Okay," she said.

6

Russ Garrett returned to his office Friday morning for the first time in over a week. He was depressed to see how little work had piled up in his absence.

He was depressed about a lot of things. The weather, for one thing. Rain fell in alternating periods of heavy and very heavy. He was depressed about the Yankees. They had lost 5 to 3 to the lowly St. Louis Browns. He was depressed about the way his own baseball career had fallen into limbo. He was depressed about the news. There was more hell to pay in the Middle East and rumors of a possible Communist takeover in West Germany. He was depressed to realize that he was just this moment thinking about Ann Devore for the first time since before he went to Kansas City. And he was depressed at how good he felt about last night.

He should feel guilty, or something. He'd wanted it to happen. Jenny had gone to the bedroom, and Garrett had sacked out on the couch. He didn't go to sleep. He lay there, his legs cramped up and uncomfortable, thinking how nice it had felt to have his arms around her. And wishing she would come to him.

When she did come to him, looking childlike and vulnerable in her flowered flannel nightgown, he should have just—

Oh, to hell with what I should have just, Garrett told himself. She came to him, sat down beside him, and started to cry; hot, cleansing tears that seemed to be purging years of fear, and Garrett could think of nothing to do but hold on tight and pretend to understand. Then she'd stopped crying and told him to kiss her, and he did, and kept doing it, and soon the nightgown was gone, and Jenny still looked vulnerable, but nothing like a child.

There on the sofa, and later in the bedroom, they had made love. She was alone and afraid, and he (perhaps) had taken advantage of her. She was (possibly) still a married woman. And she was older than he was. Which, Garrett supposed, was getting to be a habit of his.

He had not until this moment thought to compare Jenny Laird with Cheryl Tilton. He decided it was because there was no real basis for comparison. With Cheryl it had been so exciting he didn't think he would survive the night. With Jenny it had been so warm that he was sure he would.

Before he left her this morning, Garrett renewed his promise to take her son to a ball game. "As soon as this business is over," he'd said.

Now Garrett frowned. Mantle could be retired and in the Hall of Fame before Mark got a chance to meet him. Who knew when this would be over? Or if it ever would be.

Garrett was tormenting his brain trying to think of a way to speed the process up a little when the phone on his desk rang. He cursed at it and picked it up.

7

About that same time Nofsinger was reaching for a ringing telephone in a pay booth in Grand Central Station. He pushed the last inch and a half of his hot dog into his mouth, chewed hastily, swallowed, picked up the phone and said hello all before the phone had a chance to ring twice.

"Nofsinger?"

"Yes, boss?"

"Progress?" He sure is a terse bastard, Nofsinger reflected.

"All instructions carried out. I stopped tailing the Laird woman, like you said. Then I went to Boston, took care of the mail . . ." Nofsinger hoped his puzzled irritation didn't show in his voice. He'd worked very hard to get that death threat to Mantle to sound authentic. The boss had been very explicit about it. Nofsinger wondered, though, what the hell he was trying to accomplish by it. If the boss actually wanted Mantle killed, it was no skin off Nofsinger's ass, but why tip them off?

"Are you absolutely sure it has been received? There has been nothing in the newspapers here," Kennedy said.

"They generally try to keep these things quiet. If they publicize it, other nuts can get ideas. But one of the tabloid sports columnists picked it up; it was in yesterday's paper—you know, when they start getting rain-outs around the country, they've got to fill up the space with something."

"All right, Nofsinger. Have you finished the devices?"

"Yeah. I just put them in a locker here in the station. I was just about to mail you the key."

"No. Get a copy made for yourself first." That was no problem. It was supposed to be against the law as well as impossible to duplicate keys to coin lockers, but Nofsinger knew a clever locksmith who loved money.

"Okay," the fat man said. "Might take a couple of days."

"I know. Don't mail it to Kansas City. Send it special delivery care of the Ozone Hotel in Boston." He gave the address.

"That's in the *nigger* section!" Nofsinger blurted.

"I know where it is. Just send it there. Wait for further instructions. Do you understand?"

"Yes, boss, sorry," Nofsinger said.

"Good-bye."

In a darkened room in a quiet apartment in the "nigger

section" of Kansas City, Missouri, Gennarro Kennedy placed the telephone back on the hook.

He was, he reflected, once again tired of Nofsinger. As soon as this operation was over, he would be attended to.

Kennedy was tired in general, he realized. He had trouble getting interested in any project past the killing of Mantle and Garrett. Even the tracking of David Laird. Perhaps he'd just take the money he'd accumulated and leave Mrs. Klimber after Garrett was dead. Let her take care of herself. Kennedy smiled. *That* would be an amusing spectacle.

Otherwise, things were going well. Nofsinger couldn't hide his scorn over the sending of that note. Kennedy smiled. The note was nothing. It was *supposed* to be routine; it was *supposed* to be taken with less than terror; it was supposed to lead to strictly routine precautions. Most important, it was supposed to, and would, *focus attention exclusively on Boston, Massachusetts, as the site of danger.* The Boston police would go through the motions, and nothing would happen, except that grown men would play a boys' game. Then they all would congratulate themselves on their resourcefulness and courage, and the Yankees would head home.

With their guard down. There would be opportunities. There *had* to be opportunities. Things were being arranged even now so that Gennarro Kennedy would be on the scene when the best chance presented itself.

This time it would work. The failings of his recent plans, Kennedy had come to see, had been caused by his planning them too finely. He had come to treat life too much like a game of chess; to try to see too many moves ahead for pieces that carried will, if no great intelligence. This time, though, he would simply create a situation favorable to his desired outcome and manipulate events directly and immediately.

And lethally.

8

David Laird coughed, a tiny spasm of his respiratory system. Currents of pain buzzed through his head like strokes of an electric saw. The pain was never gone these days. It waxed and waned but never disappeared, and it flared into agony at the slightest jar. It was going to kill him, and soon.

There was medicine he could take to ease the pain, but he didn't dare. The medicine slowed him down and addled his brain.

If he didn't know it would hurt so much, he would have laughed. As if his brain weren't addled already. As if, in allowing Jenny to know he was following her, in trying to see her at *all*, he hadn't made the cruelest blunder possible.

In one small corner of Laird's brain, emotion held out against reason. *I had to see her*, emotion protested. *It was only an accident she noticed me at the bus stop.*

This time Laird did laugh, and to hell with the pain. Was it an accident you followed her in the first place? Was it an accident you couldn't be content with your first glance? An accident you shadowed her in every available moment? Wearing your own face? The one every policeman in the country is looking for?

I should have created a different face, emotion conceded.

You should have stayed away from her entirely! None of your faces should have set eyes on her. And you know it.

Yes, emotion said, *but I have seen my children again, albeit at a distance. And my son is a fine boy.*

Laird smiled. On that emotion and reason could agree. But was the pain worth it? The risk he'd run when he'd parked on the road and watched Jenny's house that day? He realized now that his death (the one to come) would lead to his discovery. He had, in fact, planned his actions in a way that would make that inevitable, so that history would know that the likes of Rex Simmons and Edward Bristow had been punished by someone who was entitled to mete out that punishment. How very neat. How very vain.

But he had forgotten the innocent. He sat amazed at his ability to have done that. It was the innocent who always suffered. He himself had been innocent once. Poor Ann. Jenny and the children. And others.

He should have died years ago, as he'd planned. Hell was worse when you were alive. And it was hell. Seeing

Jenny, hearing her voice, getting close enough, at times, to touch her, knowing all the time you weren't even worthy of her pity. That you had forfeited all that even before you ran away from her.

No more innocent people would suffer, even if Laird had to turn himself in and disgrace his family a second time.

David Laird felt better having made that resolve. Now it was time to act on it. With an effort he rose and forced himself to sit at the wooden table.

A newspaper lay open in front of him. Laird had the item he was looking for practically memorized, but he blinked his eyes clear and tried it again. It remained the same.

Mickey Mantle's life had been threatened. That's all the item said, really, just the bare fact and a few platitudes to the effect that baseball was just a game and it was foolish to let one's enthusiasm go so far.

But there had been a threat on Mickey Mantle's life.

David Laird, masquerading as Thane, had been given a gun and told to kill Mickey Mantle. He was supposed to have been the tool of some evil, subtle plan by the Fascist Klimber organization, the power behind Rex Harwood Simmons. Laird had, of course, turned their own plan against them.

But the fact remained that the Klimber organization wanted Mickey Mantle dead. Laird was the only one who knew that. The authorities were probably taking it as a matter of routine.

Which, after all, it probably was. But then again it might not be. Laird had to warn them. He did not want Mickey Mantle to die. He didn't want anyone to die anymore.

He had to warn them.

With sheer force of will David Laird packed the pain in his head into one white-hot pellet and tucked it away in a corner of his skull. He rose from the table, staggered from the cottage into the rain, got into his car, and drove to the closest telephone. During the ride he thought of a way to make them take his call seriously.

He knew the number he had to call. When he had seen the man with Jenny, some vestigial sense of jealousy had led him to find out all he could about Russ Garrett.

"Major League Baseball," said the voice of an operator.

"Russ Garrett, please." Laird used the same whisper he had at the ball park the day he'd killed the congressman.

"Just a moment; I'll ring him."

"Hello," Garrett said.

"Mr. Garrett?"

"Yes?"

"It would only be wise," David Laird whispered, "to take the threat against the life of Mickey Mantle seriously."

"What did you say?"

"I said, it would only be wise to take the threat against the life of Mickey Mantle seriously."

"Who is this?"

"Good day, Mr. Garrett." Laird hung up. He heaved a sigh. He had, he felt, done his duty. He drove home through the rain. When he got there, he didn't bother to dry himself. He had gotten used to being wet. He pulled his chair to the window of the cottage and watched the waves crash on the New Jersey shore, thinking of nothing until it was time for him to leave.

Chapter Seven
Hot Corner

1

Everybody was a little on edge in anticipation of Monday's Labor Day doubleheader. The Yankees, waiting out a second day of rain in Philadelphia, were nervous because they hadn't won a game since last Thursday, when they'd beaten the Browns in St. Louis, 9 to 1. They lost to the Browns 5 to 3 on Friday. Mickey Mantle, though he did his best to ignore it and concentrate on baseball, was upset to think somebody would want to kill him. Mickey'd never hurt anybody—there sure were some crazy people in the world. It was hard to believe just how many until you got to be famous. Then you were up on a hill, where all the people who didn't like not being up there, too, could see you real good. He wanted to get to Boston and get it over with.

The Boston police were wary, because even though that threat had probably been the work of a crank, you could never tell, could you? And that's all that had to happen, one of the Yankees' stars to get taken care of in Boston. It would be bad for the city, bad for the cops. Bad for the Red Sox, who were also worried. Tom Yawkey, owner of the Sox, had told the cops to do whatever they had to to make sure things didn't get out of hand. As a result, a whole lot of Boston police would mingle with the Labor Day crowd, armed and ready and warned not to get so involved in the action on the field they forgot to watch the people.

Back in New York Captain Al (Vicious Aloysius) Murphy had a couple of reasons to be nervous. For one thing, they were bringing Martin back to New York today. Murphy was even going to miss the Sunday afternoon opera broadcast to meet him. Martin was showing good progress and was going to be okay, but Murphy was still nervous about moving him. For another thing, he hoped the Boston cops would pay attention to the teletype message he'd sent without thinking he was trying to horn in. He'd warned them to take a special look at all the Fenway Park vendors (he'd had to look up the name of the ball field) to make sure they were who they were supposed to be. He assumed Garrett would remind them. Garrett was the third reason he was nervous. Here Murphy was trying his damnedest to keep that stupid kid in one piece, and now he had to go to Boston chasing after the ghost of David Laird. Murphy had included a request for the cops up there to keep an eye on him, but he doubted it would help.

Hal Keating, who was sitting in a fisherman's restaurant on the pier eating lobster with Russ Garrett, was worried that by leaving the state of Missouri, he was throwing away his chance to bring the St. Louis Browns to Kansas City. Still, some things couldn't be helped, and Keating's curiosity was one of them—a legacy from his OSS days, he guessed. Garrett had opened one king-size can of worms and found a tangle that might never be smoothed out. He liked Mantle and he liked Garrett, and Hal had come to save them any grief he could. Hal was there to help.

Gennarro Kennedy, sitting on the edge of his bed in a dingy hotel room in Roxbury, fingering the Grand Central Station locker key he'd just received, was worried, too, though he wouldn't have put it that way. Kennedy would have said he was eager; trained and ready for his upcoming tasks, whatever they might turn out to be. He kept looking at his watch, counting off the minutes until he had to meet the Yankees' train. He'd follow them to the door of the hotel, but not inside.

2

Russ Garrett was about the only one who wasn't worried. He was past that. He'd been uneasy and bewildered so long, he'd finally gone numb. He could still think and all that, but his emotions refused to exercise themselves without extreme provocation.

He'd been that way since Friday, when he got the mysterious call. He told Murphy about it; Murphy said okay, thanks. "A crank can write a letter, another crank can write about it in a newspaper, and a third one can read it and make a phone call." And even if it weren't a crank, the captain pointed out, what could he do about it? "Don't get excited," Murphy advised.

Then Garrett called Jenny Laird, because something the caller said had stuck in his memory. He recited the phone call to Jenny, and she confirmed it. "It would only be wise" was one of David Laird's pet phrases. He used it all the time; in his lectures to classes, in his writing, even in casual conversation. Garrett himself had heard Laird use it on TV, when he testified before Simmons's committee.

A little while before that news would have excited him. Now he followed Murphy's advice. Garrett was sure it was David Laird who'd spoken to him, but he doubted he could convince anyone who mattered. If Garrett had heard it on TV, millions could have heard it. Garrett wished he'd had the time to ask the voice about the dead dentist and why he'd been left to have his face eaten by the sea gulls.

Then Garrett thought about the handsome, open face of Mickey Mantle, and about the way Bristow's injuries had matched those of Simmons and the hot-dog vendor, and felt a little sick. Not excited, just sick.

Garrett had to go to Boston. Saturday had been devoted to arranging things so that he could. The first thing he did was check Jenny and her kids into a nice little hotel on the East Side of Manhattan, then have a chat with the house detective about keeping an especially good watch over them. Next he went home to pack and tell his parents he would be gone a few days. They hadn't been home when he'd gotten there—they were visiting a neighbor who was in the hospital after having nearly electrocuted himself trying to fix his own TV set. Garrett's father had chortled and said it served him right.

Finally Garrett had to deal with Murphy. He wasn't sure how he did it, but he managed to get out of town before the captain could put him in protective custody. That night he drove his Kaiser up the Post Road to Boston, getting to the hotel about midnight. He had a little talk with the house detective there, too.

Sunday morning Hal Keating had showed up. Garrett was glad to have him.

Garrett pulled a big, white hunk of meat from the lobster's left claw. "What's new in Kansas City?" he asked.

"Everything's up to date," Keating said.

Garrett said, "I'm just trying to take my mind off here and now for five minutes, Hal, okay?"

"No such luck, Russ. Nothing is going on in Kansas City right now to take your mind off this business. Hell, even your girl friend left town. Went to Washington to get the office in shape for her new boss."

"How do you know that?"

"She called me before she left. She wanted to know how to get in touch with you. I guess she figured Washington is a whole lot closer to New York than Kansas City is."

"That's not even funny, Hal. What did you tell her?"

"I told her to try the commissioner's office. I could hardly keep that much a secret. I didn't know you wanted to avoid her."

"I don't know if I do, either." Garrett sighed and pushed himself back from the table. "Boy, I'm full. Hal, I swear you know every good restaurant in the country."

"Just the American League cities. What do we do now?"

"Go back to the hotel and have a little talk with Mickey, I suppose. The Yankees ought to be in by now."

3

Gennarro Kennedy watched the New York Yankees leave the train station and get into cabs to go to their hotel. Mickey Mantle was easy to identify: tall and strong and golden haired. He did not look, Kennedy thought, like someone who was in fear for his life. Mantle was laughing and joking with his teammates.

Kennedy tried to decide the best way to kill him. An open attack was out, at least while he was in Boston. Kennedy reminded himself that he didn't *want* to deal with Mantle in Boston, and had no intention of doing so.

Besides, the circumstances weren't right. Mantle would seldom be alone, even in his hotel room—the ball players were all doubled up. And Mantle wouldn't be easy to take on. He was as big and strong as Kennedy himself, and younger. Kennedy had a gun, but he didn't think he'd use it. A gun would attract too much attention in those situations where he'd be most likely to employ it.

One idea appeared to have possibilities. The Yankees were scheduled to return to New York by train Monday night. It would be a simple matter to be at the station then, posing as a redcap. If he could get hold of Mantle's luggage, he could plant one of Nofsinger's devices in it. Nofsinger was standing by in New York to bring them to him for just such a contingency. Mantle would return to New York, open his suitcase . . .

Kennedy killed the idea just as it began to stretch its wings. What if Mantle didn't do his own unpacking? Not that Kennedy minded killing a supernumerary or two. But an accident like that would only make people more cautious and matters more difficult. Besides, as far as he could see, the ball players traveled light and handled their own baggage—it would be hard to plant the device.

Kennedy sighed. He'd be on the train to New York. An opportunity would present itself, either then or during the next few days. Mantle couldn't be protected forever, and wouldn't be, back in New York. The note had seen to that.

Still, Kennedy mused, there was something appealing in the notion of tipping them off but accomplishing his task nevertheless. More artistic. A more fitting memorial for poor little Lindy.

The cabs were loaded up and starting to leave. Kennedy had no more time for thinking. He put his rented DeSoto in gear and followed them.

He decided when he arrived that a simple peek in the lobby wouldn't do any harm. He walked by the glass doors, watching the Yankees go up the short flight of carpeted steps to the level of the front desk. Someone rose from one of the plush lobby chairs and accosted Mickey Mantle. Kennedy saw he had been right about how well Mantle was protected. Several members of the Yankees stepped between Mantle and the man who'd been waiting. Then they stepped aside. By bending a little Kennedy could see the man's face. Kennedy quickly ducked away from the entrance (the doorman had begun to eye him suspiciously, anyway) before the man could notice him. As Kennedy walked back to his car, he began to smile.

Russ Garrett. Garrett was here, in Boston. In Kennedy's hands. Mantle and Garrett. He *had* to be able to get one of them.

Soon he was on the phone to New York. "Nofsinger," he said. "Bring me one of the devices. The electric one, I think. No, I won't meet you personally. When can you be in Boston? Very well. A colored man in a short red jacket will meet you a half-hour past that time." Kennedy named a street corner outside Fenway Park for the rendezvous. It seemed appropriate, somehow. "No, he won't say anything. He is a deaf mute." That took care of any possibility of Nofsinger recognizing Kennedy's voice. "Yes, I trust him. Now I suggest you get moving."

Kennedy hung up and decided he'd better get moving, too. It was still raining on and off, and he was going to have to stand around in it tonight. He'd better find a place he could get an umbrella on a Sunday night in Boston.

4

Rex Simmons had never had much union support, and Tad didn't expect any, either. That's why he wasn't worried about any political ramifications when he decided to go to the Congressional Office Building Labor Day morning. He took his time among the holiday-weekend crowds.

He wasn't going to do much work, anyway. He was just looking for Cheryl. He didn't know what had gotten into that girl. She could never be reached at her apartment in Silver Spring anymore—he hadn't found her there since they'd left Kansas City for Washington last Friday.

At first he had suspected she was out getting laid. It would be like her to run around and rub it in that she had raised the flag on him, the bitch. But anytime he called the office, there she was, just like she said she'd be. She had a lot of work to do, she told him. Putting his brother's files in shape for him, she'd said.

Tad Simmons wasn't buying any of that crap. He'd just amble down to the office and *see* what she was up to. Maybe she had some gimmick on the phone that would send calls in the office out to wherever she was, doing God knew what. Maybe the slut was having men in the office. On the couch in Rex's—dammit, *his* office. She'd done that with Rex, Tad knew. Whatever it was he would find out and lay down the law. *He* was the congressman now. He'd be making laws. Time to get in a little practice.

Cheryl was in the office. Alone, in her proper place. She jumped when he came into the room, then smiled kittenishly at him.

"Hello, Tad," she said. "I mean, Congressman."

Tad's eyes narrowed in his foxy face. "What the hell are you doing?"

Cheryl took a puff at her cigarette, then waved her hand at a litter of items scattered on her desk top, making a smoky circle around them. "Cleaning out my desk," she said. "I was going to leave you a note. Maybe this is better."

"What the hell are you talking about?"

"Quitting. I've had enough, that's all. No hard feelings."

"No hard f-f-feelings my ass!" Tad saw Cheryl stu-
diously ignore his stutter, and that made him all the madder.
"You're not about to run out on me n-n-now, little girl."

Cheryl stubbed out the cigarette, emptied the ashtray
into the garbage, wiped it with a tissue, threw the tissue
away, and stowed the ashtray neatly in a small cardboard
carton on the floor beside her desk. "I hope that doesn't
break," she said absently.

Tad was turning red. It took him ten seconds to get past
the *g* sound of *goddammit*. It was a roar by the time it came
out.

Cheryl looked up at him. "Oh, come off it, Congressman. You've got days before Congress reconvenes. You'll find
somebody." Cheryl tilted her head as if pondering something.
"Might be a good idea if you went back to Kansas City to do
the hiring. Better politics."

Tad stood still. He clenched his fists, closed his eyes,
and bit his tongue. He *would* get control of himself. He
concentrated on it. He astounded himself by doing something
he never thought he'd do—he asked himself how Rex would
have handled this. He decided that Rex, with the way he felt
about Cheryl, would either have dissolved in hopeless tears or
strangled her by now. Or both.

Tad laughed. That put things in perspective, didn't it?
Stupid to get that worked up over a woman. Especially when
you held all the cards.

"What is it, Cheryl?" he said. "Really, I mean. Just
because we don't sleep together anymore doesn't mean we
can't be friends. Do you want a raise?"

"No raise, Tad. I'm just leaving."

Tad was still being reasonable. "You won't get away
with it. You know I won't let you."

"I know too much?"

"Something like that. Besides, I need you. You know too
damn much to be replaced, that's for sure."

"I've got copies of the files, Tad." Cheryl might have
told him it was still cloudy outside or that the Washington
Monument was tall.

"What?"

"The *real* files. The files that tell how much money we got from Mrs. Klimber and why. And what you did with it. Those files."

Tad didn't stammer. He didn't speak. His only thought was *Jesus, Rex would have killed her, and he would have been right.*

Cheryl went on. "That's what I've been doing in the office this weekend. Making photostats of the files. For insurance."

"Wh-wh-wh-wh . . ." *Son of a bitch,* Tad thought.

"Where are they?" Cheryl asked. Being helpful. Tad couldn't stand it. "The originals are in the locked drawers where they belong. Oh, here's the key." She picked something up from her desk and held it out as if she expected him to take it. When she saw he wasn't going to, she placed it gently back down.

"I'll just leave it here," she said. "The copies are all in the mail. To all sorts of places. Reporters, lawyers, friends—even one to my ex-husband. There's no delivery today, of course, but I really have to get in touch with those people and tell them not to open them unless something happens to me."

"Why?" Tad didn't try to say more than the single word. "I told you. Insurance. I want out of here, and this is my way to get it. As long as I stay unmolested, you stay in office. And out of jail. I made dozens of copies." She looked at him, eyes wide.

"You bitch," Tad said. "You're enjoying this."

"I suppose you're right," Cheryl told him. "Someone said to me recently that I get some sort of kick out of power as a thing in itself. Even sexually." She shrugged. "It could be. Maybe that's what I saw in your brother and you. But if that's the case it makes much more sense if I have power myself. Simpler. Don't you think so? Now I *do* have power. Power to leave you, and to see that you leave me alone." She picked up her carton and folded down the lid. She stood up and got ready to go. Tad was paralyzed; she had to walk around him on the way to the door. Just as she passed him, she stopped and turned around.

"Oh, and Tad?"

Congressman Simmons felt as if he were talking in his sleep. "Yes?" he said. He didn't even feel his lips move.

"You lay off Russ Garrett, too. Let the police find out who killed Rex. Leave Garrett alone. Or by the time I get through, your seat will be hotter than the Rosenbergs'. And I'll laugh while you cook. Do you believe me?"

Tad nodded, but he still couldn't believe any of it.

"Good," Cheryl cooed. She blew him a kiss. "Good-bye, Tad," she said. "It's been fun, mostly."

She walked out.

5

They turned on the lights in Fenway Park at the start of the third inning of the second game.

"About time," Hal Keating said. "Damn clouds make it look like the middle of the night."

Garrett grunted, heard himself, and apologized. He'd been spending too much time with Vicious Aloysius Murphy. "I hear it's raining again back in New York. I hope we get the second game in before it rains up here."

"Long night for the ground crew at the stadium," Keating observed. Garrett agreed and said they'd probably be getting the field in shape until dawn—assuming it had stopped raining down in New York in the meantime.

"If it doesn't stop raining the Yankees may never win another game," Garrett said glumly.

The Red Sox had won the first game of today's double-header 7 to 4, in spite of Mickey Mantle's home run. Ted Williams had done the most damage, with a homer and a single. George Kell had also homered, but to Garrett's mind, that one didn't really count. In Fenway Park a right-handed batter had an easy poke for a home run. A ball that would be a lazy pop-up in Yankee Stadium would clear the big tin-covered wall in left field here in Fenway. Center and right field were fairly normal, and Williams was a lefty, so that homer was legitimate.

Garrett was not enjoying himself today. Too many

people rooting against the Yankees in strange accents. He was tired of hearing people say "Hit it out of the *pahk!*" Garrett was also under the impression that when anybody in the crowd looked at him cross-eyed, it was a Boston policeman deciding *be* was the guy who'd sent Mickey the threatening note. At that, he supposed he couldn't blame them. He looked sour enough, and he couldn't take his eyes off Mickey anytime he was on the field.

Garrett sat and looked at the field, not seeing it. It wasn't baseball, he decided, that had been bothering him. He'd been this way ever since he'd heard from Cheryl just before he'd left the hotel.

He didn't know why that should bother him; it ought to make him happy. Cheryl had done something for him he wasn't close to being able to do for himself. Garrett felt pretty sure that Congressman Telford Simmons wouldn't be around upsetting his mother with stories of "Communist" girl friends in his past.

"Rest in peace, Annie," he said.

Hal Keating risked turning one eye away from the spectacle of Yogi Berra digging in at the plate. "What did you say?"

Yogi got a hit, driving in a run for the Yankees. "Nothing, Hal. *Way to go, Yogi!*"

Having gotten the cheer out of his system, Garrett went back to his thoughts. Maybe that was it. Over the last couple of weeks, he'd finally let go of Ann Devore. She'd been part of him so long, alive and dead, through so much—baseball, Korea, the hospital, and after—that he felt empty, somehow, kind of diminished.

Or maybe it was how Cheryl showed signs of wanting another session of whatever that was they had done out in Kansas City. He was afraid of Cheryl Tilton. She was a woman who had shown over and over that she would stop at nothing. Bedding her had been fantastic; the idea of dealing with her on a regular basis was something more than intimidating.

When she'd called him, she'd been so casual, even chatty. It seemed so out of character. "... and Tad wanted to get out of Kansas City, even though Congress doesn't convene for a while, because Mrs. Klimber was getting to be impossible. Russ, that woman calls twelve times a day. Her man Kennedy had some sort of family business, had to leave town, and she's always telling us she needs Gennarro to do this, and she needs Gennarro to do that—just the way she talks about her absurd son."

All this while Garrett had been trying to make it to his car so he could be there before the bus that was going to take the Yankees to the ball park. "I can see how it would be a nuisance, Cheryl—" he began.

She cut him off. "Anyway, I figured if Tad wanted out, so did I. Now I'm out, and you're free, too, and I want to celebrate."

Garrett said that sounded like a great idea.

"Great, I found out from the baseball office that you're coming back tonight. I'll meet your train. See you tonight, Russ. 'Bye."

She hung up. Good. Maybe she didn't know the train would arrive sometime close to three A.M. And she *certainly* didn't know Garrett was driving back.

"Damn," Garrett said.

Hal Keating was strangely silent. Something must have been going on in the game. Garrett took a look at the field, noted that the Red Sox were up and no one was on base, and thought some more about that damned phone call. Something about that call had gotten on his nerves.

Hal Keating nudged him. "The game's over, Russ. Yankees won, 5 to 3. And nobody even mussed Mickey's hair, let alone killed him."

"That's something, at least." Garrett thought about it as grumbling Red Sox fans made their way around him and to the exits. "He's not out of Boston yet, Hal."

"Yeah, well, he will be in no time. Soon as the Yankees get all showered up, they're gonna head for the train. They already checked out at the hotel. Or were you still paying attention back then?"

"Hal, what are you going to do now?"

"What am I going to do now? Well, my boy, I am going

to take you to another lobster place that's even better than the one we went to last night. Then I am going to be driven to New York by you in your fancy green car, and I am going to spend a couple of days renewing old acquaintances."

Garrett frowned. "I want to stay with Mickey." Cheryl had put an idea in his head.

"Oh, come on, now."

"No, I mean it. I'll go down to the locker room and check up on them." He reached into his pocket and pulled out his car keys. "Here. You know where my car is parked. You take it, drive it to New York. I'll meet you there tomorrow, and we can have a laugh about how silly I am. After Mickey is tucked in safe and sound."

Keating shook his head. "Russ, I'm starting to worry about you. I admire caution as much as anybody does; I wouldn't have come here if I didn't. But you're getting ridiculous. That was a *crank letter*."

"I still think I better take the train back with the team."

Keating was disgusted. "You *belong* on the goddam train. You've got a one-track mind. Only trouble is, the gauge is too narrow for any sensible idea to travel on it." He reached out and snatched the keys from Garrett's hand.

Garrett grinned. "Thanks, Hal."

"Oh, go to hell. I'm just being nice to you out of habit." Keating stuck the keys in his pocket. "I plan to take a little walk with you first, though. I might as well visit the boys in the locker room."

"Sure."

"And I plan to go to New York by way of that restaurant. No reason for *me* to pass up a good dinner because you're a goddam fool."

"I don't care if you go by way of Montreal. Just get the car to New York in shape for me to use it. It's paid for, you know."

6

". . . But I *still* say we're gonna have to play better than

we played today against the White Sox come Wednesday.
Don't you think so, Rags?"

Mickey Mantle was the most animated of the Yankees. A
lot of them were taking the opportunity to sleep. Mantle was
probably just happy to be alive—what the hell, crank or not,
a threat like that has got to get on your nerves to *some* extent.

Russ Garrett realized all that. He was glad Mantle was
alive, too. He turned away from the window of the train—he
was tired of the central Connecticut scenery, anyhow—and
answered the question.

"Just keep hitting the ball, Mick, and let Casey worry
about the rest. All you can do is your best, right?"

Whitey Ford perked up at that; probably saw an
opportunity to make a good joke. Garrett tuned out and let
them talk. Mantle had only been talking to him because he
was the only one awake, anyway.

Garrett had never learned to sleep on trains. Sleeping on
trains was a major-league skill. Some day soon, he supposed,
major leaguers would learn to sleep on airplanes. Garrett's big
skill was sleeping on buses. He'd caught on to that after only
a couple of weeks in the minors.

He still didn't feel right. He should have gone to the
restaurant with Hal. All he'd had was a couple of sandwiches
in the Yankee locker room and a few beers on the train before
they'd stopped serving. Garrett yawned. It was late—there'd
been some kind of delay in Hartford. The train had stood
there and growled for what seemed like hours. Garrett didn't
know exactly where they were now, but if the train made
Grand Central Station before 3:30 A.M., he would be very
surprised. Cheryl would not be happy.

Cheryl. What the hell had she said? He'd thought he'd
had it for a while right after the game, but it had eluded him.
He thought about it until it exhausted him, and he dozed.

He woke up with a start and with a thought in his head
he wouldn't have let come in while he was awake.

What the hell was Hal Keating doing in Boston? Could
he really have come all the way to help just in response to a
casual remark of Garrett's? In his current state of mind,
Garrett doubted it.

Garrett shook his head, trying to shake the idea out of his mind, but the little bastard was tenacious and hung on. All right, Garrett thought, let's have a look. I'll demolish you in no time.

But the idea wouldn't stay crushed. When Garrett pointed out to himself, for example, that it was impossible for Hal to be David Laird in disguise because Garrett had known him since before Laird had disappeared, the idea had a simple answer. Who says, besides you, that David Laird is really in on this?

Jenny says so, Garrett responded. Hysterical female, under a lot of pressure. You came around and put ideas in her head.

Bristow. What about Bristow? It could be a coincidence. Or it could be a cynical move to make you *think* Laird was behind it. It was Hal, after all, who said Bristow's broken jaw might be a prophecy by the killer.

Now look at Hal. Is he smart enough? Does he have the background to be shifty enough? Yes to both questions. You have to be smart and shifty to work OSS.

Does he have a motive to kill Rex Simmons? He could. He's got a defense-related industry right in Kansas City, Simmons's power base. God knows what sort of dirt can come up in the name of congressional investigations.

Garrett shook his head again, more slowly this time. Once your mind got perverse enough and you were willing to look at a friend that way, you could find indications all night.

Like how much Hal had been told by Garrett. How nobody had tried to bother Garrett until he went to Kansas City and spoke to Hal. And Hal had had ample opportunity to make contact with Chicago Ned and his boys to do any heavy work that might come up.

"Bullshit," Garrett said aloud. The ball players didn't even interrupt their conversation—he must have said it at an appropriate time.

He'd let the idea have its head; now he could forget the whole damned thing. Except he couldn't. Because he suddenly remembered leaving Martin in the care of Hal Keating's security people, and the memory was followed by a flash of fear.

That could only mean, Garrett realized, that deep down he didn't really trust Hal. And *that* meant he had to go to Captain Murphy about it. He knew Martin was getting better and had returned to New York yesterday, but that could be because Hal wasn't interested in Martin, only Garrett. He'd been pretty eager to get Garrett away from the crowds and into the car after the doubleheader, hadn't he? Garrett hated himself. What was it Hal had said? A one-track mind, with the gauge too narrow to let the sense through. Probably true, he thought.

Too narrow. That's what the girl Lindy had said, back in Kansas City, wasn't it? Just before she'd been crushed under the hooves of the cattle? Something like that?

Garrett chewed his lip and brooded all the way to New York.

7

Cheryl was waiting for him. She stood out among the drunks and drifters that populated Grand Central Station at 3:30 A.M. like a rose on a junk pile.

Cheryl was wearing a slinky number, bold slashes of black and pink. "I *thought*," she said as Garrett climbed the ramp to the main concourse, "that we might be able to go someplace to dance." Before Garrett could say anything, she put her arms around him and kissed him vigorously.

There was general appreciation from the Yankees.

"Whew, Slick," Mickey Mantle said. "I thought it was attempts on *my* life we were supposed to be worrying about."

Garrett figured he was probably blushing.

The kiss ended, eventually. Garrett pulled away to see an almost insufferable smirk on Cheryl's face. Most of the ball players were walking away, laughing, but Mickey was still there. He seemed a little embarrassed himself.

"Uh, Rags?" he said.

"What is it, Mick?"

"Talk to you for a second?"

"Sure. Excuse me, Cheryl?" She told him not to take too long. Garrett and Mantle walked off a few steps.

"I, uh, I ain't too good at this kind of thing," Mantle said, "but I want you to know I appreciate everything you did for me, coming to Boston and all. The cops, here and up there—well, I felt a lot better about things."

"You're welcome, Mick," Garrett told him. "Hell, you're a lot more valuable to the game than I am. The commissioner practically ordered me to do it."

"Goddammit, Rags, I ain't jokin'. I know it didn't amount to anything, but none of us knew that ahead of time. So thanks." He put out a hand. Garrett took it.

"Okay, then," Mantle said, as if glad to have it all over. "Anything I can do to help you out, you know, get back into playin' ball, you just let me know, okay?"

Garrett had to smile. For a split second he was going to ask for a new set of legs but choked it back in time when he realized Mantle's legs weren't in such great shape, either. Instead he said, "Sure, Mick, thanks. You go beat the crap out of the White Sox on Wednesday and clinch the pennant. That'll do for now."

"Okay, it's a deal." Mantle looked up the concourse where Whitey and Billy were standing. "Hey, Slick, wait up!" He gave Garrett a hasty wave and took off after them.

"What was that all about?" Cheryl asked.

"Baseball talk. Nice to see you, Cheryl."

"I hoped you'd feel that way."

"Only what am I supposed to do with you? I live with my parents, you know. They're stuffy about this sort of thing."

"The Commodore Hotel, Russ. I have a room in it. We can get there without even going outside—there's a tunnel right from the station."

It did sound tempting. He would have liked to be with Jenny Laird, but he didn't want to kid himself. He'd been a comfort to her when she was lonely and scared. He didn't dare hope for anything more with her. But now *he* was lonely, and Cheryl was right here, so why not? The big clock over the exit said twenty to four—the way the trains ran, Garrett wouldn't be able to get back to Port Chester until after six. Garrett still wasn't sure how he felt about the woman, but this much seemed obvious; a plush hotel room with Cheryl for company beat hell out of the sofa in his office. It was closer, too.

"Okay," he said. "I've got to make a couple of phone calls first." He pointed to a phone booth and started walking. He was waiting for Cheryl to suggest he make the calls from the hotel and was just as glad when she didn't. He didn't especially want her to hear.

Cheryl waited outside the booth. Garrett's first call went to a different hotel not too far away.

"Hello," Jenny Laird said.

"Hello, Jenny. Sorry to call so early in the mor—"

"*Who is this?*" There was terror in her voice.

"It's Russ Garrett, of course. Who else knows where you are?"

"Stop it! Don't do this to me anymore!" Jenny was hysterical.

"Jenny, what's the matter? Really, it's Russ—I took the train back to the city with the Yankees. What's wrong?"

"No," she said, as if explaining something to one of the children. "It was on the radio. In Boston. Your car *exploded*. You—your body was mang . . . It said it on the *radio!*"

Garrett closed his eyes tight and asked God and Hal Keating to forgive him, because he was never going to forgive himself.

"It's a mistake, Jenny. Honest, I'm okay."

"I thought you were *dead!*" The sobs came back.

"No, it's all right." There was something Garrett had to know. "The radio just said my car exploded?"

"It said there was a *bomb*. They—they had to identify you from your license plate."

Well, it was a tough break for Cheryl, and possibly for Garrett himself, but no Hotel Commodore tonight. He had to call Bronx Homicide, get them to find Captain Murphy and straighten him out, then go over and sit with Jenny. If she was like this, her kids were probably hanging from the ceiling. Unless they were asleep. Garrett hoped they were.

He was about to tell Jenny all this. Started to, in fact, but she interrupted him.

"I love you, Russ."

That called for an answer. It took him a while, because he'd never expected to hear that statement or anything like it from her. Garrett took stock of how he felt and decided that in spite of everything else, hearing this brave, loyal woman say she loved him made him delighted and proud. Garrett guessed that meant he loved her, too.

He didn't get a chance to tell her, though.

"Hang up the phone," said a voice.

Garrett turned to see Gennarro Kennedy. The big black man's left hand had a tight grip on Cheryl's elbow. The right held a .38 caliber revolver.

"Russ?" Jenny Laird's voice echoed tinnily in the phone booth. "Russ?"

"Hang up the phone," Gennarro Kennedy repeated. He clicked back the hammer of his gun.

"I've got to go," Garrett said as he hung up. And as he did, a lot of things seemed to fall into place.

"Hello again, Mr. Garrett," Gennarro Kennedy said. "Step out of the phone booth, please."

"You. I should have known back in Kansas City, goddammit. Lindy. She was your girl, right? She saw *you*. That's why she ran out in front of that stampede. She thought you were inside the building, and she was running to you because she saw you were safe. She was happy. She *never* said *too narrow* or *tomorrow;* I was fooled by the damned flat Kansas City drawl. She was saying *Gennarro*. Wasn't she?"

"Yes, Mr. Garrett," Kennedy said. "She was." His voice was deadly. "But we'll have plenty of time to talk about it en route."

"En route to where?"

"You, Miss Tilton, and I are going to take a little trip to the Bronx." He let go of Cheryl's arm; Cheryl rubbed the spot. "Walk ahead of me, please. A car will be waiting for us; and remember I have a gun."

Cheryl seemed unruffled. Garrett gave her high marks for that. *He* was certainly ruffled.

"Does Mrs. Klimber know about this?" Cheryl demanded, but Kennedy only laughed.

He motioned them to move along, and their footsteps echoed dismally in the marble vault of Grand Central Station.

Chapter Eight
Rundown

1

Gennarro Kennedy was really quite pleased with the way things had worked out. It just went to show there was a lot to be said for doing one's own fieldwork. Ideas came as rapidly as opportunities, once you had a little practice.

It had been a simple matter to plant the bomb in Garrett's car, once he'd found it parked not far from the ball field. He had, in fact, perhaps done too much preparatory work; calling a garage with some fictitious car trouble, knocking the driver of the tow truck unconscious, then stealing the vehicle.

He'd wanted the truck for a prop, an excuse in case anyone wondered what he was doing with his head under the hood of the car. Of course, he hadn't known how easy it was going to be, how little time it would take. Nofsinger's enclosed instructions had been excellent.

Once he'd wired the bomb, he'd abandoned the tow truck, then retreated to a spot something over a block away to wait. It was an overcast day and very near full night when the tall man had entered the car; Kennedy had just naturally assumed it was Garrett.

Kennedy had been breathless with anticipation. He remembered being angry with himself for letting his control slip so far.

The man got into the car. There was the slam of the steel door, the first grinding of the ignition, then the explosion.

Kennedy had been wise to stand so far away. Windows were broken for several dozen yards on both sides of the street. Debris clinked and clattered and rolled practically to Kennedy's feet.

Of course, a mob of curiosity-seekers gathered around the wreck. When there were enough of them (including several Negroes—Kennedy had no wish to be conspicuous), he joined the crowd to have a look at his handiwork. The results had hardly been recognizable as human, let alone as Garrett, so it was with a firm conviction that Garrett was dead that Kennedy went to the railroad station to join the baseball players on their trip back to New York.

Kennedy had gone immediately to a seat on the train away from where the ball players were likely to sit and consequently missed seeing Garrett board the train. He didn't see him, in fact, until much later.

After seeing the explosion of Garrett's car, Kennedy realized that for his purposes, one of which was making the authorities turn their attention back to "Communists" and "terrorists" and similar figments of heated imaginations, it would be much better if Mickey Mantle died in an explosion, too. He thought of ways to do it.

He came up with a magnificent plan. Not only the method, but the place would be perfect. Unfortunately, he would need Russ Garrett, alive, to make it work.

Kennedy had sighed and thought of other things. He had poison with him; he knew athletes drank lots of beer. All he had to do was think of a way to get a poisoned beer to Mickey Mantle. He took a stroll of the nearly deserted train to scout the logistics of the problem. Then he came to the coach in which the Yankees were riding. And saw Russ Garrett.

Kennedy was surprised (to say the least), but he still had the presence of mind to duck back out onto the platform between cars before Garrett saw *him*.

He stood out there taking great gulps of humid air as bewilderment gave way to elation. Garrett was alive; therefore, Kennedy hadn't killed him. Whom had he killed? Some friend of Garrett's, no doubt. It really didn't matter. The important thing now was that his magnificent idea was now possible. Even inevitable.

And it was now in progress. All that had been necessary to do was wait until Garrett was alone, then take him. Cheryl Tilton was an added complication, but not necessarily a liability. She was an extra lever to use on Garrett if he proved reluctant.

"Wait a moment," Gennarro Kennedy said to his captives. They turned around and looked at him, but he didn't mind. All he did was reach into his pocket and pull out the locker key. He opened the locker and removed Nofsinger's other bomb quickly and efficiently, without delaying long enough to give Garrett a chance to get any foolish ideas.

"All right," Kennedy said. "Just walk across the concourse and up those stairs. We're leaving from the exit at the top of them, the one where the taxicabs stop."

"Vanderbilt Avenue," Garrett said.

"Yes, that's right, Vanderbilt Avenue." If Nofsinger had followed instructions, there would be a car waiting for them there. It ought to be an interesting ride.

2

"Where am I going?" Garrett asked, though he had a pretty good idea of the answer. He was at the wheel of a bright red Plymouth Belvedere. It was a popular model and color, and Kennedy had probably done well to choose it. Still, Garrett felt about as inconspicuous as a fire engine. Not that there were many people around. This was the spooky time of the New York morning, those few hours when the city seemed empty.

At the moment he wanted to be inconspicuous, because Gennarro Kennedy was in the backseat with the .38 pointed at the back of Cheryl's head. He had no doubt the Negro would pull the trigger if anyone stopped him or if Garrett tried any funny business with the car. Besides, short of driving it off a bridge and into a river, Garrett didn't think there was much he *could* do with the car. It was big and built like a tank.

Garrett took a look at the woman beside him. Cheryl was gazing straight ahead, a completely blank expression on her face. He supposed she was trying to avoid giving Kennedy any reason to be nervous or upset.

Garrett, as previously instructed by the man with the gun, was headed north on Madison Avenue, but since Manhattan was an island, he knew he couldn't go on doing that forever. He repeated his question.

"Yankee Stadium," Kennedy told him. "I would have thought you could guess that."

"Just checking," Garrett told him. "I thought that might be it."

"You're very clever. You don't know how much trouble you've caused me."

"Sorry," Garrett said. He didn't try to keep the sarcasm out of his voice.

A look in the rearview mirror showed him Kennedy was smiling. "Don't apologize unless you mean it, Garrett. And I don't think I'm likely to forgive you in any case. I was quite fond of Lindy, you know. You've probably guessed that, too."

Garrett saw Kennedy was no longer smiling.

"The problem with you," Kennedy went on, "is that you have too many friends. That Negro policeman. That person in Boston. Unless it was a car thief."

"No," Garrett said. "It was a friend."

"It seems," Kennedy said, "that you were even able to make a convert of Miss Tilton." He reached out casually and gave Cheryl a gentle poke in the back of the head with the barrel of the gun.

Cheryl turned white. She spoke for the first time. "I don't know anything about this, Gennarro, I swear to God—"

"You know the background, though. Congressman Simmons and his 'investigations.' You were in it up to your pretty white neck. I don't see why you should be complaining now—I'm only doing my best to keep the Simmons name holy and the Simmons empire alive."

From the corner of his eye, he could see Cheryl starting to tremble. In about five seconds she was going to start screaming. Garrett couldn't blame her—he could use a good scream himself. But it was a low-percentage play, at least in this league.

"Can I ask you a question, Kennedy?" Garrett got in with the distraction a heartbeat before Cheryl would have lost control.

"Go ahead," Kennedy said.

"Is David Laird working for you or are you working for him?"

Gennarro Kennedy started to laugh. He laughed so hard, throwing his head back and closing his eyes, that Garrett was tempted to reach back over the seat and grab for the gun. He decided against it. The Plymouth was just too damn big. He'd only get one chance, and he couldn't afford to miss.

Garrett asked him what was so funny.

Just then a siren screamed behind them. Kennedy stopped laughing and raised the gun at Cheryl's head. Garrett checked the mirror.

"It's an ambulance. Kennedy, for Christ's sake, it's an ambulance." Garrett eased over to the right to let it by. Kennedy leaned back again; Garrett allowed himself to breathe.

Kennedy chuckled. "You wanted to know about David Laird. Actually, he *was* working for me, but I didn't know it. Since then I think he's been working against me."

"I don't follow you," Garrett told him.

Kennedy was silent for a few minutes, thinking. At last he said, "This has been a fascinating operation. Do you want to know all about it?"

"I would definitely like to know what this is all about."

Kennedy sighed and began to tell him. He told him everything, Nofsinger and his bogus Communist organization, the plan to kill Mantle to make Rex Simmons look good, Laird/Thane's infiltration of the operation, and all the rest. He gave names, dates, places.

He was right—it was fascinating. Garrett listened,

enthralled, piecing Kennedy's story together with his own.
Now he knew why Jenny had had the feeling she was being
followed. Kennedy had put his man on her, hoping David
Laird would contact her. There was anger in Kennedy's voice
when he told of the events at the slaughterhouse that had
ended in Lindy's death, but otherwise he was telling his story
cheerfully.

Garrett was queasy. The more Kennedy talked, the
more it became obvious what was on the agenda for Cheryl
and him. Kennedy wouldn't be spilling all this stuff if he
expected anybody would still be around to pass it on to
Walter Winchell and Ed Sullivan.

". . . but now," Kennedy concluded, "after all these
frustrations and setbacks, I'm going to accomplish my original objective. With your help, of course."

"My help?"

"Yes, I'll need you to get me into Yankee Stadium."

"What makes you think I can do that?"

"You carry the authority of the Commissioner of Baseball, Garrett. You can do it. Besides, if you don't . . ." He
shrugged and pointed the gun toward Cheryl.

"Right," Garrett said. He drove across the bridge at the
top of Madison Avenue into the Bronx. The trouble was, he
could get him into the stadium. The guards all knew him, and
the place would be powered up and lighted for the ground
crew to do their work.

They drove on in silence until the stadium came into
view. The lights made a heavenly dome in the hazy air above
the rim. The Longines clock on the outside wall said it was
4:24. The message board next to the clock said the Yankees'
next game was against Chicago, Wednesday, at two P.M.
Gennarro Kennedy said, "All right, Garrett, let's park the car
and go inside."

3

Of all the things Cheryl Tilton might have been worried
about, the one that bothered her most was the fact that she

had to go walking around Yankee Stadium again in spike-heeled shoes.

"Wait a minute," she said. She stopped, reached down, and slipped them off.

"Leave them there," Gennarro Kennedy commanded.

Cheryl looked at him. "Do you know what these things cost? Are you crazy?"

Gennarro ignored her question, but there was a tension in the silence that told her he was offended with the question.

"Leave them, Cheryl," Russ Garrett said. "Pick them up on the way out."

Cheryl shot him a look. She'd about had it with Mr. Garrett, too, the way he just rolled over and played dead for this Negro Napoleon, discussing the case on the way here as if they were *colleagues*, for God's sake. Then Garrett had sweet-talked the guard into letting them into the stadium, saying Cheryl and Gennarro were reporters for the *Post* doing an article about ground-crew workers, and how the Commissioner of Baseball had sent him along to show them around. He made her sick. Why didn't he *do* something? He hadn't hesitated to belt *her* around when she threatened him. She'd thought this Garrett was something special. He was just another coward.

Gennarro Kennedy was also disappointed in Russ Garrett. He wanted Garrett to have some appreciation of what was going on, how he was being used to get at his friend and how that would hurt his precious game of baseball. He wanted him, in short, to suffer. To lose control, maybe grovel a little.

But he wasn't doing it. He was calmly doing everything Kennedy told him. "What makes you think," Kennedy asked, "that you and Miss Tilton can pick up those shoes later? That you're coming out of here at all?"

"It's because you're not stupid. The guard knows we're in here—if we don't come out when the ground crew comes out, someone will come to look for us. And if it's Mickey you're after you can't hole up with us in here, alive or dead, because they won't let the ball players in for tomorrow's practice unless we're accounted for first. You can't kill us and sneak out yourself, because you don't know the stadium well enough. You couldn't hide our bodies where you could be sure they wouldn't be found, and if they're found, you're back in the same boat. That leads us to the package under your arm. If it's not a bomb, I'll eat it."

Kennedy decided that Mr. Garrett's death would be a lot slower and more painful than he had originally planned. Maybe the smug white bastard would watch the woman suffer first.

"You may," Kennedy told him, "eat it anyway."

"Ah, so it *is* a bomb. Maybe you plan to booby-trap Mickey's locker."

"It's the same kind of bomb," Kennedy conceded, "that took care of your other friend, except for a different means of detonation. Too bad you won't be around to see the effect."

Russ Garrett said nothing. His mind was racing, and his heart was pounding, and he was drawing on all his reserves to keep it from showing. He almost smiled. It was a baseball tradition. No matter how tense the situation was, you just spit on your hands and got down to it.

Garrett was leading them to the Yankee locker room the long way, through the curving tunnel along the first-base side of the stadium; exactly one level below the corridor where David Laird (as Garrett now *knew* him to be) had attacked the hot-dog vendor. The corridor was dark and filled with echoes of his shoes and Kennedy's; the illumination from the emergency lights was barely enough to proceed by. Cheryl's bare feet were silent.

He'd offered to take Kennedy out to the field and into the Yankee locker room by way of the team's dugout behind first base, but Kennedy had just scowled at him.

At least now he knew it was a bomb. To be placed, no doubt, in Mickey's locker and wired to something he'd use tomorrow at practice. Mickey would pick it up, and he (and God alone knew how many others) would be blown to hamburger. And the newspapers would say . . .

"All right, Garrett," Kennedy said. He pointed with the small pocket flashlight he'd been carrying. "The sign on the door says this is it. Open it."

Garrett started to laugh. "How?"

"You work out here. You use the Yankees' locker room. You must have a key."

Garrett kept laughing. "You're a genius, Kennedy—you just tend to slip up on small details. What do you think this is, a country club, for Christ's sake?"

"Shut up," Kennedy commanded.

"The *players* don't even have keys. The clubhouse boys get here early in the morning and open the place up."

Kennedy raised the gun. "I said shut up!"

"Why don't you use the bomb and blow it open?"

Kennedy's face seemed to glow with anger in the half-darkness. Sooner or later Garrett was going to have to do something about his situation, and his odds for living through whatever it was he did were very short.

Garrett told himself he knew what he was doing. The odds might get a little longer if he could goad Kennedy into making a mistake. Unless he overplayed his cards.

That's what he thought he had done when he saw the gun come up, but Kennedy merely shot the lock open. The crack and whine were a physical sensation in the concrete corridor. Garrett's ears were still ringing when the echo died away.

"Think anybody heard that?" he asked.

Kennedy motioned with the gun. "Inside."

Garrett went in, then Cheryl, then Kennedy. The man with the gun looked for a wall switch and found it. Light flooded the room, illuminating the lockers, which were really open cubicles about four feet across, each a combination closet and dressing room.

Kennedy, to Garrett's chagrin, seemed to know exactly what he was about. Before he even took a close look at the cubicle that contained the pinstripe shirts with the big number 7 on them, he grabbed a roll of adhesive tape and made Cheryl immobilize Garrett by taping him to one of the chairs. He watched her closely, making sure she didn't cheat and make it possible for Garrett to get loose. Then he put the gun down in Mickey's locker and attended to Cheryl himself, less elaborately but still securely.

Then he went to work setting the bomb.

Garrett's chair was off to the side of Mantle's locker, so he could see what Kennedy was doing. It was a trip-wire bomb, very simple, very deadly: a wire, a blasting cap, and three sticks of dynamite.

Kennedy taped the dynamite to the wall with more bandage tape, well up the wall, where the shirts would conceal it. Then he ran the wire invisibly down the joint of the cubicle, strung it over the tops of Mantle's baseball shoes, and attached it to the floor with two thumbtacks.

Garrett shook his head in despair. Kennedy was smart. One of those pairs of spikes had to be Mantle's practice pair—he'd be certain to take one of them tomorrow. Even if he didn't, he'd very likely notice the wire and give it a tug.

Kennedy finished; Garrett watched the black man's broad back as he stood with his hands on his hips and inspected his work. Kennedy was wearing a smile as he turned and started to free Cheryl.

Garrett was getting angry, very angry. This was *wrong*. Planting a bomb here was like planting one in the Vatican. Baseball was a kid's game that some lucky men got to keep playing even after they'd grown up. Garrett hated what these people had done to it—Kennedy, the Simmons brothers, even Cheryl. They were all part of it.

"You're a real mastermind, Kennedy," Garrett said. "Brilliant. What happens tomorrow when the clubhouse boy finds the lock shot off? He'll call the cops, that's what."

Kennedy freed Cheryl and went to get his gun. "Get him loose," Kennedy told her. "Keep his hands taped together." To Garrett, he said, "It was a padlock—now it's in my pocket. They might not even notice it's gone. If they do, they'll just think someone forgot to lock up."

"Yeah, that would have worked," Garrett sneered, "except you've made everybody nervous with your death-threat letter."

"I should have taped your mouth," Kennedy told him.

"It wouldn't change the facts."

Cheryl was untaping Garrett's legs from the chair. She looked at him. "Don't antagonize him, Russ."

"Oh, to hell with him; I'm sick of him. He thinks he's so goddam brilliant. He's a horse's ass."

"*That's enough, Garrett!*" Kennedy's voice cracked like splitting wood.

"What are you going to do about it? You already know you can't shoot me here. Why don't you just shrug it off as the defiant ravings of a doomed man?"

"That's just what I'll do," Kennedy said. "Stand up."

Garrett stood. He was free of the chair now, though his hands were taped together, in front of him. He kept talking. "David Laird made an idiot of you, and you don't have any idea of where he is or what the hell you can do about it. Detective Martin made an idiot of you. So did I. So did Lindy."

Kennedy's face was impassive, but his free hand was making a fist. "All right, back outside now. We'll even," he said, "pick up your shoes, Miss Tilton."

Garrett got close to Kennedy and faced him. "You know what the funniest thing is? The funniest thing is that this is all a waste of time for you. They won't even think twice about a Communist blowing Mickey up. This won't even be tied in with the Simmons case."

And all of a sudden Kennedy started to lose control, like a pitcher who's been left in the game too long. Garrett was back in business. He had to time this just right. Cheryl had to be smart, too.

Kennedy's black eyes gleamed red. He grabbed Garrett by the throat with his left hand. The right hand still held the gun. "Why not?" he demanded. "Why won't they, Garrett?"

In spite of the stranglehold Kennedy had on him, Garrett managed to laugh. "Because," he choked, "they'll pin it on *me*."

Kennedy's eyes widened. He loosened his grip a little. Garrett kept talking. "You have files on me, haven't you, genius? Okay, so do the cops. I'm a frustrated ball player, jealous of Mantle; I follow him around. I evolve theories about dead men trying to kill him. *I talk my way into Yankee Stadium in the middle of the night.* Then I either turn up dead or I never turn up at all. The same goes for the woman and the colored guy I went in with, though the colored guy just stays missing. The next morning Mickey Mantle is blown to smithereens. What do you *expect* the cops are going—*Go, Cheryl, run for it! Go!*"

While Garrett had been talking, Kennedy had been gazing at him. Garrett recognized the expression. It was the look Garrett himself had worn that day in Korea when he reached around behind his leg, then brought his hand back to see the little slivers of bone gleaming through the blood on his fingers. Kennedy was seeing something just as horrifying. Maybe his own fallibility.

Cheryl, meantime, had been inching her way behind Kennedy until she'd made it unnoticed to the doorway. She stood there a second, looking helplessly at Garrett. Garrett had tried a few subtle nods of the head to tell her it was all right, but Cheryl hadn't gotten the message. So he yelled.

Cheryl disappeared, the door banging shut behind her. Kennedy, startled, whirled around, cursing.

Garrett knew he would never have a better chance. He jumped at Kennedy, chopping down with his bound arms at the hand that held the gun. The .38 hit the floor with a clatter. Garrett managed to kick it away before Kennedy hit him.

It was a roundhouse right, powerful and fast. Garrett pulled his head back a little, but the blow still sent him staggering backward. Kennedy kept coming forward.

Garrett could use his arms to block punches, after a fashion, but he couldn't hit back. Kennedy, in no hurry, lined up each punch. Garrett shook his head to clear away the glowing spots in front of his eyes.

He spoke, primarily to convince himself that he was still conscious. "There's no future in it, Kennedy. Cheryl is halfway out of the stadium by now. She's getting the cops."

"It won't help you, Garrett." He punched Garrett in the stomach. Garrett groaned and fell backward into Yogi Berra's locker, shaking the walls of it and pulling Berra's possessions down around him. His brain gave him a brief flash of what would have happened if he'd landed in Mickey Mantle's locker, but he chased the thought away.

"You can't win, goddammit!" Garrett shouted.

Kennedy shouted back. "I'm *better* than you are! *Better! No one defeats me!*"

Garrett scrambled to his feet. Kennedy was rushing him—the patience, the control were all gone. Garrett had to do something or he was going to die. Right now.

He did something. He raised his arms high over his head as Kennedy approached. When Kennedy was close enough, Garrett brought his arms down around the black man's neck, with the tape that bound him making it a tight embrace. Then he pulled Kennedy's head toward him, at the same time ramming his own forehead into Kennedy's face. Kennedy yelled and drew back. Garrett raised a knee toward his opponent's groin, but Kennedy twisted and went down, taking most (but not all) of the impact on his thigh. He would not, Garrett knew, be down long.

Garrett took his arms from around Kennedy's neck and ran for it in the other direction, through the tunnel, into the Yankees' dugout, and out onto the ball field.

4

Darkness. The ground crew had finished and gone home. Garrett could count on no reinforcements until the police arrived. Assuming Cheryl could get away.

Garrett cursed and looked around. His eyes were adjusting—he could see the playing field stretching out like a prairie before him and the grandstand looming silently all around.

Well, Garrett, he told himself, this is where you always wanted to be. He treated himself to a sardonic snort, then got busy. It would only be a matter of seconds before Kennedy would start to follow him. The only place there could be any safety was in the stands. Quicker way to an exit, too.

Garrett ran past the dugout, then scrambled over the low fence into the grandstand. He began running up the stairs, wondering what was keeping Kennedy and if he would remember to pick up the gun.

The crack of a bullet answered his question. The

wooden back of one of the expensive box seats flew apart in a shower of splinters. Garrett threw himself to the concrete steps, crawled behind some seats. He raised his bound hands to wipe the sweat from his forehead, but when he pulled them away, the dim light from the emergency system showed him it wasn't sweat. Blood. He must have cut his temple on Kennedy's teeth when he'd butted him. Terrific. Now he'd be leaving a nice little blood trail for Kennedy to follow. Garrett's mother had always told him to carry a handkerchief. He should have listened.

Kennedy was still standing out on the field. Garrett could see him in dark silhouette, waving his arms against the purple-gray of false dawn and screaming something unintelligible. That much Garrett could be thankful for—Kennedy was not thinking clearly. If he had been he'd have gone after Cheryl for her hostage value or, better still, make himself scarce before the police showed up.

Garrett wiped away a trickle of blood a fraction of a second before it went into his left eye. That was all he needed. If he was going to get out of this, he needed his sight.

It occurred to Garrett that he might not have been thinking too clearly himself. He would have given a lot for a free pass back to the Yankee locker room, where he could at least arm himself with a baseball bat. Hell, the locker room had an exit to the street. He might even be able to get away. By his count, Kennedy had four bullets left. But somehow Garrett knew he wasn't going to get away; that this was going to come down to close quarters.

Garrett worried the tape around his wrists with his teeth until he had a good start at getting his hands free, then managed to get them loose in a matter of seconds. Now if it came to a face-to-face finale, he could at least throw a punch.

He didn't hear Kennedy shouting anymore. He put his head up above the seat and saw that his pursuer had come into the grandstand and was calmly making his way to where Garrett had gone down. Garrett cursed under his breath, wiped the blood from his forehead again, and began crawling on the concrete to the next aisle down, the one closer to home plate.

When he got there, he took a deep breath and started sprinting.

Two more shots sent him scurrying for cover. Sweat mingled with the blood that poured down his face. He lay on his back listening to the steady, relentless scraping of Kennedy's shoes on the concrete.

Garrett's feet were cold.

He wanted to cry but started laughing instead, quiet, wheezing, uncontrollable explosions of sardonic mirth.

Here it is, Garrett, he told himself. *That last workout you promised yourself. The one that was going to decide your future.* It had come a little late, that was all. Now, it was going to decide if he would ever *have* a future.

Garrett gave up the idea of escaping. It was only a matter of minutes before he became a cripple, unable to run, hardly able to walk. He looked up again. Kennedy had pulled the little pocket flashlight from his pants and was using it to follow Garrett's trail of blood. Garrett still had a significant lead, but it dwindled every second he stayed where he was.

Kennedy was talking. "Garrett, give up. You can't get away. You're hurt already—I'll put you out of your misery. And don't count on Cheryl Tilton for help," he shouted. "I've already taken care of her."

Garrett groaned softly. Kennedy had just killed a hope he wasn't sure he'd had. It was up to Garrett. Alone. Who had bad legs, a gash in his head, and not so much as a penknife to fight with. All he possessed, in fact, was his knowledge of the stadium. He'd instinctively headed for the nearest exit, but it looked inevitable now that Kennedy was going to catch him before he could reach it.

The words burned his brain. *Kennedy was going to catch him.* All Garrett could do was help pick where.

But that might be enough.

Garrett thought it over. Sure, it could work. If he could make it that far. If Kennedy didn't shoot him in the meantime.

To hell with it. He had to try. Garrett got his body up in a crouch, supporting himself with his arms on chair backs, giving his damaged legs a break—they'd need it.

He was hesitating. Come on, he told himself. This is only a matter of discipline. You've run this many steps before feeling this bad. And nobody's life depended on it then. So come on, Rags, haul ass.

Absurdly, defiantly, Russell Andrew Garrett summoned to his brain the three-part harmonies of Patti Page singing "How Much Is That Doggie in the Window." Then he started up the concrete stairs again.

Chapter Nine

Five O'Clock Lightning

1

Gennarro Kennedy saw him go. He raised the pistol but thought better of it. He only had two shots left, and he was just wasting them when he fired at this distance. Besides, Garrett wasn't moving too quickly, anyway. Kennedy merely increased his own pace and gained on Garrett at a respectable rate.

Kennedy was quite proud of the lie he'd told about taking care of Cheryl Tilton. He knew it couldn't fail to demoralize his quarry. Gennarro Kennedy was still the same; still Iago in Othello's body. He'd just had bad luck. But he'd take care of Garrett, in any case. Garrett had to die. Painfully. Then Kennedy would go into hiding, maybe leave the country. If David Laird could do it, Gennarro Kennedy certainly could. He was weary of Mrs. Klimber, anyway. He'd find something better.

He ran a course up the stairs parallel to the flight Garrett had taken and emerged onto the dim first level walkway only about twenty seconds after Garrett. He trained his pocket flashlight at the floor and quickly picked up the trail of blood spatters, little triangular smears on the concrete pointing like arrowheads in the direction Garrett had gone.

The trail was childishly easy to follow. It led him toward the narrow end of the stadium, to Gates 1 and 2, the major exits behind home plate.

Kennedy wasn't worried that Garrett might escape. The

curving hall prevented him from seeing his quarry, but Kennedy could hear Garrett's labored breathing and his scraping steps as they echoed around him. Kennedy took pleasure in the knowledge that Garrett could hear him coming, too.

There was another sign that Garrett's bad legs were catching up with him. The spatters of blood were more compact and closer together. That meant less distance covered between each one and the next. Garrett was weakening.

Suddenly the trail took a sharp left turn, up a flight of stairs. Kennedy smiled and followed. He moved cautiously, suspecting Garrett might have gotten desperate enough to have laid some feeble trap for him.

Kennedy didn't run into a trap, just Garrett's suit jacket (he'd apparently ditched it) and more blood, red and fresh. He followed it to the landing of the second deck, the mezzanine deck; then out through a tunnel and back into the grandstand itself.

Kennedy sighed. It looked like Garrett wanted to play more of that tedious hide and seek.

Then he saw him. Down below, at the edge of the mezzanine, Kennedy saw Garrett's white shirt like a beacon in the gathering light. It was just a glimpse, but it was enough. Garrett disappeared through a door into the press box.

Kennedy smiled. Garrett had trapped himself. Kennedy could taste the victory. Quietly, gun ready, he strolled down the stairs to the press box.

2

Garrett's legs were done for. He stumbled across the narrow broadcast booth to Mel Allen's desk and leaned against it, breathing heavily. He looked around, touching the TV monitor with one hand and the little refrigerator used in the Ballantine beer commercials with the other. They seemed to reassure him.

But he was wasting time. With a groan he got off the

desk and staggered back to the light switch. The lights went on; there was still power, Garrett thanked God. He got down on his knees and pulled the case of Ballantine from under the desk. There were only about ten bottles left. They would have to do.

He grabbed the little switch on the monitor and turned on the set. The electronic hum of its tubes warming up was the most beautiful sound he'd ever heard. Garrett disconnected the closed-circuit cable. He took a peek through the grillwork in the metal case and got a gratifying look at glowing filaments. Sweat and blood dripped down his forehead and burned his eyes.

He was nervous. He didn't have much time. The open part of the press box was behind him as he sat on the desk. He wasn't afraid of falling over (though he might have been) as much as he was nervous of being watched or taken by surprise from behind, which was patently absurd. He put it from his mind and began to smash the beer bottles on the floor. A warm, yeasty smell filled the booth. The sky was light enough for Garrett to see the miniature ocean form on the floor, foamy liquid waves splashing around jagged islands of brown glass.

"*Garrett!*"

Garrett gulped. Too soon! He turned over the heavy wooden beer case and let the last two bottles smash on the floor.

Kennedy fired a bullet through the door. Garrett jumped and dropped the case. Garrett needed that case. Painfully, he got down to retrieve it.

"You should know better than to think you can get me by lurking behind a door with a broken bottle, Garrett. Did I hit you?"

Garrett didn't answer. He had put the beer case back on the desk; now he was trying to pull himself back up on it through arm power alone.

The door boomed and shuddered as Kennedy started to kick it in. Garrett had planned to leave it open—he was glad now he'd changed his mind. Kneeling, he glanced back over his shoulder to see the wood around the lock start to give.

Garrett felt tendons in his shoulders pop, but he got himself upright, then leaned his belly over the edge of the table.

Kennedy kicked the door again. Garrett grabbed his pants leg and pulled his legs clear of the beer on the floor. He looked at the monitor. The small white dot had grown to a snowy gray square—no program on that channel at this hour of the morning.

It didn't matter. It was about to be canceled.

Garrett was reaching for the beer case as the door crashed open. Gennarro Kennedy, big, dark, and menacing, filled the doorway. He smiled.

"A nice run, Garrett. But it's all over." He took a step forward and invited Garrett to guess where the bullet was going to go.

Garrett took a tighter grip on the beer case.

Kennedy took another step into the ocean of beer. "I don't want to miss," he said. He raised the gun.

With a sudden shout of effort, Garrett reared back and smashed the corner of the wooden case into the screen of the TV monitor. Glass flew as the picture tube imploded. The set was knocked off the desk. It landed in the beer with a sizzle and a crack and a sudden cloud of ill-smelling steam.

All of Gennarro Kennedy's muscles contracted at once. He fired his last bullet involuntarily. His eyes rolled back; he seemed to jump suddenly up in the air and backward. He hit the wall of the booth with an audible thud, then pitched forward into the puddle of beer and glass. Garrett could hear crunching noises under Kennedy when he landed.

Garrett let the beer case fall to the floor. He lay back on the desk and allowed himself to breathe.

After a few moments he supported himself on his elbow and surveyed the damage.

The monitor's electrical cord had been long enough to reach. Garrett had been worried about that. Talks with his father had made him fairly confident the high-voltage section would still keep enough voltage to do the job even after the set had been unplugged, but Garrett was glad the juice had kept pouring in. Using the beer case, just to be sure, he knocked the plug out of the socket.

Then he looked at Kennedy. The man was dead, whether from electric shock or from landing heavily on daggerlike shards of broken bottles, Garrett couldn't say. And he didn't much care. Dark pools of blood were mingling with the beer, from Kennedy's arms, his stomach, his neck.

Garrett was sickened at that part, but he couldn't look away. Kennedy had landed facedown on a piece of glass, apparently, and its razor-sharp edge had peeled away the flesh of his jaw and neck right to gleaming white bone.

Garrett kept staring, riveted by the irony. Ever since Bristow's body had been found, Garrett had worried about someone else being killed and having his face mutilated. Now Garrett himself had brought that about.

From outside he heard voices on the upper deck. Guards, maybe. Cops. For no special reason, Garrett looked at his watch.

Eighteen minutes after five, Tuesday, September 8, 1953. Garrett closed his eyes. It figured. He'd won in true Yankee fashion. He'd called down his own bolt of five o'clock lightning.

Two bolts.

Garrett's eyes popped open as wide as if he'd been the one who'd gotten the shock. He looked again at the obscenity that had been Gennarro Kennedy's face and neck, and he knew.

"*Hey!*" he yelled at whoever was milling around outside. "*Hurry up and get me the hell out of here!*"

Because he knew. He knew what had happened to Bristow, and why. He knew how David Laird had, during hot pursuit by the New Jersey State Police, still managed to vanish like a soap bubble.

Garrett smiled. Soap bubble. Very appropriate.

He knew why David Laird had shadowed his wife but had made no attempt to see her.

He even knew how to go about learning where he was now.

3

Garrett was at the hospital having the gash in his forehead stitched and slivers of picture tube picked from his face and hands when it finally occurred to him to call home and let his parents know he was alive.

"I took care of it already," Captain Murphy told him. "You put people through a lot, Garrett. Christ. I was about half-ready to tear ass up to Boston and join the search for your killer." He growled. "Do me a favor. Don't get involved in any more crap like this. You're too dangerous."

Garrett thought of Hal Keating lying in pieces outside Fenway Park. "Yeah. How's Martin?"

"He'll be fine. Too bad he's at a different hospital; you could visit." The captain rubbed his chin. "You know, Garrett, you actually found out a lot of stuff in this case. The bitch of it is, you found out everything about it except how we can arrest the murderer." Murphy took off his hat and rubbed his head. "It was David Laird after all. And the bastard just *vanished*. I will be fried."

A policeman came in and called the captain aside. Garrett was glad; it meant he didn't have to lie. He wasn't ready to share his ideas with the captain just yet.

Murphy returned. "Okay, the bomb squad called in. The Yankees can practice on schedule. Happy?"

"Ecstatic," Garrett said and grimaced.

"Yeah, you look it. Okay, Garrett. I've got most of your story—this Kennedy was something else again, wasn't he? Talk about uppity. Big mouth, too. We got his pal Nofsinger this morning, and I've been on the horn to K.C. telling them to take a nice long look at Klimber Industries."

"What will that accomplish?"

"Nothing. I just didn't want them to feel left out. Listen, after you're done here, I want a statement from you, a formal one. I mean, I know you, but nobody else is going to believe your story unless you're under oath. Take a cab over when you're finished—I'll be at headquarters organizing the search for David Laird."

"Hold it," Garrett said. The captain stopped halfway to the door. "I thought I was in custody."

"For what?"

"I killed a man."

Murphy made a noise with his lips. "Self-defense. The Tilton woman—she's waiting outside for you, by the way, you lucky bastard—backs up everything you say. So does the physical evidence. So consider yourself on your own recognizance."

"Would it be all right if I came in tomorrow for that formal statement? I—I'm pretty beat." That was no lie. Too bad he couldn't rest.

"Sure. Take care of yourself, Garrett. I'm sorry about your friend."

Garrett gave him a feeble wave as he left.

Before long they were done with him, and Garrett and Cheryl left the hospital.

It was about nine o'clock now. The sun was starting to burn off the haze. The worst of the morning rush hour traffic had passed the Bronx, but there were still quite a few cars honking along southbound.

Cheryl had spent the morning renting a car. Garrett never found out how she'd managed to get one so early. Congressional know-how, he supposed.

Cheryl herself was radiant, as though last night had been the time of her life. Then it struck him that it probably had been. Her evening clothes didn't seem inappropriate. Cheryl had the air of someone who was celebrating the discovery of something. Even when she wasn't smiling. Even when she was apologizing.

"Russ, I'm sorry it took me so long to get help this morning. I couldn't find my way out! And all the time I expected Kennedy to grab me from behind. And I was afraid for you; I couldn't think straight. I must have run past the exit three times. Finally I ran into one of the guards. They came in to look for us when the ground-crew people left, just like you said they would. You must have been terrified."

"I was."

They had reached the car. A Buick LeSabre. Garrett

knew that right away because it had four portholes in the side instead of just three. "Poor Russ," Cheryl said as she slipped behind the wheel. "Anyway, it's all over now."

"Practically."

Cheryl looked at him strangely, then shrugged. "Well, it's all over for me. I'm through with Tad, and I'm through with his brother, and I'm *especially* through with his brother's murder. I've got plenty of time to figure out what I'm going to do next."

"Don't you know?"

Cheryl started the motor, looked over her bare shoulders, and pulled out into traffic. "Which way are we going here?" Garrett pointed. "And no, I don't know. You sound like you *do*."

"Of course I do." Garrett was leaning back with his eyes closed. "You're going back to Kansas City."

Cheryl laughed. "Whatever for?"

"Job opening," Garrett said. "A certain rich widow is going to need someone to take care of her. Good pay. Fringe benefits include congenial home, with board. And the chance to wield more economic and political power than practically anybody in or out of government."

Cheryl said nothing for a few moments. Then in a small voice she said, "The old lady *does* like me . . ."

Eyes still closed, Garrett grinned. Cheryl cursed him at first for putting the idea in her head, almost crying at times. She said she had wanted them to be together, at least for a while, but now—well, if she was going to do it, she'd have to do it right away. She hoped he'd understand.

Garrett understood. He wasn't equipped to deal with a woman like Cheryl. He couldn't, off the top of his head, think of any man who was. Besides, Mrs. Klimber's pattern was set; *someone* would be using that woman's power; if not Cheryl, maybe somebody worse.

And Cheryl would have such fun. She might even do some good. She wasn't bitter and twisted, as Kennedy had been. Who could tell? Power was power, whether you used it to kill somebody or to buy a kid a hot lunch. Besides, after the current mess people would be watching the Klimber empire more closely.

Garrett directed Cheryl back to the hotel. She would call Mrs. Klimber, then check out and catch the first available plane to Kansas City. Garrett volunteered to take care of the rented car.

When they arrived, Cheryl leaned over and kissed him passionately. "Thank you, Russ," she said when she had finished.

"For what?"

"For understanding me better than anybody ever has. And for not judging me."

"Oh, don't be ridic—" Another kiss cut him off. He began to be sorry he wasn't going to Kansas City with her. Then it was over, and Cheryl left the car. Garrett slid into the driver's seat and drove off.

He was tempted to go to the hotel where Jenny was staying, but he decided against it. He called instead, reassuring her he was all right, saying he'd explain everything later. She told him she loved him; this time he got to answer her. He felt good about that.

But he was frowning as he got back behind the wheel.

4

Garrett got the address from the day manager at the Samuel Tilden rest area of the New Jersey Turnpike, the scene of David Laird's miracle of three weeks (only *three weeks?*) ago. Now he was driving north in the rented Buick. Up the shore, past the oil tanks. To one little cottage on the beach. He stopped the car and got out, shaking his head. He should have been afraid—the man, after all, was a convictable killer—but Garrett just couldn't believe he was in any danger.

Garrett touched the small bandage on his forehead, took a deep breath, and knocked on the door.

The whole cottage seemed to jump in surprise. Garrett

could hear scratching and rustling within. The occupant wasn't used to callers.

A voice rasped from inside. *"Go away!"*

Garrett knocked again. Now the voice wanted to know who was there. "Russ Garrett," Garrett said. Then he couldn't resist adding, "It would only be wise to open the door."

And about five seconds later the door was opened, and Garrett saw the puckered, ruined face of the dishwasher, the man he knew as Joey Hart, blinking in the sunlight.

"Mr. Garrett." It was stated as a fact. No emotion.

"Yes," Garrett told him. "It's about time we had a talk. Should I call you Joey, or Professor, or Mr. Laird, or just David?"

5

He was to call him David. Gravely the man waved Garrett into the room and closed the door tight behind them. It was dark inside; it might have been nighttime.

"I hope you don't mind the shades being drawn," David Laird said. "The light hurts my eyes."

"No," Garrett said. "I don't mind." Garrett's eyes adjusted quickly. He looked across the room to see "Joey" putting something in his mouth. False teeth, he thought, only more elaborate, heavier. It had to be something like that, of course. Garrett should have known.

Garrett had the only chair; his host sat on the edge of the thin cot. And his face was totally different. This man was now David Laird.

"Thank you for waiting," Laird said. "I speak better with the appliances in, though it's more comfortable without them."

"Excellent disguise, too," Garrett said.

Laird nodded. There seemed to be a sad, painful slowness to everything he did. "Oh, yes," he said. "I wouldn't have been able to kill Simmons without it."

Despite the fact that the voice was rough, Garrett found the man incredibly congenial, under the circumstances. He'd expected a shouting match. Or something.

"So you've found me," Laird said. "I expected it would happen, but not quite so soon."

"I got lucky," Garrett told him.

"How did you figure it out? I thought my performance as 'Joey' was quite good. *Joey* is circus slang for a clown, you know. Did I give myself away at any time when I was talking to you?"

"No, not at all. Not even when I showed up there with your wife. You just got angry and sloughed us off."

"That was difficult. You can't imagine what torture it was to see Jenny again. That time she came to the restaurant by herself—well, I'd been in the New York area for some time, and I'd managed to control my desire to see her. But after she came to the restaurant, I couldn't help myself. I began to follow her. In this face. I think I wanted her to see me. Unconsciously. I think perhaps I hoped *she* could find some way we could be together again . . ."

Garrett nodded. That was the time Jenny had been "aware" of her husband's presence. She'd looked into the kitchen. Unconsciously, she'd undoubtedly recognized his posture, or his walk, or something else that said *David*. Maybe even what was left of his voice.

"You see, I'm trying to be honest with you, Mr. Garrett—"

"Russ. If you're David, I'm Russ."

"Russ, then. I hope you'll be as honest with me. Please tell me how you found me."

Garrett put his hands on his knees, leaning forward in the wooden chair. "I cut a man's throat this morning. Laid his jaw open to the bone."

Laird didn't turn a hair. Either he had gotten used to violence or he knew the details from radio reports. "I see," he said.

"It made me think of Bristow."

"My old friend."

Garrett nodded. "It made me think of him and of the way he died. It made me think of faces." Garrett scratched at the corner of the bandage.

"It's going to be hard to explain this, because it didn't

come to me in any sequence. It hit me all at once, like . . ." Garrett tried to think of a different word, but couldn't. "Like lightning."

Laird nodded sagely. Like a professor, Garrett thought. "I understand," Laird told him. "That was how my plan came to me in the first place."

Garrett resisted the impulse to ask him what time of day that had been.

"It made me think of faces. Now, you killed Bristow first, and he looked like practice. He was punched the way the hot-dog vendor, Vitiello, was punched. He was shot twice, like Rex Simmons and like the Jersey cop."

"I shouldn't have shot the policeman," Laird said. "I panicked. I wish I could tell him how sorry I am. I'm glad to hear he's recovering."

Garrett went on. "All those similarities. But then Bristow's jaw was broken, and he was left in such a way that his face would be eaten by birds. I decided that was a prediction, too, or practice. That you were going to ruin somebody's face. I kept dreading it and, frankly, hoping it wasn't *my* face you had in mind.

"Then looking at what I'd just done to a man, it dawned on me that maybe it wasn't practice, like the rest. Maybe it was *revenge*.

"And I thought of Joey Hart."

For the first time, David Laird showed anger. "He deserved it. I should have put him in those rocks while he was alive." Laird was making fists in the thin blanket. "He was a coward, and he was a traitor, and he was going to destroy my life—he *did* destroy it, with those lies he told Simmons's committee. *And he was an incompetent dentist!*"

It was ludicrous, of course, but Garrett heard the passion in the words and saw the anger on David Laird's face, and the thought of laughing never crossed his mind.

Laird touched his jaw, the famous square jaw, restored by the plastic appliance inside his mouth.

"Cancer," he said. "I had pains; I went to Bristow. He never found it. Never *thought* about it. Just let it grow, and cleaned my teeth!"

Laird's eyes were wet. "He killed me, Russ. He murdered my body with his incompetence, and he destroyed my soul with his treachery. By the time I went to another doctor, after Bristow had testified, it was too late to do anything about the cancer. That was what got me started. That and . . . and something else. I didn't want to burden Jenny anymore. Ann was dead. I couldn't take it . . ."

Laird told Garrett the story—how he'd decided against suicide in favor of revenge, and how fate put the old derelict in his way.

"I found a place in Canada doing experimental oral surgery. I volunteered. They removed the bad part of my jaw—that had been the original site of the cancer—but by then it had spread to my throat. That's why I talk this way. I—I don't know where else it's spread. I have terrible pains in my head."

As he spoke, he took a pill bottle from his pocket, removed a capsule, and swallowed it without water. He gave Garrett a sad smile. "I don't know why I bother. They don't work too well anymore."

Laird resumed his story. How the people in Canada had given him the appliances to wear. How he'd realized what a perfect disguise he now had. Several disguises. "Sometimes I'd wear both appliances, sometimes just the uppers—I did that when I was Thane—sometimes nothing at all. I used to dye my hair, too, but after I was done being 'Thane,' I soon realized it wasn't necessary. My hair is the kind of blond that looks dark brown when it's wet. When I was washing dishes, the steam took care of it. The rest of the time I just made sure I had plenty of hair oil."

Garrett already knew from Kennedy how Laird had infiltrated Nofsinger's phony Communist organization. He mentioned it; Laird supplied the remaining details.

Garrett looked at the man. He'd expected to feel some sort of triumph around this time. He felt only sadness, and frustration.

"That was an interesting trick," Garrett told him. "Using their own gun to get Simmons. Sort of a trademark of yours, isn't it?"

"What do you mean?"

"Turning things around. Twisting things. Using a plan thought up by supporters of Rex Simmons to kill Simmons himself. Using *your own face* as the perfect disguise.

"And your famous disappearance. The police of two states went crazy trying to figure out how you pulled that off. I waltzed around with it myself. The only explanations—that you'd walked off or driven off—had so many holes in them they could be used for nets. You even tried to help us out, didn't you? That time you told us 'Joey' heard somebody go through the kitchen and out to the county road.

"But once I *suspected* Joey, it was simple. Simple. Because it wasn't your disappearance at all that caused the problem. It was your *appearance*.

"You shot Simmons when you were masquerading as the hot-dog vendor, dressed in restaurant white. You were still dressed that way when the cops stopped you on the New Jersey Turnpike. And you were *still* dressed that way when you arrived at the rest area. All you had to do then was *walk in the door and show up for work*. You were *supposed* to be there, and you were *supposed* to be wearing white clothes. *All* the employees there wore them. That state trooper, Johnson, said he almost shot the first one he saw dressed that way. You were home free. You took out your teeth as soon as you stopped the car, hid them somewhere—"

"I dropped them in the dishwater."

Garrett raised an eyebrow. "Weren't you afraid they'd melt?"

"They're built so you can drink coffee while you're wearing them. Besides, after I'd killed Simmons I could have gotten along without them."

"Oh," Garrett said. "Anyway, there you were. You didn't look the same. Nobody had reason to suspect you. You stuck your head in the steam and went to work."

"It wasn't supposed to be that way, you know. I had no idea I would be stopped by the police so soon, chased by them. My original plan had been simply to have the chain of stolen cars I'd been using end there, at the restaurant. They'd assume I'd switched to a car of my own and driven on. They might have even continued to check down the road and not come into the restaurant at all. But even if they did come in, I wasn't worried. In there I was just . . . Joey."

Just Joey, Garrett thought. But he'd set off a chain of misery and violence that had left people dead and maimed across half the country. Had made a killer of Garrett himself.

Then something occurred to him. "How did you get home that night?"

"Excuse me?"

"After work. How did you get home from the rest area? You certainly didn't drive the stolen car you'd come there in."

"Of course not. I simply left through the back door and walked home on the country roads. I often did that when I couldn't get a ride to the nearest turn-off with one of the other employees."

"Long walk," Garrett said.

"My pains don't let me sleep much. Sometimes the walking helps."

"I see." Garrett looked around the shabby little room. At the ragged man sitting in the darkness; this man who'd come back from the dead for revenge. Tried to hate him, but couldn't.

"Any regrets?" Garrett asked.

Laird thought it over. "As I said before, I'm sorry I shot the policeman. And I'm sorry your friends were hurt, though that was really the fault of the Simmons faction. And I am deeply, deeply sorry for hurting Jenny and the children again. I hope you will tell them that."

σ

The sun outside had climbed above the shade rollers, and now two bright strips of light lay on the floor like mammoth glowworms.

Garrett sighed. "What the hell am I going to do with you, David?"

There was surprise in the rasping voice. "I—I don't know. I must admit I was surprised when you arrived without the police."

"I haven't told the police."

"Why not?"

"I'm in love with your wife. I don't want her to be hurt anymore, either."

"I see," Laird said. Again he touched the diseased jaw. "Because she reminds you of her cousin?"

"No! Not anymore. Because she reminds me of herself, which is pretty damned terrific. You have three great kids, too."

Laird looked down at his hands. "I know. I don't deserve any of them. Russ . . ."

"Yes?"

"You took Ann's death badly, didn't you."

"You must know I did."

"It wasn't your child. It was mine. We . . . we had a short affair. When things were darkest for me. Ann was merely being kind."

Garrett was angry. "What the hell difference does *that* make now? I still loved her, and she's still dead."

"She loved you, too. She would never have tried to abort your child. That was the 'something else' I had alluded to before that got me started this way. It ate at me worse than the cancer. I . . ."

"It's over with now," Garrett told him harshly. In a way it made sense. It explained, as nothing else did, why Ann had left him. She was ashamed. Poor Annie. "And it still doesn't answer the question of what I'm going to do." A voice inside him kept saying, *what's the goddam use, anyway?*

Laird's face showed a look of infinite weariness. "I'm dying, Russ," he said. "It's a matter of weeks now."

"I have to talk to the police again tomorrow. Under oath."

"I see." He closed his eyes and lay back on the bed. "If I could only stop the pains in my head, maybe I could think of something." He took the bottle of pills from his pocket and held it in front of his eyes. "These things are worthless to me when I take them one at a time. I wonder, if I took all of them at once, whether the pain would finally go away."

Garrett rubbed his eyes. There it was—he'd talked the

man into killing himself. For Jenny's sake, he kept telling himself. For Mark, and the twins. He didn't like it. He started out wanting to play baseball and wound up playing God.

He got up to go.

David Laird sat up. "Wait! What are you going to do?"

"Tomorrow I'm going to tell the police how it came to me in a dream that David Laird and Joey Hart are the same person. And I'm going to try to get them to keep it quiet. For Jenny's sake."

Laird looked at him intensely. It was strange, but Garrett got the impression Laird was worried about *him*, and that he understood. God, he hoped so.

"And today?" Laird asked him.

"I'm going to go to your wife and hold her hand, and tell her everything is going to be all right. I'm going to write letters to law schools and get applications. I'm going to get in touch with Mickey Mantle, and the Yankee ticket office."

"I don't understand," Laird said.

"A promise I made," Garrett told him. "I've got to make arrangements to take a kid to a ball game."

"I see," David Laird said. He closed his eyes, then opened them again. "Take care of her, Russ."

"I'll do my best," Garrett said. A ball player—even an ex-ball player—was expected to do his best.

The two men looked at each other for a long moment. Then Garrett opened the door and stepped blinking into the bright September sunshine.